FIRST KISS

"I learned some interesting things yesterday," Sofia said.

"This should be good. Like what?"

"You never want to get married."

"False," Ben said easily. "What I said was—I'd never get married *unless it was for keeps*."

"Oh."

Ben smirked. "What else did Charli say?"

"She said that you're like Warren Beatty before Annette Bening—lots of women, no commitment. A real playboy."

"Not true."

Sofia leaned in closer. "Why would Charli make up such wild stories?"

Ben met her gaze and held it with a smoldering intensity. "I have no idea."

"Maybe she's trying to discourage me from getting involved with you."

"Is it working?"

"I'd say just the opposite."

"So you're encouraged."

Sofia sucked in a tiny breath. "Very."

And then Ben claimed her mouth with his, gently at first, but the hunger was there. She could feel it, taste it . . .

BOOK YOUR PLACE ON OUR WEBSITE AND MAKE THE READING CONNECTION!

We've created a customized website just for our very special readers, where you can get the inside scoop on everything that's going on with Zebra, Pinnacle and Kensington books.

When you come online, you'll have the exciting opportunity to:

• View covers of upcoming books

• Read sample chapters

• Learn about our future publishing schedule (listed by publication month *and author*)

• Find out when your favorite authors will be visiting a city near you

• Search for and order backlist books from our online catalog

• Check out author bios and background information

• Send e-mail to your favorite authors

• Meet the Kensington staff online

• Join us in weekly chats with authors, readers and other guests

• Get writing guidelines

• AND MUCH MORE!

**Visit our website at
http://www.zebrabooks.com**

FLY ME TO THE MOON

Kylie Adams

ZEBRA BOOKS
KENSINGTON PUBLISHING CORP.

http://www.zebrabooks.com

ACKNOWLEDGMENTS

This romp is dedicated to my holy trinity of fiction pals who keep me sane in what can be a crazy-making business. . . .

Stephanie Bond—We met at the Moonlight & Magnolias conference in Atlanta and were thick as thieves in five minutes flat. If there's a smarter girl in the business, then bring her to me. I'll bet a little farm in Montana that she's a twit compared to Steph. What a brilliant darling. Love her.

Lisa Jackson—We met at the *Romantic Times* conference in Toronto and were thick as thieves in five minutes flat (again!). If there's a zanier girl in the business, then bring her to me. I'll bet a day at Elizabeth Arden that she's a hopeless bore compared to Lisa. What a fun gal. Adore her.

Karen Young—We met at a little conference in Jackson, Mississippi, and were thick as thieves in five minutes flat (is there a pattern here?). If there's a sweeter girl in the business, then bring her to me. I'll bet a shopping spree at Neiman's that she's a real bitch compared to Karen. What an absolute angel. Worship her.

She had only one fault: She was perfect. Otherwise, she was perfect.

—Truman Capote

Prologue

"That girl would make a beautiful bride if she'd just show up for one of her weddings," a woman announced to the seat occupant on her right. "Is this number three, or am I counting wrong?"

"It's number three," another woman confirmed from the row behind them. "I knew she wouldn't show. I started to skip it, too, but then I remembered how fabulous the food is at these things."

The first woman bobbed her head with unbridled enthusiasm. "Best cake I've ever tasted."

Debi Cardinella, sister of the missing bride and reluctant maid of honor, fixed a smile on the talkative guests. Here she was, miserable as hell, girdled in gold satin, and craving something sweet. Why did that loudmouth have to go and mention the word *cake*? At the last wedding, Debi had eaten a whole tier— the chocolate one with the vanilla buttercream filling and sugared champagne grapes. In one word, *ecstasy*.

All of a sudden her frantic father was in her face. "Where's your sister?"

"I don't know, Papa," Debi replied calmly. "Just like I didn't know when you asked me that same question thirty seconds ago."

Forcing a gung-ho grin, Joseph Cardinella thrusted a thumbs-up sign to Vincent Scalia, the catatonic groom in the single-breasted midnight blue suit. "Don't worry, son. This time she'll be here. I can feel it." He ambled down the aisle in search of his daughter, smiling to the doubtful-looking gatherers as if the ceremony were right on schedule.

"The Wedding March" played on. And on. *And on.* Debi stifled a groan and briefly considered knocking out the organist. With a certain nod, she decided to eat the lemon tier with the white chocolate mousse filling and pink pulled-sugar ribbons. In one word, *heaven.* After three consecutive months of matrimonial meddling on the part of her father, not to mention the indominable avoidance on the part of her sister, she deserved at least that much.

Debi turned to offer Vincent a comforting smile. Three fancy weddings. Three no-shows by the bride. It had to be murder on a man's ego—especially a short man's. Part of her . . . well, actually all two hundred seventeen pounds of her . . . wanted to step up to the altar, take her place beside him, and tell the priest to get on with it.

But the fantasy exited her head as fast as it had entered. Facts were facts. She'd been in love with Vincent Scalia since grade school, yet he was scarcely aware of her existence. His eye had always been on her sister. The younger one. The stylish one. The bone-thin one. Hell, let's face it, as far as most people were concerned, the *only* one. They went ape for her high chic and high spirits. When she wasn't in a room, the anticipation of her arrival kept it buzzing.

Everything her sister did took on a profound state of grace—the way she stood, the way she signed her name, the way she gave custodians and corporate presidents equal standing in an unequal world. The girl's presence was almost geothermal. In one word, *perfect.*

Did Debi hate her? No, that would be too clichéd. She loved her sister, cherished her, in fact, as a best friend. But the woman definitely had an annoying streak. Allowing all these people to gather for a wedding that she had no intention of showing up for was that quality in peak form.

"Oh, not now," Debi muttered under her breath as Mr. Pickles, her sister's Yorkie, pranced into view. The yappy little thing expressed his displeasure by urinating in strange places. With his owner otherwise engaged and the rest of the family too busy to fawn over him, the teacup-sized tyrant was anything but content.

But this time it wasn't a new couch or a new pair of shoes to get angrily whizzed. Mr. Pickles marched to the altar, hiked up his leg, peed down Vincent Scalia's leg, and scampered away.

The groom stood as immobile as a statue in the park. "You know, this day's a real pisser," he grumbled to no one in particular.

With his menacing fist swinging in the air, Joseph Cardinella stood over the organist, shouting, "Keep playing! She's coming this time. I just know it."

Debi covered her face in her hands. Her father was holding on to this wedding idea like a pit bull to a sweaty sock. In one word, *denial.*

Chapter One

"Do it, Raymond. You know how much I want it."
Sofia Rose Cardinella stared defiantly at the brooding
artist. Nothing about him, not his intense eyes,
Mohawk, or gothic garb could intimidate her.

"It's a big step for us. Are you sure?" he hedged,
Scottish-accented words tripping off his tongue like
powdered sugar.

Sofia loved his beautiful voice and decided that in
a perfect world Raymond McLaren would narrate
every audiobook ever produced. "I'm begging you
to take it off."

He sighed dramatically, lifting her wild mane of
jet-black curls with both hands as he leaned over to
bury his face in it, moaning with agonized rapture.

Sofia laughed. "Don't try to talk me out of this. I
want you to take that special tool of yours and work
me over good. If I scream for you to stop, ignore me.
In this case only, *no* means *yes.*"

"OK. It's your decision," Raymond said with an air of finality.

"Thank you!" Sofia gushed, punctuating her thunderous response with two hands in the air, as if conducting a full orchestra. "It is my decision. *My decision!*"

Raymond gave her a puzzled look.

Sofia glanced at her watch. "Do you know where I'm supposed to be at this very moment?"

He allowed a beat to pass. "On your therapist's couch?"

With a sly grin, a purse of her lips, and a tilt of her head, Sofia accepted the harmless jab. "No, Raymond, my wedding reception," she replied in singsong.

"Your wedding reception?"

"That's right."

"So you said, 'I do' and ditched husband, family, and friends to come here and cut off all your hair?' "

"Actually, I said, 'I don't think so,' window-shopped in SoHo, and came here to cut off all my hair."

"Then it could just be prewedding jitters making you do this."

Sofia smiled. She loved the way Raymond's inflection went up at the end of a sentence. "If that's the case, I would've been asking for this *three* weddings ago."

"Three weddings?"

She nodded.

"Surely not to the same bloke?"

She nodded again.

"Is he a masochist?"

Sofia giggled. "My father is obsessed with this idea of a family merger, and the fiancé in question is the first son of a very prominent one."

Raymond started to hum *The Godfather* theme. It was common knowledge that the Sicilian born Joseph Cardinella was far less than six degrees away from the Mafia.

"Stop it!" Sofia protested with good humor. "Neither family has ever been involved in drugs, prostitution, or illegal weapons," she said proudly.

"Hey, that's no fun," Raymond cracked with an exaggerated pout.

"Anyway, I've told my father over and over that I have no intention of marrying that man! *Me* marry Vincent Scalia? Honestly! But you have to understand my father—he's the most stubborn man in the history of stubborn men on this planet."

She let out a deep sigh and shook her head. "Refuses to listen. So I save my breath, let him go through the charade of planning all these ridiculous weddings, and then I just don't show up. Actually, it's worked out quite well. He hires a very fine caterer, so no one really complains that much."

"What about this guy Vincent?"

"Oh, he's just as stubborn as Papa. Plus he's five-foot-two, so he comes prepackaged with enough short-man issues to earn that therapist you mentioned a summer home in the Hamptons. It's hopeless."

Raymond swiveled the styling chair so that Sofia faced the mirror. His expression was grim as he fanned out her long, silky tresses. "Please don't make me do this," he begged softly.

Sofia's mind was made up. The Rapunzel look was history. Through the mirror, her exotic green eyes blazed into Raymond's. "Start cutting."

He bit down on his knuckle. "It hurts to say goodbye."

When Raymond was finished, the transformation

was total. Sofia glanced down at the garden of thick hair on the floor, then up to the stranger in the mirror. She looked thinner, older, more sophisticated. Gooseflesh sprang up all over her body. It was, indeed, a dramatic turnaround.

All the stylists at Bumble and Bumble, one of New York's top salons, thought so, too. Like planets around the moon, they moved in orbit, passing by Raymond's station, *oohing* and *ahing*. Every bit of attention seemed to thrum in Sofia's direction, and this left a young and famous Oscar-winning actress glowering in her chair as she waited for a color treatment to do its work.

Raymond captured one of Sofia's surreptitious glances to the surly starlet. "Don't mind her," he whispered. "She wants to be left alone, yet she wants all the focus to be on her. Typical Hollywood type. To tell you the truth, I don't like to do her hair. I prefer real people like you. Besides, she made five million on her last movie, and she's a lousy tipper. Let her bleedin' hair turn green."

Sofia grinned, running her fingers through her suddenly slick, gamine-short locks. It was cropped so boyish and carefree, she loved it. "This is the new me," she whispered, still trying to get used to her own reflection.

Raymond rested his hands on her shoulders. "I can't believe I gave you shit about doing this. You're beautiful."

Sofia fluttered her eyes self-consciously. "My eyebrows are too thick, my teeth are uneven, and my feet are enormous. So don't call me beautiful. I'm just a skinny broad."

"Oh, you're way more than that, love," Raymond countered.

Sofia traveled several blocks before finally shaking free of the feeling that she'd left something behind. She walked with a new purpose and energy, feeling supremely confident in slim white capri pants and a black midriff top. Her eyes eclipsed by large Gucci sunglasses, she carried a classic Chanel handbag adorned by a beautiful Hermes scarf tied carelessly around its leather strap. More than a few passersby did a double take, as if she were a celebrity they couldn't quite place. Sofia hated to disappoint them, but she was just a girl from New Jersey.

She skipped across Fifth Avenue seconds before impatient traffic lurched forward. Planning a great look was simple, she mused. All one had to do was ignore trends, pay no mind to silly In and Out lists, and watch every Audrey Hepburn movie ever made.

It took much less than a million to look like a million. Sofia's secret was cleaning out her bank account for fine accessories and going cheap on basics like shirts, jeans, and undergarments. After all, a top-dollar handbag lasts forever and fools wardrobe watchers into thinking the pinpoint Oxford you scooped up at a discount store is haute couture.

Just ahead was Berrenger's, the exclusive specialty store where she worked in the beauty department for Aspen Cosmetics, a luxury line of skin-care, makeup, color, and fragrance products. Her counter did boffo business, the kind of numbers that put it in the top five of Aspen retailers worldwide.

The moment she hit the employee entrance, Ricky Lopez exclaimed, "I almost didn't recognize you!"

Sofia gave her coworker and best friend a megawatt smile. He was gay pride walking, a fiercely flamboyant creature of sass and sweetness.

"What are you doing here? Didn't you go to my wedding?" Sofia blurted accusingly.

Ricky cut a snappish glance. "I learned my lesson after the first two, honey. I'm not showing up to another one of those unless it's Antonio Sabato Jr. you're marrying, in which case I'll bop you over the head on your way down the aisle and assume the bridal position myself." He fell into step beside her, shamelessly checking out a new management trainee.

She laughed, getting out a quick, "You're awful," before spinning around, giving him all angles of her daring new style. "You like?"

Ricky murmured a lascivious, "Oh, yes. I like a lot." His heat-stoked gaze was still on the trainee, a dead ringer for boxing dreamboat Oscar De La Hoya.

Sofia slapped Ricky's arm. "He's married," she hissed.

"A minor obstacle. Give me two martinis and a blindfold. He'll be subscribing to *The Advocate* this time tomorrow."

Sofia scanned the rack for her time card and shoved it into the big, industrial clock, grimacing at the loud click. It made her feel like a factory worker. "I was referring to my hair."

Ricky stepped back to sweep her up and down with an assessing gaze. "*Sabrina.* After Paris. Perfection."

Sofia grinned. "Audrey or Julia Ormand?"

"Oh, please," Ricky said, dismissing the thought with a hand gesture. "Some nights I still wake up screaming about that remake. Don't bring back the horror."

She gave him a pleading look. "We need a place to stay for a few days."

"And this *we* includes Mr. Pickles," Ricky surmised. "Now that's a different kind of horror."

"You won't even know he's there."

"Until he pees in my closet again."

"He was upset."

"That makes two of us. My Ferragamos still smell like a fire hydrant." Ricky sighed. "The couch is already made up, and I rented *Roman Holiday.*"

Sofia hugged him tightly. "Oh, Ricky, you know me so well. Mr. Pickles will be an angel this time. I promise."

Ricky raised an eyebrow. "Don't make promises that little shit can't keep."

"Ricky!" Sofia protested hurtfully, moving into the lounge, not ready to face shoppers just yet.

He covered his mouth in mock shock. "Did I say that?"

"Mr. Pickles adores you."

"Correction—Mr. Pickles adores *you.* He merely puts up with the rest of us." A beat and a sigh. "I'm kidding. Of course he's welcome."

Sofia beamed. "It's just until Thursday's family dinner at Villa. By then Papa will have calmed down, and it'll be safe for me to return to the fold."

"That is until the next wedding," Ricky put in dryly.

Sofia shook her head. "The next one will be on *my* terms."

"Do you really think your father is capable of letting go of this Vincent Scalia thing?"

She took an angry step back. "Why don't the two of them just leave me out of it and marry each other?"

"Not a good idea. My people feel much more at ease with Joseph and Vincent in the heterosexual camp."

Sofia groaned and fought the urge to reach into her purse for a cigarette. She limited herself to six a day, and already down to two left, she decided to tough it out. "What time did you get here?"

"At opening," Ricky answered with a diffident shrug. "Sales are so-so."

She grimaced. So-so wouldn't get her to Carmel, California. Aspen Cosmetics was sponsoring a national in-house contest for its newest fragrance, Honesty, and the associate with the highest sales for the month would win a three-day trip to that sunny West Coast paradise. Given her status as one of the company's best product movers, Sofia definitely had a chance. And she had less than a week to make it happen.

Without fully realizing it, cigarette number five was lit and between her lips. *Screw it*, Sofia thought, taking a drag. It was, after all, her wedding day. She shot a glance at the time clock. Half past one. Too early to call Debi and find out how angry Papa was this time. On a scale of one to ten, Sofia's guess was an eight— severe but manageable.

"I'm not doing enough with my life, Ricky," she announced with sudden philosophical directness.

"We can't all be Suzanne Somers," he said.

"Seriously, there's got to be more than avoiding the weddings my father plans and hawking perfume and lipstick. I'm bored."

"What's happening with that idea to start your own beauty company?"

Sofia blew out a puff of smoke and watched it curl up to the ceiling. "Not a thing."

There was a hard and fast knock on the open lounge door. Howard Berrenger stood there, eyeballing them crossly. "Is there a reason why the two of you are clocked in but not on the sales floor?" He was the designated bad cop of the retail dynasty, a numbers cruncher who tracked sales per square foot with more precision than Papa's bookies did point spreads.

Sofia stubbed out her bad habit and rose gracefully. "We were strategizing for the Aspen contest, Mr. Berrenger. It'll be great PR for the store if one of us wins."

Howard's grim face relaxed. "You cut your hair," he observed.

Sofia ran her hand through what used to be, then smiled. "I wanted a change."

"It suits you." He clapped his hands. "Now, let's hit the floor and get on the fast track to a record sales day."

Sofia and Ricky shared a look.

"What are we on?" Howard demanded with infomercial-host fervor.

"The fast track," Sofia and Ricky replied in unison, having attended enough sales meetings where they were forced to repeat the mantra.

Saturday business picked up, and Sofia managed to close an Honesty perfume sale with almost every customer. Time passed quickly. Before she knew it, her dinner break was upon her.

Berrenger's anchored a minimall, which featured a cluster of intimate shops, small restaurants, a center court for special events, and a single screen art-house theater. Sofia ordered a fruit salad to go from a delicious little spot called Gina's, then strolled toward a gathering crowd.

There was always something going on in center court. Last weekend it'd been a man in full Scottish regalia playing the bagpipes, the week before that a lesbian choir. She squinted to make out today's placard. . . .

THE ROMANTIC STYLINGS OF BEN ESTES

Intrigued, she weaved through the bystanders for a closer look. Right away, Sofia liked what she saw. Finally, a man who knew how to wear a tuxedo! His shirt cuffs extended half an inch from his jacket sleeves, and his pants broke just above his freshly polished shoes. Add the brilliant splash of orange provided by the pocket handkerchief, and this chap could do no wrong. Except, of course, ruin the whole look by saying something stupid. Men were so talented that way.

Sofia noticed a hormonal wave rippling through the mostly female gaggle of onlookers, and it was no secret why. Assuming this was Ben Estes, he did, indeed, have *romantic stylings*. Tall and lean, he had a good haircut, a long, handsome face, a strong jaw, and alert, intelligent brown eyes.

She spotted a vacant seat right in front and claimed it immediately.

A few moments later, he plugged a microphone into a machine that resembled a boom box, pressed a few buttons, and spun around to face the crowd.

"Good afternoon!" he bellowed.

Even with all his swooning good looks, the response from the crowd was anemic, but it didn't faze him. He charged on, still upbeat.

"My name's Ben Estes, and I'm thrilled to be here at Berrenger's Market. Any Sinatra fans out there?"

Another tepid reaction.

"I thought they were having funny dog tricks today!" a woman cried.

Sofia spun around angrily. *The rudeness!*

The heckler's outburst generated a low rumble of chuckles.

Ben shrugged and managed an adorable, self-deprecating grin. "I don't know about the funny dog tricks, ma'am, but I promise to roll over between songs."

The crowd roared.

He pointed to the woman expecting an animal show. "And this first number is just for you, baby." Jaunty, horn-laden music exploded from the machine, and Ben began snapping his fingers in true crooner style. He sang in a rich, melodious voice. Definite shades of Harry Connick Jr.

Sofia recognized "The Lady Is a Tramp" immediately and fell into a fit of giggles. This guy was good. This guy was *very* good. She ate her fruit salad while he performed his set, which was made up of Sinatra signatures like "My Way," "Fly Me to the Moon," "Strangers in the Night," and the showstopper "New York, New York."

Suddenly it dawned on Sofia how much her father would hate this guy. He wasn't Italian, he had the audacity to sing standards made famous by Frank Sinatra, and he did so in a cheesy mall setting of all places. Oh, yes, Joseph Cardinella would definitely have a problem with Ben Estes.

But no man had ever appealed to Sofia more.

Chapter Two

The crowd dispersed as quickly as it had gathered, and Ben was left alone to take down his one-man Vegas-style show. He gave Sofia a look and a smile as he wrapped the microphone cord around its base.

She rose to dispose of her fruit salad container. "You're very entertaining. Much better than this venue deserves."

He tilted his head to one side, regarding her with an appreciative nod. "Thank you for that."

"May I offer a suggestion?"

He arched his brow. "Sure."

"You're a little heavy on the Sinatra worship. Perhaps you could mix up your act with other singers."

His shapely lips fell out of their curve and into a firm line. "There *are* no other singers."

Regarding him curiously, Sofia took a few steps down to join him in the center-court square. "What do you mean?"

"Just what I said. There *are* no other singers. It begins and ends with Sinatra."

"That's ridiculous. What about Michael Bolton?"

Ben pulled a face. "He's not a singer. He's a primal screamer."

"I love Michael Bolton!" Sofia protested lightly.

"You should get some help for that."

"You're like one of those people who love *Star Trek*. What do they call them?"

"Thirty-five year-old virgins who still live with their mothers."

"No." Sofia laughed. "There's a name for them. . . ." She traced her lower lip with her thumbnail as she scanned her brain for the answer. "Trekkies!" she erupted. "You're like a Trekkie, only you have it bad for Frank Sinatra. You're a *Frankie!* I bet you even have a short black friend named Sammy."

"Actually, his name is Taz. But he does look like Sammy Davis Jr. Ten points for you."

She extended her hand. "My name's Sofia Cardinella."

"Card-carrying *Frankie* here." His shake was firm, and he made solid eye contact, followed by a flirtatious wink.

Sofia experienced a rush of adrenaline. He was so unbelievably clean—the way he dressed, the way he smelled, the closeness of his shave. Plus he was a bonafide hunk. "Is this your first time at Berrenger's Market?"

"Yeah, the juggling dog canceled, so I filled in. I figure you have to start somewhere."

"Can you make a decent living this way?"

"Yes—in Chile. It's much tougher living in New York. But I manage to scrape by, mostly by avoiding my landlord."

Sofia looked up dreamily. "That sounds so exciting and passionate."

"Interesting you should say that. My ex-girlfriend found it tiresome and immature."

"Where's her sense of adventure?"

"With a professional hockey player."

"I'm sorry."

"Don't be. I've got better teeth and can read without moving my lips."

Sofia stood there, smiling, completely enchanted by this man's quick wit, masterful style, and inner confidence. He didn't take himself seriously, but he definitely took his singing seriously. Of that she was certain. And despite his flippancy, there was genuine pain regarding the ex-girlfriend. She saw the flash of hurt in his eyes when he mentioned her. The complexities were piling up. Ditto her interest.

"I have to get back to work," she murmured regretfully.

"Where's that?"

"The cosmetics department at Berrenger's."

"I'll walk you. I catch the train at that exit."

"Great," Sofia chirped, purposefully walking slowly to prolong the moment. "So tell me, Ben, why Sinatra?"

His eyes sparkled, and he began to speak in an excitable tone. "Because he knew how to live. He worked hard; he played hard; he was the straw that stirred the drinks. Plus he was fearless. I like that about him."

"Are you fearless?"

"I'm trying to be. I used to be scared of my parents, of not living up to their expectations. So I finished law school like they wanted me to and got a job with a big firm. *Dullsville*. I wasn't into it, and the partners knew it. I gave it a year, then quit a few months ago to give singing a go. It's always been a dream of mine. I've seen worse guys than me make it, and one day I thought, why should I sit around like crabgrass and fantasize? So here I am, grateful to be subbing for a yellow lab. But, hey, it beats nine-to-fiving at a job I hate."

"I've got a dream," Sofia said, caught up in Ben's chuck-it-all daring.

He stopped and peered down at her. "Tell me about it."

She looked up at him—all six-feet-five of him. For a moment she said nothing, struck by how addictively watchable he was. His expressive cheekbones were vintage-thin Brando, and his long arms and square shoulders smacked of strength and virility.

There was an earnest look fixed in his brown eyes— genuine interest, the kind that can't be faked. He wasn't humoring her in hope of getting her number and in greater hope of getting her into bed soon after that. Ben Estes actually wanted to hear about her dream. Suddenly her heart was sending a message to her brain: *like this guy.*

"I want to start my own beauty company," she heard herself saying without a hint of self-consciousness.

"So what's stopping you?"

"Oh, the usual—discipline, ambition, the fact that it'd be hard work."

Ben laughed heartily, gripping Sofia's shoulders with both of his large, nicely manicured hands. "You and me, baby . . . We're *way* too honest about ourselves."

She felt the heat of his touch through the cotton of her top, and wondered briefly, illicitly, what it would feel like on the rest of her. "You've inspired me."

He smiled his delight and started walking again. "That should be worth your phone number, at least."

"Oh, at least," Sofia agreed.

"And maybe ten percent of that company once it's up and running."

"You're pushing it."

"Can't blame a guy for trying." He reached inside his jacket pocket and pulled out a pen and a little black book. "The digits, please."

"I'm hard to reach. Ask me out now."

He stopped again, his eyes bulging incredulously. "A take-charge dame. I like that."

"The fifties are over." Sofia smiled. "Didn't you get the memo?"

"I've got gigs every night over the next several days," he said, visibly torn.

"Tell me when and where. I'll show up in bobby socks and make like a swooning fan."

"Will you squeal and faint and do anything to please me after the show?"

"I'd only do that for Michael Bolton, but I'll clap real loud for you."

"Gee, thanks." He bit down on his lip and flipped through the calendar section of his little book. "I'm doing a gig at an Italian restaurant called Villa on Thursday. Are you free?"

Sofia covered her face with her hands. "This is too bizarre." She faced him now, eyes gleaming. "I eat dinner there every Thursday. It's a standing family ritual."

"What a gas! So you know Costas?"

Sofia nodded enthusiastically. "He's like an uncle to me."

Ben fingered the cleft in his chin. "He booked me . . . Very reluctantly, I might add. Maybe you could put in a good word."

"Consider it done."

"So I'll see you Thursday. We'll have dessert together; a drink, too."

"That sounds great."

"It's a little soon to meet the family, but since they'll be there . . . what the hell?"

Sofia giggled. "I should mention that in my father's great Sicilian pecking order, Frank Sinatra stands right next to the Pope. On principle, he'll probably hate you."

Ben shrugged. "Not a problem. I'm used to parents hating me. Right now even my own parents hate me."

They stood there, smiling, looking away, then into each other's eyes again, both resisting the idea of saying good-bye.

"I should go," Sofia said finally. "My break was over a long time ago, and someone in my department is likely to tattle."

He leaned in and kissed her cheek. "I'm going to learn a new song and sing it just for you," he whispered.

Sofia watched him go, lugging his karaoke machine, looking very much the overdressed vaudevillian. Somehow he pulled it off and came away looking like a matinee idol.

She returned to the counter just as her break time had gone thirty minutes over. And there stood Howard Berrenger, pointing to his watch like some angry father to a teenager who'd missed curfew.

"Our dinner break seems to have gotten away from us, Sofia," he said.

She dashed into her beauty prison and slipped into

the white lab coat that made her look like the dermatologist she wasn't. "I know, Mr. Berrenger. But I
met this fabulous guy, and I haven't had a boyfriend
since Karl, and . . . Well, let's not talk about him.
Anyway, my love life has been a nonevent lately." She
shook her finger at Howard in a scolding gesture.
"And part of that's your fault. Sometimes you put
me on the schedule all weekend long! How's a girl
supposed to find a man under those conditions?"

Howard opened his mouth to speak.

Sofia silenced him with a little "Stop! In the Name
of Love" choreography. "And please don't suggest
that I try my luck with the men around here. They're
either married, gay, or sleeping their way from department to department like we're still in the seventies
and Berrenger's is Studio 54. By the way, the women
in shoes could use a lamppost, if you know what I
mean."

Howard had no idea what to make of Sofia's rant,
and his disgruntled look quickly metamorphosed into
a perplexed one. "I see . . . Well, carry on," he said,
straightening his tie as he ambled away.

Ricky shot up from organizing the lipstick drawer.
"Forget those sluts in the shoe department. What's
this about a man?"

Sofia twirled with adolescent glee. "I just met an
amazing guy. He was singing in center court."

Ricky lost interest—fast. "Ooh, he's going places.
Paging Carnegie Hall." He swooped back down, this
time to see about the nail polish.

"Don't be such a snob. He's going to be a star. I
know it."

Ricky cracked a smile, still unconvinced. "Well,
there's no place to go but up."

Sofia captured some fingerprints on the counter

and reached for the glass cleaner to wipe them away. "Just wait until you meet him. He's gorgeous; he's funny." She threw the damp cloth at her friend and counter mate. "You'll be wishing he had a brother."

Ricky, so handsome that he was pretty, suddenly looked intrigued. "He must be. I haven't heard you carry on like this since Matt Damon came into the store to buy underwear a few months ago."

Sofia's mouth dropped open in disbelief. "I believe that was *you* who carried on. In fact, you came close to being slapped with a restraining order."

Ricky shrugged. "Whatever." His hand shot up to wave excitedly. "Here comes your maid of honor."

Sofia spun around to see Debi approaching. Her sister trudged forward, swathed in gold satin, Mr. Pickles prancing alongside. *She looks heavier than ever,* Sofia thought sadly, always concerned about her sister's health and self-esteem. Sometimes just walking was an effort, and when Debi reached the counter, her breathing was labored.

"Your hair looks great, but Papa's still going to recognize you," Debi said.

Sofia placed her hands together in prayer and cautiously inquired, "How is he?"

Debi delivered a grave expression. *"Very quiet."*

"Yikes. That's not good." Sofia shifted focus and gave her sister a puzzled once-over. "Why didn't you go home and change clothes?"

"And ride back with Papa? No, thanks. I'd rather walk around like I don't have a date to the prom. Which I never did. Am I typecasting myself?"

Sofia smiled. She loved her sister's wicked humor. "How's Vincent?"

Debi splayed out her hands on the counter to inspect her nails. Some were long, some short, some chipped, some perfectly polished. She never could be bothered with manicures. "Vincent's an eternal optimist. He thought you were coming. But he didn't call it rain when Mr. Pickles pissed down his leg. I guess there's a limit."

Sofia tried to fight back the laughter but lost the battle. "That's awful," she managed between guffaws.

"Yeah, I can tell it's real painful for you." With an amused smirk, Debi waited out the giggle fit. She turned to Ricky and tilted her head to indicate Mr. Pickles. "I've got one word for you: galoshes."

Ricky leaned over the counter for a closer look at the furry creature. "No," he began in a baby voice. "Mr. Pickles is my house guest. He won't pee on me."

Mr. Pickles growled.

Ricky stood up straight. "I swear that dog is the spawn of Satan."

"Don't say that!" Now Sofia leaned over. "My little baby comes straight from heaven! Isn't that right?"

Mr. Pickles's tail swished into action, and he whined with devoted delight.

"Same routine?" Debi asked.

Sofia hooked her arm through Ricky's, drawing him closer. "I'm staying with this darling man for a few days, and I'll keep underground until the family dinner on Thursday."

"Plenty of time for Papa to get over the catering bill, treat his ulcer, and ask God why he didn't have sons," Debi remarked. She bounced a look to Ricky. "Then we start all over again."

"Not this time," Sofia countered. She could feel her own eyes sparkling. "I met a guy."

Debi's lips parted in wonder. "Shouldn't your maid of honor at least be out of her dress before you make such announcements?"

"He sings in malls," Ricky put in.

Debi looked worried. "I thought only children did that. How old is this guy?"

"He's going to be famous," Sofia said confidently.

"Like Tiffany?" Debi wondered in her glib way.

Ricky nodded. "That's right! She started in malls." He broke into the teen sensation's first hit, "I Think We're Alone Now."

"The two of you are impossible," Sofia scolded.

A customer approached, breaking up the huddle. Sofia talked her into a bottle of Honesty and sent the woman on her way. She jotted down the sale in the contest book. Even with all her goofing off, it'd been a good day. The chance to win the Carmel trip was definitely there.

"Debi!" she called from the terminal the moment the thought hit her, "I'm starting my own beauty company, and you're going to be my partner."

"What about me?" Ricky asked.

Sofia mulled it over a few seconds. "You're my vice president of marketing," she said cheerfully.

Debi took in the area with a circular glance. "Anybody else need a job?" she said to no one in particular.

"It'll be great!" Sofia said, rushing back to join them. She reached over to clasp Debi's hands. "You're a whiz when it comes to science. Combine that with my beauty and style sense, and the sky's the limit."

"What about me?" Ricky asked again.

Sofia didn't have to think this time. "You're a fabulous artist and the best interior decorator I know. With you in the mix, we'll have *fierce* packaging."

Ricky beamed.

"What does your husband say about all this?" Debi asked. "Oh, that's right. You didn't get married."

Sofia fixed a pleading look on her. "Sis, I'm serious about this. Really, I am. Look at us. Ricky and I aren't exactly climbing the corporate ladder at Berrenger's. We're glorified shop girls." She glanced at him. "No offense."

"None taken," he said. "But I prefer shop *queen.*" Debi cackled.

"And as for *you,*" Sofia went on, looking back at her sister, "that chemistry degree is just collecting dust. Doing Papa's payroll and the bookkeeping for the gambling parlors isn't a challenge. You can do that work in your sleep. None of us are focused. We're just drifting along."

"Is this your idea of inspiration?" Debi asked. "Now I'm depressed."

"Me, too," Ricky added. "I feel like a loser."

"Tomorrow's a new day. Only *you* can change your life," Sofia said.

Debi gave her a look. "Are you channeling Oprah Winfrey?"

Sofia released Debi's hands and propped both elbows onto the counter, noticing more fingerprints but ignoring them. "Ben—he's the great guy I met— made me realize how important dreams are. No more thinking about it. I'm going for it! But I can't do it alone. And I don't want to. What do you say?"

"I'm in," Ricky said. "Can I tell Howard Berrenger to shove my time card up his—"

"Not yet!" Sofia interrupted. "We should probably, I don't know, *make our first dollar* first!"

"We need a business plan," Debi announced.

Sofia furrowed her brow. "What's that?"

"I'm definitely in," Debi said. "If nothing else, it'll be an adventure."

Chapter Three

Thank God it's Thursday, Sofia thought as her eyes fluttered open to greet the new morning. The waiting was over. Tonight she would finally see Ben Estes again. Just thinking about it made the butterflies take flight.

She massaged an ache in the back of her neck. Five nights on Ricky's couch was all she could take, and five nights with Mr. Pickles was all *he* could take. Definitely time to shove on before the friendship hit a snag.

Ricky lived in a cramped one-bedroom apartment in the Chelsea area. His bathroom had just enough space for a tub and a commode, leaving the only sink in the kitchen. Brushing her teeth with the dirty dishes took some getting used to. No matter, the big picture window provided great sun and an extraordinary view. At fourteen hundred dollars a month, the place was considered quite a deal, especially taking into account the popular location.

Just as Sofia began to wonder how Ricky managed to swing the rent without a *permanent* roommate, her gaze fell upon a check littering the living room floor. She picked it up and returned it to the Pottery Barn coffee table, anchoring it with an Enrique Iglesias CD. The five hundred dollars was from Ricky's mother, Cynthia. Suddenly the morning fog of Sofia's mind began to clear. There was a story behind this money, a story that broke her heart.

Ricky Lopez came from a working-class Latino family in the Bronx. His mother commuted into Manhattan every day to clean rooms at the Charade, one of the city's most exclusive hotels, and his father delivered produce for a local distributor. Ricky grew up never feeling like he belonged. His superior English skills upset the family order and caused tension, especially between father and son. Another thorny issue was Ricky's pride in his Latin heritage. His father was a Puerto Rican immigrant who thought being Latino was working against him in the United States, so he wanted to get as far away from it as possible, yet he resented Ricky's polished command of English. There was no winning with Juan Lopez.

Ricky's penchant for all things feminine didn't make things any easier. His early passions were dolls, makeup, dancing, and putting on elaborate shows for his mother. He idolized Marlo Thomas, watching reruns of *That Girl* over and over again. Classmates and neighborhood kids taunted him cruelly with fag jokes, and his father did the same when he got drunk, which happened almost every night.

But Ricky took it like a man. He had no tolerance for his father's lunkheaded machismo and hated the way Juan openly cheated on his mother while expecting her to do everything for him. On Ricky's seventeenth birthday, Juan Lopez kicked him out of the house. *That was ten years ago,* Sofia thought sadly, and she knew Ricky hadn't seen or talked to his father since that night.

"Good morning. It's National Ben Estes Day," Ricky said groggily, emerging from the bedroom in a pair of Calvin Klein boxer briefs. His physique was gay male iconography personified: a bronzed, hairless, perfectly triangular form with corded arms and a diamond-hard stomach. He blew her a kiss on his way to the john.

Sofia got up and started the kettle for some tea, her mind still whirling with thoughts of Ricky. What a lonely, isolating situation it was. Sometimes it brought tears to her eyes. Yes, her own father could be insufferable, and granted, occasionally it was best to avoid him for a few days. But when it came right down to it, the safety of his arms was right there to protect her. No matter what. To not have that . . .

"I'm throwing a box of condoms into your Chanel bag before you leave tonight," Ricky said, grabbing a bottle of Evian from the refrigerator. He looked at her and shrugged. "You never know."

Sofia smiled. She loved him like the brother she never had. "Be merciful—don't start in before I drink my morning tea."

"Come on, let me," he teased. "This is probably the last time I'll wake up with you until the day after your *next* wedding."

She regarded him warmly. So often he used humor and bravado as masks to hide the hurt, and Sofia couldn't fault him for whatever deals he needed to make to preserve himself. But for the most part he was happy and whole, a special person who knew how to give and receive love.

Impulsively, she embraced him, and he seemed to be reading her mind because he squeezed tightly in response. "I'm always here for you," Sofia whispered.

"I know, honey," Ricky murmured. "I know."

Ben Estes loped down Fourteenth Street wearing yesterday's clothes and wraparound Oakleys that cloaked heavy-duty party damage. He imagined his eyes were about as clear as the Hudson River. Last night had gotten *way* out of control.

The evening had started like most evenings do— sitting at the bar of Swifty Morgan's with his two best pallies, Taz Jackson, a budding screenwriter, and Kitty Bishop, a promoter who can work a product like a stripper can work a roomful of frat boys—very easily. They'd just started getting loud on a second round of martinis when Charli Grant walked in. *The* Charli Grant.

Ben and Taz had gone completely loco. Seconds into her arrival, they'd been reduced to horny teenage-boy status. They'd bugged out their eyes, elbowed each other, and stared catatonically.

"Jesus Christ, guys," Kitty had complained. "She's *old*. One more face-lift and her eyes will be sitting on her forehead."

"Speaking of Jesus," Ben had replied, raising his gaze to the heavens. *"Thank you, Jesus."*

"Amen, brother," Taz had agreed.

Ben had raised his martini glass in salute. "I had my first orgasm with that woman." He'd punctuated his announcement by downing the rest of his drink.

"I notice you didn't use the word *virginity*," Kitty had pointed out.

"Ah," Ben had begun smugly, "I didn't say she was there. I just said I had my first orgasm with her."

Kitty and Taz had doubled over with laughter.

"What about you, Taz?" Ben had inquired.

"Pam Grier, baby. Foxy Brown made me feel like a man!"

The guys had turned their eyes on Kitty.

"Let me guess," Ben had ventured, scratching his chin to mull the thought over. "Rick Springfield."

Kitty had laughed and shaken her head. "It's not the same with girls," she'd informed them. "You guys can grow orchids out of your birds with a Sears catalog. We're more complex sexual creatures."

"Who were you thinking about?" Ben had pressed, not about to let it go. "Somebody was in that lusty head of yours."

"OK," Kitty had caved. "It was Alan Thicke, the father on *Growing Pains*. But most of the thanks should go to Duracell batteries."

And then they had collapsed into laughter and ordered another round. Kitty had been militant about moving on to other subjects, but Ben hadn't been able to stop stealing glances at the object of his teenage fantasies.

A cacophony of horns blasted in protest to a stalled garbage truck. The noise blasted Ben to consider more urgent matters, like the fact that he was starving. A man couldn't survive on martini olives alone. He decided to duck into a diner and fuel up on eggs, bacon, toast, grits, and pancakes. Besides, he still felt a slight buzz and needed something to soak up the alcohol.

Chowing down, his thoughts drifted back once more to the wild night. He didn't agree with Kitty. Charli Grant looked damn good for her age. Certainly she was in her mid-forties by now. But she didn't look a day over thirty-five.

Back in the eighties she'd been the It girl for a spell, starring in *Malibu Undercover,* a television series about a trio of female agents with special skills. Charli had been the blond martial-arts expert, and there'd also been a brunette disguise artist and a redhead computer genius. But somehow they'd always managed to end up on the beach in bikinis for most of the show.

The first season had been a ratings bonanza, with Charli Grant emerging as the breakout star. Next came the obligatory swimsuit poster that sold in the millions. Ben scooped up some egg yolk with a quarter slice of toast and grinned. He could picture it even now.

Charli in a candy-apple red bikini. Hands on hips. Lips pouty. Hair windblown. Body glistening wet. That poster alone had taught him more than an entire semester of sex education with Mr. Carroll, his eighth-grade gym teacher who hadn't known shit about the subject.

But as fast as she'd risen to the top, Charli Grant had hit rock bottom. At the end of the first season she'd tied the knot with a Svengali twice her age, who tried to muscle the show's producers into doubling her salary—or risk losing her. In a nanosecond the network suits replaced her with another blonde. Shortly after that, Charli's marriage had ended, and since then, there'd been very little written about her. She was just another Hollywood has-been.

Ben's curiosity had been slowly killing him all night. Charli had walked into Swifty Morgan's in a short green number that proved this beyond a doubt: her fame might've headed south, but her body was still in the same place. She'd taken a small table in the corner and immediately began knocking back drinks like a woman who wanted to forget.

"Go talk to her," Taz had encouraged.

"Yeah, don't keep Mrs. Robinson waiting," Kitty had cracked. "The collagen in her lips is down for the count."

Ben had shot Kitty a warning look. Sometimes she had a mean streak that wouldn't quit. Then he'd approached Charli's table with a certain cool, not wanting to come off like some starry-eyed fan or lecherous creep. Small talk turned medium, then large. Suddenly Ben had ditched Taz and Kitty to escort Charli to Copacabana, an ultra-hot dance club where the salsa beats shake the interior like exploding scud missiles.

It'd been total mayhem—throbbing bodies in feverish motion, drinking until flashing strobes were the preferred lighting. They hadn't stopped until dawn. Charli had made it clear that if Ben took her home, his teenage fantasy would become adult reality. He'd been tempted. *Very tempted.* But his inner voice had kicked in with this bit of sexual wisdom: *never sleep with someone who has more problems than you do.* Charli Grant had struck him as a woman with issues he couldn't even begin to comprehend. So as tough as it'd been, he'd hugged the sex symbol like an old school chum and put her in a cab.

Watching the taxi roll away, Ben had known that Taz would never let him live this down. He'd just said no to a lockup with Charli Grant, an opportunity most men would've given up a kidney for. Taz, who viewed sex as a sport and advocated scoring big and often, would definitely have a hard time accepting this turn of events.

"Some fresh biscuits just came out of the oven. I can get you one on the house."

Ben looked up to see a cute waitress smiling down at him with a glint in her eyes that translated, "I get off in an hour." He wiped his mouth with a napkin and shook his head. "No, thanks, baby. I can't eat another bite."

She lingered for a moment.

"Pick up!" the short-order cook cried.

"That's me." She rolled her eyes and giggled.

Ben craned his neck to read her name badge. "You serve up a good breakfast . . . Tiffany. I appreciate it."

"Let me know if you want anything else." Her parting glance left nothing to the imagination.

Sex. Most people assumed Ben had a lot of it. With a lot of different women. But that wasn't the case. In fact, CZ was the last partner he'd had. CZ Rogers, the bitch who'd ripped out his heart, tossed it onto an ice rink, and encouraged her shit-for-brains hockey-playing lover to knock it around like a goddamn puck. But he wasn't bitter.

Ben often wished that he could jump into bed with a willing chick to kill a lonely night, but for him sex had never been so simple. That connection was emotional, intimate, a soul expedition that made him feel naked in every sense of the word. It could be the greatest thing in the world; it could also be the worst.

Even though he couldn't afford it, Ben left Tiffany a twenty-dollar tip and took off for his apartment. His entrance there had to be low profile because he still owed his landlord last month's rent. Tonight's gig at Villa would settle things, and then he could start worrying about this month's rent.

Poverty. It sucked. But being a lawyer sucked

harder. Therein lied the comfort that what he was getting was worth what he was giving up. He loved singing Sinatra's classics. Whenever a performance went well, he left feeling eight-feet tall. And it was worth all the scrapes and hard knocks and lean times to feel that way. Nothing beat it. Nothing.

He ducked into his building in the East Village, his eyes peeled for the landlord. The dishwasher had been broken for two months, so Ben didn't feel too bad giving the guy the slip. The place was a dump. Sometimes he felt like the landlord should pay *him* to stick around. Spotting a shadow turn the corner by the super's office, Ben darted up the stairs, taking them three or four at a time. His long legs made it easy, but he was out of breath by the time he reached the fifth floor.

"Is that you, Estes?" the landlord bellowed.

Stealthily, Ben reached for his keys without jangling them, unlocked the door, and slipped inside. Once safe, he let out a deep breath. This was not his proudest moment. But he couldn't allow that to get him down. Life was full of moments. Better ones were on the way.

He showered, shaved, and slept most of the day, resting up for his evening performance at Villa. As Ben drifted in and out, he remembered setting up a date with that fetching girl he'd met at Berrenger's Market. He decided to add "The Way You Look Tonight" to his set and sing it just for her. No doubt she would turn up looking like a million.

Sofia Cardinella. He liked her style, humor, and attitude, not to mention her looks. What a beauty. Just having her around was good for the environment. Plus, she was sharp—a classy, intelligent broad. A date with her wouldn't be a staring contest.

Cardinella . . . Something about that name rang a bell. He'd heard it bandied about, but he couldn't place the reference. Kitty would know. She knew every name that mattered in the tristate area. Ben made a mental note to ask her as he gave himself up to total sleep. REM sleep. He dreamed about knocking them dead at Villa.

The fact that Ricky was stuck pulling a double shift at Berrenger's mattered not. Sofia didn't need a second opinion. She looked good. One glance at her and Ben Estes would be singing his heart out.

Earlier that day, she'd maxed out her Berrenger's house account for a sexy pair of black lace bell-bottom pants by Gucci—sprayed on from the knee up, flared and billowy from the knee down.

Standing in Ricky's tornado of a bedroom, she checked herself from all angles in the full-length mirror. Her father would freak. The white tube top left her shoulders bare and stopped about an inch above her belly button. Much was on display tonight, and the strappy silver hologram heels pushed her night-vamp ensemble over the edge. It screamed, "Look at me!" And she knew that Ben Estes would do just that.

At the last minute, Sofia decided that she needed a splash of color, so she slipped on a few beaded lounge bracelets and switched her Chanel bag for an orange Miu Miu patent-leather clutch. Transferring contents from one to the other, she came across that box of condoms Ricky had promised to arm her with. The discovery made her laugh. The package was too bulky for the smaller purse. Giggling mischievously, she opened it and tossed in a few, returning the box to Ricky's nightstand.

Before she realized it, Mr. Pickles had upended the stash of rubbers and was darting out of the room with one of the mylar-wrapped love gloves clamped between his teeth. Sofia shook her head. Once that dog set his mind to something, he was impossible to turn around, and right now she didn't have the time to try. But at least Mr. Pickles was into safe sex.

Sofia hailed a cab and instructed the driver to drop her at East Fifty-fourth Street between Madison and Park Avenues. From there she swung out and tottered half a block to Villa, a two-story trattoria with mustard-sponged walls and colorful banners of hardwood trees bearing orange-red fruit draped all around. Hand-made pottery and baskets were stacked and displayed everywhere, giving the place on old-country atmosphere.

Every time she went there, a wave of bittersweet feelings erupted inside her. Villa was Jacqueline Cardinella's favorite restaurant, and Joseph made it a top priority to take the family there each and every Thursday night. Sofia remembered how much fun she and Debi used to have there as children, feasting on baked clams, fried calamari, beef-filled ravioli, cheesecake, and apple tarts. And listening to their mother's sweet, melodious laugh.

Sofia calculated the years in her head, sighing wistfully. She'd been thirteen when her mother passed away, twelve when the cancer took such a toll that Jacqueline preferred not to leave the house. That meant Sofia had spent more years coming to Villa without her than with her. But that didn't matter. It was still her mother's restaurant.

Costas Roselli, whose father had operated Villa

before him, caught her coming in the door and opened his mouth for a thunderous greeting.

Quickly, Sofia placed a finger to her lips before he made a sound, positioning herself behind one of the thick drapes, then motioned him over.

"You cut that lovely hair," he observed in a loud whisper, embracing her warmly and kissing her on both cheeks. "But you're still the most beautiful girl around."

"Thank you, Costas."

"Why are you hiding? Everyone's here."

"I just wanted to observe them for a moment," Sofia explained softly. "Papa's mad at me again."

Costas shook a finger. "Three times, Sofia!" he scolded. "What are you so afraid of?"

"I don't love Vincent!" she hissed. "If my father wants to marry into the Scalia family so badly, then let *him* do the honors. I'll even book their tickets to Vermont. Wouldn't the ceremony be legal there?"

Costas clutched his potbelly and laughed heartily.

"I hear you've added music to the menu. What time does Ben Estes perform?" Sofia asked silkily.

Surprised, Costas merely arched his brow.

"I saw him play at Berrenger's Market. He's *very* good. You should consider a long-term booking before he gets too big."

Costas didn't take the bait. "He talked a good game, just like you're doing. We'll see how tonight goes. He starts in a few minutes. I'll leave you to your spying." He winked and took off to seat an older couple.

Sofia parted the drapes ever so slightly to get a view of the main room. There they were, firmly ensconced at the center table like always, wine flowing, conversation lively. She saw Papa, Fat Larry, Little Bo, Debi, nutty Aunt Rebecca, and . . . Please no . . . It couldn't be . . . *Vincent Scalia!*

The anger started at her toes and blazed a trail straight up to her head, where it began to throb. What was he doing here? *Look at him,* Sofia seethed silently. His short body was sitting in the chair so low that she had a good mind to order up a high chair and have it sent over.

"Pssst," Sofia uttered faintly, knowing Debi would pick up on it as sure as Mr. Pickles picked up on the faintest rustle of a Doritos bag.

Debi looked up from her plate of calamari, spotting Sofia's location immediately. Her sister's sibling radar was state of the art. She muttered something ridiculous about powdering her nose and quickly found her way behind the drapes, doing a double take at the sight of Sofia's outfit.

"Is it too much?" Sofia asked, doubting her attire for the first time.

"No," Debi assured her sincerely. "You look fantastic. Very Heather Locklear."

"Thanks." Sofia snuck another peek at the table, gritting her teeth. "How many times do I have to leave him at the altar before he gets the message?"

"Papa talked him into coming."

"Switch seats with me. I don't want to sit next to him."

"That might be too obvious. I've been here for half an hour."

"Not any more obvious than me skipping our wedding."

Debi opened her hands as if to accept the logic. "This is true."

"I have my first date with Ben later. I don't want to fight with Papa tonight."

"Don't worry. Aunt Rebecca ordered a Long Island Iced Tea, and you know what that means."

Sofia rolled her eyes. "She'll talk about her three ex-husbands and announce that all men are cheating pigs."

"And Papa will demand an apology because he was faithful to Mother."

"And Aunt Rebecca will refuse to give him one; they'll stop speaking, and the evening will be over," Sofia finished.

Debi smiled like one of the Stepford wives. "I love it when the family gets together."

Sofia took in a deep breath, preparing to make her entrance. Then she put a big happy grin on her face and simply went for it.

Papa erupted from his chair immediately. Sure, he was happy to see her, but he was *redressing* her with his eyes, too. Sofia couldn't read his mind, but she knew it had something to do with a higher neckline, pants that weren't skintight and a long, heavy coat.

"Baby bunny!" he exclaimed, wrapping her up in his arms. "I didn't think you were coming."

She kissed him lightly on the lips. "I'd never miss a family dinner. You know that."

He placed her head in his hands and studied her for a moment. "Your sister told me you cut off all your hair."

"It's the new me."

"I love both versions." He released her and extended his hand toward Vincent. "Hey, look who's here—a man who should be on a honeymoon cruise with his wife right now."

"Papa, don't start. *Please.*" She gave the perpetual groom a quick smile. "Hi, Vincent. I hope there are no hard feelings."

Before Vincent could answer, Joseph inserted himself between ex-bride-to-be and ex-groom-to-be, throwing an arm around both. "What are you talking about? There'll never be any hard feelings between the Cardinellas and Scalias. Fuhgeddaboudit!"

Sofia shot a look to Debi, firing a laser beam gaze to Aunt Rebecca's Long Island Iced Tea, already three-quarters down.

Debi picked up on the message and rocketed into action, surreptitiously flagging down the waiter to order a second one. Right now Aunt Rebecca was *almost* looped; pretty soon she would be *all the way* looped.

"Doesn't Sofia look beautiful?" Joseph prodded his dream son-in-law.

Vincent swept her down with a rakish glance, and considering the fact that he was eye-level with her chest, it didn't have far to travel. "Oh, yeah."

Sofia pulled a face.

Joseph turned red. "You've seen enough, Vincent," he snapped. "Sit down and eat."

The Mafia prince reacted as fast and furious as a dutiful soldier.

"Stop trying so hard, Papa," Sofia said. "It's such a waste of time. I'm *never* going to marry him."

"Never say never," Joseph replied tightly.

"I'll choose my own husband, thank you. And for your information, I've got a date tonight. Maybe I'll marry *him*."

"How come I don't know anything about this?"

"For starters, I graduated from high school twelve years ago."

"What's this guy's name?"

"Ben Estes."

"He's not Italian."

"For me that's a plus."

"What kind of work does this Ben do?"

"He's a singer. In fact, he's performing here tonight. Costas was smart enough to book him before he became a big star."

Joseph sighed, shrugged, and contemptuously muttered, "So when's the big date?"

"After dinner."

"Some date. He takes you out after *I* pay for your meal."

Sofia prayed for calm. She could either stand here to squirm and bitch with her father all night, or pig out on beef-filled ravioli. The waiter had just brought her choice to the table. "Guess I better eat your money's worth." She slipped into the seat beside Fat Larry and started to dig in.

"You look like a movie star, Sofia," Fat Larry whispered bashfully.

"You're sweet to say that."

"Hey, Sofia!" Little Bo called from the other side of Fat Larry. "You look like a movie star."

She smiled. "Fat Larry was just—"

"I already told her that," Fat Larry interjected.

Suddenly a flush started at Little Bo's neck and painted his entire face red. "You stole that from me! I told you she looked like a movie star the second I saw her tonight."

"Get outta here!" Fat Larry argued. "I was thinking that before you opened your big mouth."

"Not a chance!"

"Oh, so you're one of them telephone psychics? You know what I'm thinking, now?"

Sofia turned back to concentrate on her food, knowing those two would be arguing for the rest of the night.

Before Papa took them on to run errands and see about family interests, Fat Larry and Little Bo had been fired from every Mafia family on the East Coast. With their buzz cuts and old suits that smacked of the seventies, they were the laughingstock of the underworld. But these goons were devoted to her father. In fact, there was nothing they wouldn't do for him. Fat Larry was short and skinny, and Little Bo was tall and rotund. They'd been around for as long as Sofia could remember.

The lights dimmed, a spotlight hit the floor, and Costas stepped into the beam. "Ladies and gentlemen, have I got a treat for you tonight. Please welcome, Mr. Ben Estes!"

After a moment of hesitation came a smattering of applause.

Ben sauntered into view.

There were several gasps—all female. Sofia was one of them. *He looks incredible,* she thought. Oh, God, did this man have charisma! And it hit her like a blowtorch.

"I want to sing this first number to a beautiful little baby I just met. I've been watching her from the bar, and let me tell you, that's nice work if you can get it. This one's for you, Sofia."

Lush strings filled the restaurant.

Sofia stopped breathing.

Ben began to sing slowly, with perfect pitch and on-the-sleeve eroticism, "The Way You Look Tonight."

She felt swept in, like a powerful wave had crested and broken and thrown her onto some magical beach.

"You've got a date with this creep?" Joseph shouted.

Sofia was horrified. *"Shut up!"* she hissed, trying to keep it down but ending up just as loud, if not louder.

"He's trying to be like Frank Sinatra!" Joseph continued.

This time Debi turned on him. "Papa, this isn't *Showtime at the Apollo.* Show some respect."

"He sucks," Vincent chimed in.

Sofia shot over a venomous look.

Suddenly Aunt Rebecca's fist hit the table with an almighty crash. "Those bastards had no shame! They brought their whores into my bedroom all those years while I was caring for my sick mother! Men are cheating pigs!"

Sofia shut her eyes. *This isn't happening,* she tried to convince herself.

"Take that back! I never cheated on Jacqueline!" Joseph screamed.

"This is *so* happening," Sofia whispered miserably.

Ever the trouper, Ben plugged along, finishing up his dedication to Sofia and moving on to "My Kind of Town."

That's when Joseph went ballistic. "It's the musical equivalent of flag burning! Frank Sinatra is sacred! Who is this poser? I want that son of a bitch to put a stop to this crap right now. Where's Costas? Go get me Costas!"

Fat Larry and Little Bo were up and on the hunt.

Sofia wanted to crawl under the table.

Costas showed up with a bottle of wine.

"How many years have I been bringing my family to Villa?" Joseph demanded.

"At least twenty-five," Costas answered.

Joseph jabbed his finger toward Ben. "That cheap lounge act makes me never want to set foot in here again!"

"For you, Joe, he's history," Costas said. "He'll

never sing here again. I won't even let him eat here. I won't even let him get takeout here."

Joseph nodded. "We all make mistakes." He patted Costas's cheek. "Stop that piece of shit right now, eh? Let a man's family eat in peace."

"Papa, this is awful!" Sofia protested.

"You're damn right it's awful!" Joseph countered.

Slicing his finger across his neck, Costas mouthed the word, "Cut," and stepped directly in front of Ben. Seconds later the music stopped, and they ended up in a hushed huddle at the bar.

"Thank God this family doesn't love opera. Can you imagine us at the Met?" Debi wondered.

Seething, Sofia turned to her father. "That is the rudest display of behavior I've ever seen!"

Joseph slapped his chest and glanced around as if to address the whole restaurant when he said, "She doesn't show up for her own weddings and *I'm* rude! Ain't that a kick in the ass!"

"Who cares if that kid wants to sing Sinatra?" Aunt Rebecca put in. "Frank Sinatra was a cheating pig, too!"

Fat Larry and Little Bo finally returned. The shuffling lunks ambled over to Joseph's chair. "We can't find Costas nowhere, boss," Fat Larry announced.

Joseph shook his head. "It's taken care of, fellas. But thanks."

Sofia stood up. Damn Papa and his religious worship of Ol' Blue Eyes!

"Where are you going?" Joseph demanded.

"On a date, I hope, assuming Ben hasn't fled the city. Don't think I'm not considering it."

"You're still going out with that lowlife?"

"Papa, Ben Estes is going to be a star, so you better get used to him belting out songs made famous by your precious Sinatra, because he'll be doing a lot of it!''

"He'll never sing in this town again!" Joseph threatened.

"What are you going to do? Blacklist him from your bingo parlors?" Sofia taunted.

"You should put out a hit on that jerk," Vincent put in. "You know, make him sleep with the fishes."

Sofia reached out and slapped Vincent on the back of the head. "Oh, shut up. The only reason you don't like him is because he's six-foot-five."

Joseph Cardinella scratched his chin, taking the suggestion into serious consideration. "Vincent's right," he said finally. "That guy needs to disappear."

"Papa," Debi began dryly, "we have a few gambling interests and construction companies. The seediest thing you get involved in is a nice contribution to the right councilman's campaign."

"What's your point?" Joseph asked.

"This isn't *The Godfather,*" Debi said.

"More like *One Flew Over the Cuckoo's Nest,*" Sofia scoffed.

"Are you saying I ain't got the balls to rub somebody out?" Joseph asked angrily. "That singer's days are numbered. Just you watch."

Sofia walked away, hoping the death-threat hemorrhage would stop with her out of the picture. She felt strangely unsettled, more than usual after a family dinner, which always ended in a ruckus, though usually not as bad as tonight. The look on Papa's face, the sound of his voice . . . It was very troubling. He had something to prove, and that could be dangerous.

She found Ben at the bar. He was flanked by a handsome black man and a saucy-looking redhead. They were all making martinis disappear.

"Hey, baby," Ben said. He tried to be cool, but there was genuine hurt in his languid bedroom eyes. "These are my best pallies, Taz Jackson and Kitty Bishop."

The introductions went back and forth. Sofia liked Taz immediately. He was warm, and his excitement about the screenplay he was writing, an all-black science-fiction film that he described as *"Shaft* meets *Star Wars,"* proved infectious. Kitty, on the other hand, came off as icy and disapproving. But Sofia knew the type. The platonic female buddy of a cluster of guys was a potential new girlfriend's worst enemy.

Once the conversation hit a lull, Sofia navigated Ben over to the side for a private exchange. She couldn't believe it. He'd just been yanked off the stage in the middle of his second number, yet his raw intensity, sexiness, authority, and sophistication were still so potent. His appeal was like a drug.

"I'm sorry about my family. What can I say? They're nuts."

"Don't worry," he assured her. "Rotten gigs build character. One day I'll look back on it and laugh."

"My father wants to kill you," Sofia said abruptly, thinking there was no good time to make such announcements.

Ben shrugged. "Not a problem. I'm used to parents wanting to kill me. Right now even my own parents want to kill me."

"No. He *really* wants to kill you."

He paused a beat. "I should've opened with 'Luck Be a Lady.' "

Chapter Four

"Wait a minute," Kitty bellowed accusingly, elbowing her way between Sofia and Ben. "Now I know where I've heard your name." She turned to Ben now. "This girl's a *Cardinella*. Her father's a gangster!"

Ben looked at Kitty, then back at Sofia. "Is this true?"

Sofia blanched. "She says it like he's Al Capone. Forget everything you've seen on *The Sopranos*. My father is no more dangerous than the Teletubbies."

Ben's eyes went wide. "So he is a gangster."

Sofia shot an annoyed glance at Kitty. Honestly! As if the night wasn't bad enough. *"Discreet businessman.* Think of him as Mafia lite."

"But you just said he wants to kill me."

"He does, but he put Fat Larry and Little Bo on the job, and those two couldn't rub out a suicidal man ready to jump from the World Trade Center. Trust me. There's nothing to worry about."

Costas approached, his face long with apology. "I'm sorry tonight didn't work out." He placed a comforting hand on Ben's shoulder. "I need you and your friends to get lost. Nothing personal. One of my important regulars is making a lot of noise." Reluctantly, Costas made eye contact with Sofia.

She seized the moment. "Ben is talented, and you know it. I got chills listening to him tonight."

"If I were in an outfit like yours, I'd get chills, too," Kitty cracked.

Sofia glared.

Costas shrugged as if to say, "What can I do?" Then he sighed heavily. "He's got a real singer's voice, that's for sure. I'll make a few calls, see if I can scare up a gig at another joint."

Ben nodded his thanks. "That'd be great. You're a pal."

Costas gestured toward the exit. "Now make *my* life easier, kid. Don't drag your feet on your way out of here."

Ben took Sofia's hand. "So, Mafia princess, what are your plans for the night?"

The tingle that his touch triggered took her by surprise. "I'm supposed to have a drink with this swell guy."

"Is that so?" His smirk was cocky, but not too cocky. "I'm taking you to Swifty Morgan's—my third favorite place on earth."

"What's your first?"

"Any stage with a spotlight and a microphone."

"And your second?"

"My bed." He made deliberate eye contact.

Sofia's cheeks glowed with a slow, warm heat.

"Let's go." And then he swooped his arm around

her waist, ushering her toward the door for a speedy
escape.

Sofia spun fast, locking a defiant, triumphant gaze
on her father.

Ben held the door and checked her out as she
passed through it. He was such a guy. She loved that
about him.

With Taz and Kitty several steps ahead, Sofia leaned
in to whisper, "I don't think Kitty likes me."

"I don't think Kitty likes anyone," Ben said easily.
"She's a tough broad; grew up hard. Her mom's a
wacko, her dad's a deadbeat, and she got passed
around by one sorry relative after another."

"That's awful."

Ben shrugged. "It's the hand she was dealt. But
Kitty's done OK for herself. She's a survivor."

"Like Cher," Sofia offered earnestly.

Ben laughed. "Yeah, like Cher. What's the old joke?
The only things left after a nuclear holocaust will be
cockroaches and Cher. Well, add Kitty Bishop to that
short list."

Sofia slipped her arm through his, giggling softly.

"Hey, Taz!" Ben shouted. "Hail us a cab!"

"What do think this is—*Mission: Impossible?* A black
man can't get a cab in New York!" Taz fired back the
sad truth with such good-natured, self-deprecating
humor that everyone laughed with him.

Just then Kitty hit the street with a hip-sprocket
gait, letting out an ear-piercing whistle.

"Shazam!" Ben exclaimed, just as a taxi screeched
to a *halt.*

"You guys are fun," Sofia *raved.*

Ben winked. *"Baby, this is only the warm-up show."*

* * *

The bleary-eyed patrons of Swifty Morgan's greeted Ben like a soldier returning from a long war.

"You lousy drunks," Kitty blasted them. "Where's your sense of time? He just left this dump a few hours ago."

They all cracked up, jazzed by the ribbing. A stool warmer giving off strong Buddy Hackett vibrations shot off at the mouth with, "A lot of nerve you got calling us drunks. What are you here for—the food?"

Kitty gestured to the bartender with a familiar wink. "My job is to make sure Jilly here stays current on his martini training. It's important work. And they say party girls don't contribute to society."

Jilly eyed the ballsy dame with equal parts lust, fear, and hurt.

Kitty turned to Sofia. "Can you handle a martini, honey, or should we start you out with a banana daiquiri?"

Sofia glowered. Friend of Ben's or not, this bitch had gone too far for one night. "Make that two," she answered sweetly. "One for me and the other to pour over your head."

Kitty sucked in a breath, momentarily speechless.

Ben and Taz lost it. So did the rest of the regulars.

"Baby, I think you're going to fit in just fine," Ben murmured, wrapping an arm around Sofia's waist and pulling her close.

Kitty's glare promised retaliation. But for now she spun quickly to face the bartender. "You're not pretty enough to just stand there like scenery," she snapped. "Make us some drinks."

"Didn't you get my messages?" Jilly asked. "I left several on your machine."

"No shit," Kitty said. "By the way, leaving more than two qualifies you for stalker of the week."

"I thought we had a good time."

"You sound like a lovesick girl, Jilly."

"I just thought!—"

"I never imagined a twenty-six-year-old bartender with a big dick would think so much. Where I come from, men like you just want to serve liquor and get laid. My mistake. I got the only sensitive one in New York."

"Damn, Kitty," Taz admonished her. "Give the man a break."

"Oh, please. Like you gave *your* class ring to any of the girls *you* took home last week. At least I pass along a real phone number."

"That happened once," Taz protested weakly. "Well . . . maybe a few times." He shrugged, then offered a guilty grin. "Hey, I'm dyslexic."

"Yeah, right," Kitty challenged. "That's a pretty convenient disability, wouldn't you say?"

Sofia leaned in toward Ben to whisper, "Are they always like this?"

"No," he assured her. "Sometimes they're mean to each other."

She felt her eyes grow big.

Ben smiled, splayed out his large hand to manage two martinis between fingers, and with his free one piloted her to a cozy banquette in the corner.

Almost on reflex, Sofia slipped stealthy fingers inside her Miu Miu clutch to retrieve the pack of cigarettes nestled inside. Quite suddenly, she thought better of it, peering up at Ben. "Maybe you should kiss me now."

His forehead creased. "What?"

She flashed the cigarettes—exhibit A in her stylish court of silly reasoning. "I'm dying for one of these, and one might lead to two, maybe three. Yes, I've got Altoids, but there's a limit to what those can do for a girl. Close your eyes and you might think you're kissing the Marlboro Man. Now that would work for my friend Ricky, but I'm thinking you're completely straight." She drew back. "You're not bisexual, are you?"

He seemed amused. "No, I'm not."

"Just checking."

He laughed.

"What's so funny?"

"You are. Don't worry. I only get my kicks with chicks."

"In all honesty, I'm of the opinion that bisexuality is just . . . I don't know . . . *greedy*. Not to mention the indecisiveness of it all. Think about it. Say I was a single, bisexual woman. Are you with me?"

Ben smirked. "I'm getting a picture."

She narrowed her gaze suspiciously for a moment, then moved on. "OK, here's the scenario—I'm at a party with Brad Pitt and Charlize Theron and they're both hitting on me. How do I make that choice? I mean, before going out tonight I had a whale of a time just picking out a handbag. Imagine trying to decide between Brad and Charlize. It would drive me to madness!" She took a sip of her martini and paused earnestly. "Have you ever known a bisexual person?"

"I don't think so," Ben said. "I've known some confused guys. And Kitty went home with a swinging couple once. Does that count?"

Sofia rolled her eyes with good humor. "No, I'm talking about a full-fledged bisexual."

"Are you leading up to some kind of announcement?"

She did a double take. "What? No! Don't be silly. I've seen the movie *Personal Best* with Mariel Hemingway. That's the closest I've come to being with a woman." By habit, she realized, a cigarette had been rescued from the pack. The lighter had been retrieved as well.

Ben's gaze bounced from her bad habit to her sparkling eyes. "Are you going to smoke that?"

"I might."

"What about my tobacco-free kiss?"

"There seems to be a holdup on that, and I'm not the kind of girl who likes to sit around like furniture." She snapped her fingers. "I want things to happen."

He inched closer. "If you'd shut up about bisexuals long enough, maybe something would happen."

She closed her eyes. "OK, this is me pausing romantically."

And then Sofia felt the incredible heat—one hand on her waist, another hand cupping her cheek, a soft kiss trapping her lower lip for a very deliberate, very sensual prolonged moment. The warmth of his hand burned through her black lace Gucci pants, his fingertips like flickering flames on her inner thigh. She wanted the erotic sensations to stretch on and on.

In the background party people laughed and drank. From the jukebox Tony Bennett sang about leaving his heart somewhere. Indianapolis maybe. It really didn't matter. Because inside Sofia's chest, her heart was going chitty chitty bang bang. *Wow. This guy can kiss. Like a champ.* If the singing career hit a snag, he could always set up a booth in Times Square.

There was no clumsy positioning, no awkward negotiations of head tilts and body alignments. Oh, yes, this was meant to be. Sofia Cardinella had been born to make out with Ben Estes. Guys in the past had squashed her nose, or slobbered on her chin, or used their tongues like an offshore drilling rig. Not this one. He did everything to perfection. And even better, it was effortless.

The playful little bites to her lower lip were still going strong. She played along, using her lips to capture his upper one. It was an intricate, delicate dance, the pleasure heightened by the occasional sweep of hot, disciplined tongues.

His hand dropped from her cheek to cradle the back of her neck, yet his other one remained in position, secure in its hip-to-thigh placement, making no move to up the ante. Relaxed like never before, Sofia entered a hypnotic, trancelike zone. As far as she was concerned, he could have this kiss forever.

Tony Bennett's song was over, and Dean Martin had already crooned. So had Ella Fitzgerald and Peggy Lee. Even Mel Torme had done his thing. Frank Sinatra, of course, had belted out a few numbers, too. How long, she suddenly wondered, had they been canoodling like this?

Ben seemed to sense her distraction. He kissed her nose and pulled back, ever so slightly, letting out a little laugh, revealing gorgeous teeth.

Oh, God, was he prettier than she was? Quite possibly, yes. But he didn't seem to be aware of it. That was good. She made the quick decision to file this realization under THINGS HE SHOULD NEVER KNOW.

He looked around the bar, then moved in to playfully nip at her earlobe. "We don't have to stop," he whispered seductively. "Nobody's watching us. They're all getting drunk and having a great time."

Just as she began to check things out for herself,

he slipped his tongue into her ear. The wonderful feeling triggered an involuntary gasp. Ben was right about nobody watching. She saw Taz in the corner, chatting up a tall redhead with enormous boobs. Kitty, meanwhile, had joined a group of old-timers for what looked like strip poker. The poor codgers were shirtless. She was fully clothed and draped in the supremely confident attitude that she wouldn't have to doff so much as the Escada scarf around her neck.

Speaking of necks, Ben had moved to hers now in a way that was driving her crazy. So much for her personal policy against public displays of affection. The right candidate had come along and changed her view on the issue. After tonight, she could see herself marching for PDA rights.

Ben stopped for a moment to nurse his martini. "I barely need this. You're intoxicating enough." He grinned. "But I hate to see a good drink go to waste."

She regarded him with something close to awe. "Is your whole life a party?"

"Most of it. I don't count the being too broke to pay my rent, of course. That part is pretty much a drag."

A vision of her father's horrible histrionics flashed in her mind, followed by a torrent of guilt. "I'm sorry about the fiasco at Villa tonight."

Ben looked around, as if spooked. "Should I get some muscle to shadow me for a while?"

"I'll protect you," Sofia said, aping a fierce stance. Then she turned serious. "Costas doesn't toss promises around casually. If he says he's going to line up another engagement for you, he will."

Ben didn't look convinced. "We'll see." He finished off his martini and pensively ate the olive. "You don't seem too hung up on success and money and all that jazz."

She fingered the stem of her glass. "How can I be? All I do is work behind a makeup counter."

"So we're a good match," Ben joked. "The struggling lounge singer and the lipstick girl."

Her mouth fell open. "I didn't mean it that way."

"I'm teasing you."

"I really think what you do is amazing. It takes more courage than putting on a suit and showing up at an office like the rest of the world."

He reached for her hand and squeezed it. "Thanks. But keep what I do in perspective. I'm not suffering for Bosnia."

Sofia shook her head resolutely. "It's incredibly brave. That awful woman in Berrenger's Market would rather have seen a dog chase his tail than hear you sing, and my father thought you were so distasteful that he forced Costas to make you stop."

"OK, it's been an off week," he deadpanned.

"My point is that you put yourself out there. You expose yourself to those potential humiliations. Most people don't do that. They keep all their little dreams locked up inside. At least you give it a shot."

His stare was long and approving. "When can I see you again?"

She decided to play coy. "You're seeing me right now."

"Yeah, but I'm already looking forward to the next time."

A nervous feeling officially set in. Why? Because the complications were stacking fast. A fun, easy first date. Maybe too good to be true. Kissing that was off the charts. Again, too good to be true. Early talk of a second date. What about the part where she's supposed to wait around, wondering if he'll call? And then there were the external forces—her father hating him, his best friend hating her. Those last two developments were so very *Dawson's Creek.*

Sofia needed a cigarette. Bad. She lit one and took a drag before he had a chance to talk her out of it. Then she apologized. "Sorry. I know it's gross. But I limit myself to no more than six a day. When you think about the people who smoke a couple of packs, it doesn't even count really." She knew her rationalization was lame but let it ride anyway.

His gaze fell on the pack.

Sofia knew the look—covetous. She displayed it every time she passed a store that sold Manolo Blahniks.

"Mind if I bum one of those?"

"You smoke, too?"

"Actually, I quit about a year ago."

"But I'd feel terrible if you started up again."

"Then maybe you should quit, too," he reasoned.

Sofia took a serious drag on that one. "I haven't had *that* much to drink. But nice try."

Ben reached for the pack and tapped out a cigarette.

She watched him light it. She watched him bring it to those talented lips. "Wait!"

"For what?"

"Have you really been clean for a year?"

He merely smiled.

"You can't start again."

"Why not? I promise to stop if I get pregnant."

She laughed and moved quickly to stub hers out before the weaker part of her demonstrated its will. "OK, you win."

"Do you mind if I enjoy just this one? It's been so long."

Sofia searched his incredible eyes and saw laughter in them. "So you guilt me into quitting and then you cave in?"

He snuffed it out. "Have another drink with me. A real one."

She glanced at her martini, almost empty. Its effect had hit her already, hence the little buzz humming around her. "I can't keep up with you."

"Don't sell yourself short, baby. You can keep up with anyone." Ben raised a hand to catch Jilly's attention, showing him two fingers and the thumbs-up sign in a single ice-cool movement.

"Jilly seems like a neat guy," Sofia ventured, watching him work on Ben's order with all the precision of a nuclear scientist. "Kitty should give him a chance."

"No way," Ben said. "Kitty's a barracuda. Jilly's a guppy."

"Oh, I don't think that's true. Maybe she just wants somebody to love her, to treat her nicely."

He regarded her with mild amusement. "Kitty eats the Jillys of the world for a midnight snack. In ten years he might be able to take her on, but he needs some experience first. A broken heart wouldn't hurt. Look over there."

Sofia followed his gaze. The strip poker game was down for the count. All the geezers were in their boxers. Kitty had only lost a shoe. The mere sight brought on a fit of giggles.

Ben smiled at her, leaned back, and stroked his lower lip with his thumbnail. Then he reached into his right coat pocket and pulled out a loose cigarette and a little gold Dunhill lighter.

She gasped incredulously. "You told me that you quit a year ago!"

"I did quit a year ago," he said easily, opening the flame and artfully lighting the stick. "I also quit last week. I quit every night, actually." He shrugged, took a drag, and grinned. "It just doesn't take."

Sofia reached for her pack and lit up, too. "I can't believe you!" she roared. "I wasted a perfectly good cigarette."

"These are my rules—never smoke before nightfall and never take more than four drags."

"Oh, listen to the surgeon general over here."

Ben chuckled. "You're funny. And you're beautiful. That's a killer combination. I could fall hard for you."

The words knocked her out. She felt a strange sensation, as if oxygen had been removed from her lungs.

Thankfully, Jilly showed up with the drinks. "Just the way you like it," he said, landing two traditional rock glasses on the table. "Two fingers of Jack Daniel's, four ice cubes, and the rest water."

"You're a pal," Ben said.

Sofia reached for her drink. After his last announcement, she needed one.

But Ben put a hand over her glass. "Let it die down. Once the ice sinks in the flavors blend."

Jilly hovered, grinning at Ben with something close to hero-worship. "Who's the girl?" he finally asked.

Ben brought a proprietary hand to Sofia, massaging the back of her neck. "Sofia Cardinella." He turned to her. "Did I say that right?"

She nodded eagerly, feeling like a fan, too. This man had major league charisma.

Jilly leaned in to Ben with this review, sotto voce: "She's money."

"Any girl that sweetens up a group shot can be money. This chick's the federal reserve," Ben said.

Sofia merely sat there, feeling a bit dim. Working without a glossary, she could only assume that being compared to the system that regulated the nation's money supply was a good thing. It sure beat a piggy bank.

What was Ben? she wondered, attempting to turn the tables in her mind. Suddenly it hit her. This guy was Wall Street. And considering the fact that only days ago she had been booked to marry Vincent Scalia, trading was definitely up.

Chapter Five

The shrill ring of the telephone blasted him awake. He rented one of those old-fashioned numbers— ugly, loud, and from decades past. It never gave him static or ran low on battery juice like those cordless toys. As he crawled across the bed toward his nightstand, he wondered who the hell it could be. Nobody he knew used a phone before noon. Except bill collectors.

On that thought, he considered letting it ring. But he couldn't take the noise another second. "Hello," he managed, his voice thick with last night's good times.

"You can't say I'm not a man of my word. This is Costas from Villa. I've got a gig for you."

Ben rubbed his eyes and tried to focus on the clock. It was nine. Jesus. Didn't people sleep anymore? He sighed. "Let me guess—Carnegie Hall."

"Show some gratitude, wiseass."

"First things first. Where is this gig?"

"A club called Chalkboard. Ask for Manny."

Ben's eyes did an instant roll. "That place is a dive. I could get *you* a gig there."

"I don't sing," Costas said hotly.

"Exactly my point." Ben rolled over onto his back and stretched. "Every night is amateur night there. I bet it doesn't pay much, if at all."

"Manny said he'd negotiate."

"I know Manny. That means a free beer. I couldn't even get a real drink out of the deal. Forget it."

Costas fumed in a long second of silence. "You've got a lot of nerve, kid."

Ben didn't skip a beat. "So do you, pops. A good sleep was interrupted for this. Now round up a decent gig. Then we'll be even."

"Even?" Costas spluttered. "I don't owe you shit!"

Ben zeroed in on the envelope of cash sitting on his dresser. "You shorted me last night. I didn't want to say anything in front of Sofia. She thinks the world of you."

"You sang one song! Why should I pay the whole booking fee?"

"One and a half songs to be exact. But that's beside the point. *You* pulled the plug. I would've done the whole set."

Costas muttered something in Italian. Whatever it was, it sounded profane. "Come to the restaurant and get the rest of your money."

"Cool. Now don't put off finding me a gig. I've got bills to pay."

"Hold on, kid," Costas began incredulously. "I'm settling up on your fee, and you still expect me to hunt you down a job?"

"Hey, it's the decent thing to do," Ben reasoned.

"After all, you cheated me last night, and I covered it up so you wouldn't look like a rat in front of Sofia. Obviously, I'm a nice guy."

"You're a pain in the ass!"

Ben shrugged. "By the way, I prefer Manhattan. Don't line up anything in Jersey. The train's murder on my tux."

Costas screamed something in Italian again. Then he hung up.

Ben replaced the receiver and just remained horizontal, revolving the closing events of the previous night in his mind. The image of Sofia brought on a smile, not to mention an early morning erection. He was officially up now. The sheet covering his body looked like a tent. He threw it off and lay there naked, remembering.

After two drinks, the girl had been looped. But she was a cute drunk—thank God. Some broads turned into Godzilla's sister when they tied too many on. He'd hailed a cab, listened to Sofia sing "I Will Survive" (the tone-deaf version) in the cabin, walked her upstairs, and smiled through a cool reception from the gay best friend. Then he'd gone back to Swifty Morgan's for more action, deflected envious praise from the regulars about his latest cuddle up, and cleaned out Kitty's poker winnings in one game of five-card stud. He'd been motivated on account of the fact that she'd been a bitch to his date. Yeah, it'd been a good night. A real gas.

He sighed, considering the day ahead. By the time he got going it would be too late for breakfast and too early for lunch. But he'd better scram before the landlord started pounding on the door. Unfortunately, the rent would have to wait until he got the rest of his cash from Costas. A minor delay.

Ben jumped into the shower. He took no fewer than two a day. Sometimes more. That's what a guy had to do to stay clean in New York. With his favorite towel looped around his waist, he headed for his tiny but meticulously organized closet. Everything hung together in categories. Sweaters were carefully folded on shelves, shoe trees lined the floor, and an impressive collection of conservative Sulka silk ties neatly filled a rack affixed to the back of the door.

Taz always gave him hell about his closet. "Damn, you must be the only cat in New York who doesn't own a pair of jeans!" he'd exclaimed once after running a quick inventory.

"Jeans are for boys," Ben had told him then and would tell anyone now. "I'm a man, and I dress jazzy, snazzy, and razmatazzy!"

He selected an orange sport shirt and slipped on a pair of khaki slacks—steamed (he owned a professional one), pressed (best thing his mother ever taught him), and pleated (mom again, a real peach) to perfection. Nothing went to the dry cleaners. It was an evil industry. The tobacco companies were pussycats by comparison.

His black shoes—a great pair of slip-ons by Jil Sander—were freshly shined (every Monday courtesy of Sam on Fifty-eighth Street) but needed a final buff before stepping out. He took turns rubbing his feet under the couch cushions until satisfied. Then he hit the door, a thing of beauty if he did say so himself.

One polished toe outside his apartment, he heard heavy steps on the stairs. The sound smacked suspiciously of impatient landlord. He swung back in for cover, taking a peek to make sure.

Two lunkheads landed on the top. Something about them rang a bell. Holy shit! They were the same guys who had been flanking Sofia's father at Villa last night. What the fuck were they doing here? Suddenly Ben put it all together, his stomach falling faster than Planet Hollywood stock.

They stopped in front of the door across the hall, looking like two wrestlers in bad suits. Unfortunate either way. So being down on both counts was just tragic.

Big sigh. Maybe all this was just a coincidence.

But what could they want with Connie Patterson? She didn't get out much and seemed to live on a steady diet of bad Chinese food (from Golden Temple down the street) and bad talk shows (Maury Povich and Montel Williams).

The three knocks were so loud he could feel them in his chest.

"Who the hell are you?" Connie was never big on idle chatter.

"I'm Fat Larry," the short one announced. "This is my associate, Little Bo."

"Why should I care?" Testy.

"We're looking for Ben Estes. He's a singer. Tall guy," Fat Larry explained.

"Do I look like a Ben Estes?" Testier.

"Could you point out his apartment? A neighbor downstairs said he lived on this floor."

"Some eggrolls might help me remember. Otherwise, it's a total block." *Stupid. Eggrolls are what, a dollar?*

Little Bo craned his neck closer, as if seeking to understand. "Are you saying we should buy you some Chinese food to get this information?"

"Damn, you oughta go on that millionaire quiz show." *Better.*

And then the door slammed shut, followed by the click of the deadbolt.

Ben sucked in a breath.

"We might want to talk to the boss," Fat Larry said.

"Yeah, make sure he don't object to us spending that kind of money on information," Little Bo agreed.

Ben felt disbelief register on his face. These guys had to get permission to fork out two dollars? He knew toddlers with bigger budgets.

"Who won the toss?" Little Bo asked. "I forgot."

Fat Larry grinned. "I did."

"You nervous?"

Fat Larry displayed no outward signs of it. "I shoot. He falls down. We run like hell. Piece of cake."

Ben's heart seemed to freeze midbeat.

"Did you bring the silencer?" Little Bo inquired.

Now the rest of his body turned to ice.

"I want my lips to have that Jennifer Lopez look."

Sofia massaged her temples with her fingertips. "Not so loud, honey." But the throbbing thundered on. At least the nausea had passed. Maybe Kitty was right. Banana daiquiris had never done this much damage.

"And I want my eyes to have that Ashley Judd look."

Sofia tossed an annoyed glance to the woman whose face had that Regis Philbin look. *I sell makeup, not denial.* It was in her head, almost out of her mouth, but in the end, her edit button came through.

"How does Gwyneth Paltrow get those cheekbones?"

Sofia gave up a dumb look. "Not with blush."

"Huh?"

She could spot a counter-squatter at twenty paces.

They talked incessantly, asked too many questions, played with all the testers, and never bought a damn thing. An Aspen girl needed commission to make her world go-round. Why couldn't this dreamer park it at Estée Lauder?

"Can I put this on your Berrenger's charge?" Ricky asked in a triumphant singsong, stealing a glance at Sofia. He whizzed past her on the way to the register. *"Huge* sale."

The little shit.

When the telephone jangled, she lurched for it immediately, thankful for the diversion. "Aspen Cosmetics."

"Hi, I'm in a cab. I should be there in a few minutes." It was Debi.

"Oh, look for my silver compact. I think I lost.it in the taxi last night."

"I'm sure this isn't the same car. We're in New York, not Petticoat Junction."

"What's your driver's name?"

"I don't know, but it has at least fifteen consonants. And apparently his shifts last longer than his deodorant."

Sofia giggled.

"How was the rest of your date?"

"Amazing. We kissed for almost an hour. Then he got me drunk."

"Now that's romance."

"It *was.* It *is.*" Sofia sighed dreamily. "I can't wait to see him again. Can you imagine going on a first date and *not* spending the entire night listening to a guy talk about himself?"

"I can't even imagine the first-date part."

"Oh, stop it," Sofia insisted.

"Hey, noticing behavioral patterns requires frequency."

"Well, trust me then, most guys—and Ben is the rare exception—can talk about themselves all night."

"That reminds me of Irving Grey. Remember him?"

Sofia tried to place the name. "The police officer you dated that summer?"

"Not quite. But I guess he *was* in law enforcement. He worked as a security guard at Tiffany's. One night he said, 'Enough about me. Let's talk about you. What do *you* think about me?' "

"How awful. Why do men think they're so fascinating?"

"I blame the blow job," Debi said. "If they believe women find *that* interesting, they'll find merit in anything."

Sofia laughed again. She adored conversations with her sister. "I want you to meet Ben. You'll love him. He'll love you." Then she got quiet as a familiar anger bubbled up. "Papa won't be part of the lovefest, of course. God, he was insufferable last night."

"Since you brought it up," Debi ventured carefully, "Ben is going to be a hard sell, no matter how wonderful you think he is. Papa had fewer issues with Luke Romano."

"But that thug robbed a convenience store!" Sofia exclaimed. And then she downloaded a mental image of her tattooed, bad-boy, high school love. In the classroom—dumb as a stump. In the kip—valedictorian. Besides, at seventeen, who cared about a guy's ability to hold his own at a party if Marxism came up? Yes, roughnecks definitely had their place in a girl's life. Preferably, a brief one, but a place nonetheless. "Papa needs to see a pharmacist."

"We've known this for some time," Debi pointed out.

Sofia groaned.

"When are you moving back home? It's been almost a week."

She glanced up at Ricky to see him talking trash with the girl across the aisle at La Prairie. "Soon. Last night I threw up on Ricky's couch after Ben dropped me off. And this was after Mr. Pickles made a mess on his favorite rug. He didn't mean to. I think it was separation anxiety."

"So what's your excuse?"

"I obviously have a drinking problem."

"Do you mind if I hang up now? This call has probably cost me twelve dollars. Anyway, the driver just cut in front of a garbage truck to let me off at the door. Now he's giving someone the finger. There should be a law against raising that arm. He could take out the whole block."

"Oh, just pay the man and get in here," Sofia demanded, laughing and shaking her head as she hung up. Finally, her hangover seemed to be subsiding. She could actually imagine eating food again.

The telephone rang once more. This time it didn't sound like a sonic scream inside her head. How did Ben and his crew do what they did *every* night? "Hello," she said very casually, quite absently.

"Sofia, don't you mean *Aspen Cosmetics?*" Oh, shit. It was Rachel Martin, the company's national account representative. All she cared about were sales per hour. A real number cruncher. Total bore.

"Sorry, Rachel. I was distracted."

"How would you like to be *distracted* for several days?"

"What?"

Rachel paused a beat. "On a beach in Carmel."

"Oh, my God!" Sofia felt a wonderful tingling all over. Adrenaline surged. Thoughts of the Honesty fragrance contest had completely slipped her mind.

"You won by a healthy margin," Rachel informed her. "The runner-up was seventy-six units behind. Excellent work."

"I'm in shock," Sofia gushed. "I've never won anything! And you know what? I've never been to California, either. This is fabulous! It's more than fabulous!

"Carmel is beautiful. It's also home to one of Aspen's most profitable counters."

"Oh, really?" Sofia attempted, trying to appear interested. Who cares about business? Fast forward to the good part! "I'm dying to get away. How soon can I go?"

"There's an open date on the tickets. Anytime, I guess."

Tickets. The plural usage caught her off guard. She'd never considered who she might take along.

Ricky was still gossiping with La Prairie girl.

Debi was in the store now and shuffling toward the counter.

How could she possibly choose between them? The realization of her dilemma ameliorated her excitement over the news. After all, she had just won big, but someone she loved would definitely lose.

"Don't forget to send me a postcard. And when you get back from Carmel, keep up the great sales work."

"I will. Thanks, Rachel," she said without much vigor, feeling a funk coming on as she quietly returned the receiver to its cradle.

Debi arrived just in time to see her weighted expression. "What's wrong? I haven't seen you look this distressed since the day you had to decide between two great pairs of Jimmy Choo shoes.''

Sofia reflected back. "Oh, it's much worse." She mulled this a moment longer. "Wait—I take that back. It's about even. But awful just the same.''

Ricky joined the fray. "What's awful?"

"Something terrible happened to my sister," Debi explained.

"Worse than your father taping over a whole week of *Passions?*"

Sofia thought this over, too. "Oh, I was so mad! And all for those terrible late-night Cinemax movies.''

Debi nodded, as if familiar with the tale. "Shannon Tweed has quite a body of work when you think about it.''

Sofia decided to just blurt out her good fortune. "Rachel just called from the corporate office. I won the Honesty contest.''

"We're going to Carmel!" Debi and Ricky shrieked in unison.

They stopped. They regarded each other. They glowered.

"You're not going to Carmel," Ricky said sharply.

"Oh, really?" Debi fired back. "Well, I wouldn't pack a bag if I were *you.*"

And then they both turned expectantly to Sofia.

"I need a cigarette," she said, pulling open a drawer to fetch her purse, a darling little Louis Vuitton number that had gobbled up half a commission check last month. Shoes, handbags, and smoking. A girl could have worse vices. At least she'd be well accessorized on her way to an early death. Lighting up, she considered the situation, her brain going into heavy-duty analysis mode after the first puff.

Ricky might be an easy rejection. How could *both*

of them get time off for days at a time? To just steal
a night or weekend together often required advanced-
level manipulation, the kind that only years of watching Donna Mills snake around *Knots Landing* had
taught her.

On the flip side, was a beach really Debi's idea of
a vacation? Her sister avoided swimsuits like Carmen
Electra avoided decent boyfriends. Speaking of Carmen, why did *Entertainment Tonight* give her the time
of day? All she could do was tan nicely, squeeze into
tight clothes, and run around with jerky guys. The
state of Florida was chockablock full of that kind of
girl.

Anyway, back to the real conundrum. It occurred
to Sofia that Debi was just hooked on the *idea* of
going. In practice, she'd be a serious drag. Anyone
who hated flying, loathed beaches, and thought shopping a bore would be advised *not* to board an airplane
destined for California.

"I can't believe you're smoking behind the counter,"
Ricky said.

Debi toyed with the lipstick display. "She always
wanted to be a Pink Lady."

Sofia rolled her eyes. "Call me Rizzo." Puff number
three. One more drag and the cigarette was history.

La Prairie girl looked on with implicit disapproval.
The urge to tattle was all over her face. Ditto too
much eye makeup. Raccoons had a more subtle look.

"You're going to get busted," Ricky warned.

"Ben hates fresh air," Sofia announced. "He's lived
in the city so long that he can't think straight without
a cigarette, cigar, or pipe blowing in his face. Isn't
that *cute*?"

Debi looked perplexed. "He's propollution. Since
when is that cute?"

"He got you drunk on the first date," Ricky said. "I say proceed with caution."

"I had *two* drinks! They were strong, yes, but who knew the Olsen twins could hold their liquor better than me?"

Ricky and Debi laughed. Finally, her sister spoke up. "OK, enough stalling. Who's going on the trip?"

And then she saw him—Ben Estes—bum rushing toward the Aspen counter, his trademark cool replaced by an almost frantic, on-the-sleeve anxiety. Something was wrong. He pointed his finger at her accusingly. "You told me not to worry about your father."

Alarmed, Sofia turned to Debi, then back to Ben. "I meant that. He's harmless."

"Then explain the two thugs who showed up at my building." He threw down the challenge like a gauntlet. "The only reason I'm not dead right now is because they forgot the silencer and had to take the train back to New Jersey to get it." He paused a beat. "Plus, they knocked on the wrong door."

Sofia and Debi traded knowing looks. "Fat Larry and Little Bo," they said together.

"This is my sister, Debi, by the way," Sofia offered. "Debi, Ben Estes."

He nodded politely.

"Those men are incapable of carrying anything out," Debi tried to assure him. "Even with them on this full time, you have a greater chance of dying in a motorcycle accident."

"I don't ride a motorcycle."

Debi bobbed her head slowly. "The incompetence level is that high."

He glanced from one sister to the other. "So these

two goons have a lousy track record. Say I turn out to be their lucky break. What then?"

Sofia experienced a tiny panic. It was a good question. She didn't have a good answer.

"What if I duke these bums a hundred?" Ben suggested. "Will they get lost?"

"You mean give them one hundred dollars?" Sofia asked.

Ben turned to Debi. "Your sister's quick. That's why I dig her."

Debi grinned.

Sofia put a finger to lips, considering the bribe. Whatever made Fat Larry and Little Bo tick, it sure wasn't money. They both lived with their mothers, dressed poorly, and never traveled. It was sad, really. Maybe she should duke them a hundred, too.

"This isn't a brainteaser, baby," Ben said. "If you can't answer right away, I'm obviously screwed." He gave her a once-over. "Jesus, you're a troublesome broad. I've known you less than a week and already I'm losing gigs and running from killers. And we haven't even made a little hey-hey yet."

Sofia felt a flush of warmth.

"Dullsville it's not," Ben went on. "But I'm not ready for the big casino in the sky yet. I'd better disappear for a spell and give these walking indictments a chance to forget."

Sofia gasped as the perfect solution flashed in her mind. "Pack a bag. We're going to California."

Chapter Six

"You're taking *him*?" Ricky roared. "After less than a week? My relationship with my cable guy goes deeper."

"Do you make out with your cable guy?" Sofia demanded.

"He's straight," Ricky said. "But curious, I think. It could happen."

"Hello?" It was an outraged Debi now, hands on ample hips. "Put songbird here in a safe house. Sisters come first."

Sofia covered her ears and closed her eyes.

Ben had no clue what to make of this. He mulled it over. *Crazy.* Yeah, that said it all for this group. And the fuss about him taking their place on a trip to California was a waste of time. After settling his rent, he'd have trouble coming up with subway fare.

He reached over to remove Sofia's hands from her ears. "Hey, it sounds like a party, baby, but no use fighting over me. I'm busted. Swifty Morgan's might run me a tab, but I'm a nobody on the West Coast."

"You don't understand," Sofia said. "I *won* this trip to Carmel. It's free. All expenses paid."

"This puts a new spin on things," Ben remarked. Travel gratis to a heavenly beach with a gorgeous honey or stick around to be clobbered by Frick and Frack? A no-brainer if ever there was one. "Count me in."

Ricky waved a dismissive hand. "You're not even in the running, Wayne Newton."

"Hey," Ben shot back, instantly offended. "I'm straight, and Debi's related. I think *you're* the odd man out." Suddenly "Danke Schoen" and "Red Roses for a Blue Lady" were playing inside his head. Shit. It'd take all day to chase out those tunes. *Wayne Newton.* What a kick in the teeth that was. He'd rather be called Michael Bolton.

Sofia turned to her friend imploringly. "Stop making this so hard. You know we can't take off at the same time."

Reluctantly, Ricky seemed to concede that fact.

"And Debi," Sofia started next, turning to her sister now, "since when do you want to bask in the sun on some beach? You hate bathing suits. You hate the sand even more."

Debi held up both hands in mock surrender. "He's over six feet, he sings romantic ballads, and he dresses well. A fat sibling can't compete with that."

Ben smiled at Ricky and Debi. It was a little smug, but he couldn't help it. "We'll send a postcard. Promise."

"This is merely a safety measure," Sofia pointed out. "It's the least I can do since my father is trying to kill you. So before you get any fresh ideas, know this—we'll be sleeping in separate beds."

Ben shrugged. "Maybe the first night. You'll come around."

Sofia laughed . . . But she didn't protest. He noted that.

"The trip sounds great. Catching up on sleep would do me good. I haven't been well rested since . . . 1982, I think. But what happens when we come back?" Ben steadied a gaze on all three of them. "Going to Carmel is a Band-Aid. I need a *permanent* solution to being chased by Skinny Larry and Big Bo."

"Fat Larry and Little Bo," Debi corrected.

"Whatever," Ben said, irritation growing. "Let's make it easy and give them both a single Native American name, like in *Dances with Wolves.* I vote for Wearing Bad Suits."

"How about Having No Clue?" Ricky suggested.

Sofia reached over to take both of Ben's hands in hers.

The gesture came unexpectedly, unnerving him. His palms were sweating something fierce. Though he was trying to play it cool, the truth was, those two goons had him scared. Maybe they weren't smart enough to find him right away, but they sure seemed dumb enough to do harm once they did. Bill collectors were one problem. Jerks with guns was quite another.

Sofia was staring into his eyes. *Earnestly.* God, she was beautiful. But he tried to concentrate on her script.

"A week is a long time. Papa will forget all about this by then, and Wearing Bad Suits will forget before he does."

Debi jumped in. "She's right. Someone will give

Papa the finger on the turnpike, and you'll be a distant memory."

Ben wanted a unanimous jury. He looked to Ricky.

"I once told him that I thought his appreciation for Stallone movies bordered on homoeroticism. He forgave *me*. All *you* did was sing."

This would have to do, Ben decided. "How soon can we split?"

Sofia released his hands, then squeezed one tightly, patting it with affection. "Go home and pack. I'll call you later with the flight information."

He couldn't get over how incredibly soft her skin was. In a nanosecond he canceled the idea of catching up on rest during this trip. Any man who ran with a hot number like Sofia Cardinella and chose to sleep was a definite Harvey. Ben sorted out a quick packing list: mints, condoms, Viagra (for the jet lag). No reason to waste a night. Besides, eighteen was a long time ago.

A gaggle of state-of-the-trend teenagers bumped into view and began circling the counter. "I thought you wanted to get that new lipstick we saw in *In Style.*"

"How can I get a look? That fat lady is beached in front of the display like some whale."

Ben grimaced. The cruel words had arrived sharp, fast, and without warning. He watched helplessly as Debi's face registered the hit. Hurt. Shame. A longing to blink and disappear. It was all right there.

Realizing that they'd been heard, the teenagers collapsed into fits of laughter and moved on, impervious to their psyche damage.

The painful moment stretched on for long seconds. No one quite knew what to say or whether to acknowledge the incident. It occurred to Ben how lucky he was. His life had been full of breaks. Great looks, natural athletic ability, an easy way with girls, always the center of a cool clique of friends—everything that made life easy for a guy. He didn't know what it felt like to be the object of ridicule. Debi knew. He sensed that Ricky did, too.

Finally, Debi broke the silence. "Just when you think you're rid of the high-school experience, they pull you back in." She did a spot-on Al Pacino from *The Godfather III*, modifying his infamous line.

Everybody laughed. The tension instantly dissolved.

Ben read the discomfort in Sofia's eyes. It was poignant, this naked yearning to shield her sister from outside hurts, this silent appeal for the world to love her for just being Debi, no matter how heavy she was. But the rest of the story was in Debi's own eyes. Instinctively, he sensed that she couldn't meet those terms, that loving her own body just because it was hers went beyond her scope of self-acceptance. It was sad. Because no amount of love could rescue a person in that place. Those were personal dragons to slay.

Ricky moved fast to change the subject. "Since you're running off to Carmel, I suppose I'm stuck with Mr. Pickles."

Sofia slapped the counter. "Wait a minute! Doris Day owns a hotel there that's pet friendly." She turned to Ben, her eyes wide with the implicit expectation that he also find this bit of news exciting.

Guess what? He didn't. "Who or what is Mr. Pickles?"

"My darling little Yorkie. He's an angel. You'll love him."

"Bring your rain boots," Ricky said. "He likes to piss on men's shoes."

Ben looked to his feet, then back at Sofia. "We should talk about this. I'm not a big fan of dogs."

Sofia waved away the concern. "Oh, don't listen to him."

Ricky sensed the divide and paddled toward it with both oars. "Listen to her fiancé then. He got pissed on. In more ways than one."

"Fiancé?" Forget the little dog. Ben was genuinely stunned.

Sofia glared at Ricky, then gave Ben the benefit of her most innocent smile. "It's a long story."

He put on a serious face. "Make it short."

"My father—"

"Imagine that," Ben interjected.

Sofia pursed her lips. "My father wants me to marry the oldest son of a family he does business with. He won't take no for an answer."

"The father or the potential husband?" Ben asked.

"Both," Sofia said. She rolled her eyes. "Anyway, Papa plans these big, elaborate weddings, and I simply don't show up. Why encourage him? It's an ongoing drama."

"You can always count on good food, though," Debi said. "That's why people keep attending."

Sofia nodded. "The catering really is top-notch."

Ben tried to make sense of it all. "It sounds like you're engaged then, at least technically."

"I'm not engaged to anyone," Sofia replied indignantly.

"But obviously there's a man out there who thinks he's engaged to *you,"* Ben pointed out.

"That's *his* problem," Sofia maintained. "These things happen. Look at Ethan Hawke. He thinks he's a writer. Madonna thinks she's an actress. Victoria Principal thinks she's a dermatologist. I could go on forever."

Ben raised a hand. "Please don't. I get the point."

He surveyed the scene. Store traffic appeared slow. "I haven't eaten all day, and attempted murder makes me hungry. Can you take a break?"

Sofia concentrated hard, brow furrowed, mouth tightly clamped. "I really want to . . . but there's still the matter of Howard."

"Is he the fiancé?" Ben asked.

"No, Vincent is the fiancé, or rather fiancé *wannabe*. Actually, I prefer delusional. That distances me. Don't you think? Anyway, Howard is one of the Berrengers. He co-owns the store and stands guard over the schedule. Labor cost is a big worry in retail. Did you know that? Well, since I'm taking off for a vacation without notice, I'll have to sweet-talk Howard. Then I need to make our travel arrangements. Oh, goodness." She cut herself off, suddenly overwhelmed. "A break just won't do. I need the rest of the day off!"

Ben smiled something wild. He had it bad for this dame. Real bad. A trip with her would be anything but dullsville. "Take care of your business, baby. And let me know what time the big bird takes off. No flights before noon, though. I'm sleep deprived as it is."

Debi just stood there, staring at them in marvel. "You come from there, too," she said.

"Where's that?"

"The planet of the me, myself, and I people."

Ben grinned again. He liked the sister. She didn't sit around and collect sympathy. The girl was clever, and a clever girl made for good company. Impulsively, he slipped a hand through hers. "You're a kick. Grab a bite with me. Eating alone is lousy. Besides, the newspaper's a downer, and I don't like to read much."

"It's a good thing you're handsome," Debi said.

With an easy gait he started off, taking her with

him. "So what are you in the mood for? I could go for almost anything. Nothing healthy, though."

There was inward retreat. He could sense it. Debi looked down at the floor when she said, "Haven't you heard? It wouldn't kill me to skip a meal."

"Don't let those kids tear you down. You're a woman of substance. Like Camryn Manheim."

"Come on, Ben," Debi scoffed quietly. "Does any man really sit around fantasizing about the overweight star of *The Practice?*"

"Maybe not. But there are loftier pursuits than the male fantasy. Trust me, it's not a high-rent district. Darva Conger made it into mine."

"The TV millionaire bride?"

Ben nodded, putting a finger to his lips in the universal sign to hush. "I really dug the white hair and fake tan. Don't ask me why."

"You're such a man." Debi snickered. "What does it feel like to walk around and always think you're the right size? Give or take a few beers, of course."

"It's not the cakewalk it used to be. Guys are under pressure, too."

"Oh, please. Do men really say to each other, 'I would kill to be a size thirty-two in Levi's?' "

"I don't know. Some of Ricky's friends might."

"Doesn't count. They're not having wet dreams about Darva."

"I still think men are under the gun," Ben argued. "Next time you pass a newsstand, stop a minute and take a look. There's *Men's Health* and *Men's Fitness*. Billboards of half-naked underwear models are all over Times Square. I even know guys who spend two hours at the gym every day and *still* feel like they're slacking off."

"Are you one of them?"

"Me? No way. I don't like to lift anything heavier than a highballer with Jack Daniel's and four ice cubes. And I hate to sweat. Unless I'm going at it hot and heavy with a chick. Then I can see the reward."

Debi shook her head, laughing. "It's still not the same. Take Elizabeth Taylor and Marlon Brando. Two stars who personified male and female beauty in their prime. When she got fat, everybody talked about how gorgeous she used to be. But when he packed on the pounds, all I heard people say was, *'Brilliant actor.'* "

They were nearing the food court now, still holding hands like old friends. He stopped and faced her. "Maybe you're right. Men do have it pretty easy."

Debi cracked a smile. "Shocking revelation. We should arrange a press conference."

After a minirush died down and they were able to talk again, Sofia pounced. "So, what do you think?"

"About what?" Ricky asked.

Sofia gave him a dumb glance. "About Ben!"

"He's a step up from Vincent."

"That's the understatement of the century."

"I give him extra points for wit. Most guys who look that good should have their larynx removed."

As she considered the trip to Carmel, anxiousness spread across her abdominals. "I hope it's not too soon for us to vacation together."

"How long have you known him?"

"About a week."

"How many dates?"

"Just one."

Ricky shrugged. "I slept with a guy once just after talking in a line at Tower Records." Then, quite suddenly, he grabbed her arm. "This isn't happening."

Sofia remained immersed in her own thoughts. "Yes, it *is*." She frowned a moment, but brightened just as quickly. "Why am I thinking about this like it's a problem? I'm going on a free vacation with a hot guy. A girl could be in a worse situation."

Ricky's grip remained tight. "Don't forget—your father wants to kill this hot guy and make you marry a short man of his choice," he said, unleashing the words in rapid-fire.

Sofia gave Ricky's hand a studied look. "Why are you holding my arm like this?"

"I might fall down."

"And what—break your hip? *Let go*. You're cutting off my circulation."

"I know that's her," he said, as if in a trance.

"Who?"

Ricky gestured with his head. "The woman browsing the Bobbi Brown counter. It's Charli Grant."

Sofia stole a look. The name rang a bell . . . vaguely. So did the woman who apparently owned it. And like a rock from the sky the memory hit her. *Malibu Undercover*. Three cool, beautiful, and smart crime-fighting girls. Growing up, she and Debi had *loved* the show. "Whatever happened to her?"

"I don't know. The *E! True Hollywood Story* hasn't covered her yet."

Sofia was officially staring now. Rude, yes, but this was Charli Grant! "She looks great. Almost twenty years off has been good to her."

"Remember that episode when she got kidnapped?"

"That was *every* episode. The writers never really stretched themselves."

"I'm talking about the all-time best show. The bad guys stuck her in that cave. She had to dismantle a bomb, wrestle a shark, and swim to safety—all in two minutes.''

"Oh, I remember!" Sofia exclaimed. "I wanted to *be* her. I got in so much trouble for unplugging Papa's alarm clock. Debi and I were playing *Malibu Undercover*, and I pretended it was a bomb. I think he overslept for a meeting that morning."

Ricky watched the scene unfold, glowering. "That twit in Bobbi Brown doesn't even know who she is. Are you witnessing this? She's treating Charli Grant like a normal person!"

"That bitch!" Sofia hissed, teasing him.

He cracked a smile. "I know it's ridiculous, but I have good reason to be mad. Quentin Tarantino came in last week, and she acted like Prince William had paid a visit."

Charli Grant shopped. Sofia and Ricky watched. There was talking. Some head bobbing. The sales associate pointed at the Aspen counter. And a star from yesteryear smiled and stepped in their direction.

"Is she coming over here?" Ricky wondered, equal parts excitement and fright. "I would love to do her lips. She'd look great with Ice Storm liner and Avalanche hydrating lipstick from our new Cold Mountain colors."

"I bet she hears that from all the guys."

Charli Grant was heading straight toward them.

Ben and Debi were back, moving on them from the side.

Sofia saw Ben first.

Ben saw Charli Grant first.

And then Sofia watched in disbelief as the singer and the semicelebrity greeted each other with big smiles, a warm hug, and an ambiguous kiss. Charli's mouth was parted slightly as she planted one low on his cheek, catching the corner of his lips, her arm holding his elbow in a gesture that whispered at an intimate history.

Suddenly Sofia wanted Charli Grant back in that cave. Right now, as a matter of fact. How could she compete with the star of *Malibu Undercover*? Her only credit was Scruffy Orphan Number Four in a sixth-grade production of *Annie*.

"You didn't call," Charli said, admonishing Ben with faux sternness, relegating Debi to windshield bug status.

Ben went through the formalities of an introduction.

Charli surrendered a brief nod to Debi, but no eye contact. Her interest was Ben—exclusively. "We should get together again."

Ricky leaned in to whisper, "I know you're going to disapprove, but I still love her."

Debi joined them at the counter. "Hi, I'm chopped liver."

"Do you know who that is?" Ricky asked. "You just got snubbed by Charli Grant from *Malibu Undercover*."

Debi turned back around. "This will be a great water-cooler story. Does anyone know where I can find a water cooler? Preferably one with people who watched a lot of bad eighties TV gathered around it."

Sofia shushed them, straining to hear.

"I've never met a straight man who could move his hips like you," Charli was saying.

"It's all in the music, baby."

"I'm game for another all-nighter," Charli purred. "Are you up for it?"

"No can do, doll. I'm pulling a disappearing act for a few days. Trouble's brewing."

This intrigued her. "What kind of trouble?"

"The worst. It involves me in a coffin, parents wondering where they went wrong, chicks weeping—the whole shebang."

Charli moistened her lips with her tongue. "Sounds dangerous."

Sofia stared lasers.

"I could call Fat Larry and Little Bo," Debi offered. "There's something to be said for the efficiency of killing both of them at the same time."

"Do you think he slept with her?" Ricky asked. "If so, even *I'm* jealous."

Ben sauntered over, Charli attached to him as if she were a sidecar.

"I'm your biggest fan," Ricky announced.

Charli laughed a little. "Well, thank you. I didn't realize that I still had fans."

"Oh, you should see all the sites dedicated to you on the Internet. And then there's eBay. Charli Grant merchandise goes for big bucks!"

"I had no idea," she said, cutting a rakish glance at Ben.

Sofia didn't buy the false modesty *or* the ignorance about her presence on the Web. Charli Grant struck her as a woman hyperaware of *everything* around her. "What brings you to Berrenger's?" Sofia asked. Then, before she could stop herself: "Perhaps I can interest you in our *age-management* skin-care system."

Debi nearly lost it.

Ricky gasped.

Charli just stared.

And Ben took Sofia's arm with a certain show of force as he said, "Perhaps I can interest *you* in a private conversation right over here." He guided her to the other side of the counter, behind the register, just out of earshot from the others. "What was that?"

Sofia jutted a defiant chin forward. "She was rude to my sister. You were too busy drooling to notice."

Ben took offense. "Hey, I don't drool, baby. Drooling means trying too hard—something I don't do." He regarded her carefully. "You're jealous."

"Jealous?" Sofia spat incredulously. "Now you *are* trying too hard."

"I'm not into that broad. Her skirts are too short, and she wears circus-tent type makeup. But we partied together one night, and I realized how lonely she was. I thought I owed her a little kindness. That's all. And here you go kicking her Achilles' heel. Age is a major hang-up for women like her—especially if their biggest claim to fame is how they looked twenty years ago."

Sofia felt like crawling into one of the cabinets, somewhere between the exfoliants and self-tanning creams, and just hiding. It wasn't like her to overreact, especially when it came to a guy. But her general refusal to admit wrongdoing suddenly reared and bucked. Yes, he made a fairly convincing argument, but it still didn't address Charli Grant's dismissal of Debi. Ben was good, but he wasn't Johnnie Cochran.

"Let me get this straight," Sofia said. "I'm supposed to feel sorry for this woman because she's no longer young, beautiful, and famous? Next to her, you must think the homeless are just plain whiny."

He laughed. A big laugh. "You know what? You keep a guy off balance. I can't wait to get on that plane and fly across the country with you. We're going to have a ring-a-ding-ding time."

Sofia felt swept in. There was something about his gorgeous, playful eyes. She didn't know what the hell it was. But his gaze was riveting. And his words were right on target.

A ring-a-ding-ding time it would be.

Chapter Seven

Go to sleep, Debi chanted silently. *Just close your eyes and go to sleep.*

Her inner voice was fierce, but as the hour approached midnight, a burning compulsion kept her wide-awake. She had been so good all day long—eating small portions of reasonably healthy foods. Yet now, alone in the dark, her willpower began to crumble.

Is this how an alcoholic feels when she reaches for the bottle after a long day of sobriety?

Finally, Debi gave in, dressed quickly, grabbed her purse, and ran down the stairs, out the door, and up the street to the all-night deli. At this hour, she never bumped into anyone she knew. The habit was a secret she shared with the deli's Asian clerk, a tiny woman whose sympathetic smile always translated into something along the lines of, "You poor, lonely, fat woman. How sad that junk food is your surrogate lover."

Debi tried not to think at all as she paid the thirteen dollars and rushed back home to her comfortable bed, where she could flip channels and indulge in the illicit pleasure that was not just a snack but a *mission*. No ordinary foods would do. This was a *fix*. Cheetos, crispy M&M's, Crunch & Munch toffee-glazed pretzels, Ben & Jerry's World Class Vanilla, snack-size Butterfingers, and a giant Coke to wash everything down.

She consumed the forbidden calories and fat grams as fast as her body could take them in. Joy turned to numbness. Bloated lethargy turned to almost nausea. Only then did she stop. What did it matter anyway? The scale had tipped past the two-hundred-pound mark a long time ago. That had been her point of no return.

After the sick feeling passed, a damning sense of shame pricked away at her like a thousand needles. The empty bags, wrappers, and containers littered on the floor intensified the self-loathing. She was the binge-eating equivalent to a sloppy drunk. Debi considered this and decided that the country needed a fat First Lady, a woman who would do for heavy eaters what Betty Ford had done for heavy drinkers—make them respectable.

An infomercial had her hypnotized. Two B-list television actors were praising the benefits of a new ab-rolling machine. Debi didn't dare change the channel until she found out how much it cost. Then—and only then—could she get on with her life.

Five easy payments of thirty-nine ninety-five.

OK. She flipped over to VH1. Toni Braxton was gyrating to one of her silky, pop-soul hits. The singer had obviously splurged on the ab roller. Her stomach was flawless.

A wave of drowsiness rolled over her. The sugar high was working in reverse now. Debi's eyelids felt weighted down, her thoughts scattered. She had to stop this abusive cycle of midnight binges. She needed to exercise more. She needed to consider the stomach surgery made famous by Carnie Wilson. She needed to mail her Discover Card payment. She needed to find out who really killed JFK. The list went on and on.

And then the telephone rang. With a start, she rose to answer it.

"I have the best idea." It was Sofia.

"I hope it's better than this one—calling after midnight."

"Were you asleep?"

"Almost."

"Then no harm done. Anyway, it's only nine o'clock in California. That's early."

"We don't live in California."

"But I'm going there tomorrow, and I've already set my watch for Pacific time."

Debi had to smile. In the world of Sofia, this was sound logic. "What time do you leave?"

"Early. Seven, I think. Ben's already grumbling. He wanted to sleep. But the airline doesn't give you many choices once they find out you've got free tickets."

Debi would genuinely miss her sister over the next several days. This got her thinking. What would happen if Sofia married Ben and moved to Manhattan? She'd be stuck in New Jersey with their father. How tragic. She could see how things might spiral down. Instead of once a week, her late-night binges would increase to once a day.

Oh, God, she could imagine herself really packing on the pounds. Until she was one of those freak cases—a fat woman so big that leaving the house required strategic planning from heavy-moving specialists. Her meals would become grist for the tabloid mill. JERSEY GIRL EATS ENOUGH FOR SMALL VILLAGE. Richard Simmons would come for a visit. Together they would cry and talk about inner beauty and dreams coming true. Then he would give her a free *Sweating to Broadway* exercise video.

"I told Papa about the trip to Carmel," Sofia was saying. "He thinks I'm taking Ricky with me."

"I'll pretend that I'm mad at you for not asking me. Just to reinforce the lie."

"You're not, are you?"

"Mad at you?"

"Yeah."

"Of course not. Ben is great. In fact, I'd like to take him on a vacation with *me* after you get back."

Sofia laughed. "I know that he'd go. He thinks you're very intelligent, not to mention hilarious."

Debi paused, taking in the high praise. It wasn't often that people looked past her weight to the substance of her personality.

"Anyway," Sofia went on, "I've got an idea that will help you find a guy just as fabulous as Ben."

Debi stifled a groan. "If this has anything to do with matchmaker.com, I'm hanging up."

"WWJD," Sofia said.

Debi was perplexed. She'd seen the bracelets. She knew what the acronym stood for. But the point was lost on her. "What would Jesus do?"

"No, even better," Sofia corrected grandly. "What would the *Jews* do? SpeedDating. It's all the rage with the Jewish singles crowd. Aren't they an amazing people? Great with money. Now great at finding the perfect mate."

"You're stereotyping."

Sofia sighed. "If you had an extra thousand dollars, would you hand it over to a Rosenbaum or a Johnson?"

"Neither. I'd first want to know the credentials and experience of both."

"Say there's no time for that. You have to make an instant decision or you lose the money. Who's it going to be? Rosenbaum or Johnson?"

"This is ridiculous," Debi protested.

"Rosenbaum or Johnson?"

Debi gave in. "Rosenbaum, I guess."

"My case is rested," Sofia said, sounding very pleased with herself. "I think this SpeedDating is going to catch on in a big way. It's the best invention since . . . I don't know . . . Dryel. Here's how it works—a girl shows up at a place, pays twenty-five dollars, and goes on about eight dates with available, straight men. The best part of all—each date is only seven minutes long. That way if you get stuck with a loser, there's an end in sight."

Debi wasn't sold. "So instead of being rejected by just one man in a single night, the potential is there to be rejected by eight."

"Stop being so negative. This is a great way to meet eligible guys. Anyway, I've already signed you up and paid your fee. Show up at the Starbucks down the street from Berrenger's tomorrow night. The fun starts at seven-thirty."

Debi closed her eyes. Fear of inadequacy was building now. She would never get to sleep. "I believe this concept is based on the idea of encouraging marriage within the faith. News flash—I'm not Jewish. And if the mothers of these men happen to show up, things could get ugly."

"Don't worry about that. This is a knock-off version of SpeedDating. I think a group of Episcopalians are behind it. By the way, they're good with money, too. Big earners."

There was silence.

"I've already talked to Ricky. He'll escort you there," Sofia said.

"And probably fare better than I will, too."

"Well, better to know about closeted homosexuality after seven minutes than after seven years. Remember my friend Michelle from high school? She caught her husband with her tennis coach. Anyway, Ricky's going to do your makeup, too. Be at the Aspen counter no later than six-thirty."

"Sounds like you've got it all planned. Who's picking out my clothes?"

"Wear the black pantsuit." A pause. "And promise me that you'll show up. At least give this a try."

Debi resigned herself to the potential humiliation of SpeedDating. After all, when Sofia got her mind set on something, it was easier to surrender than to stay in battle. "Are you sure I'm ready for Speed-Dating? Keep in mind that I've been stuck in a rut called NoDating."

"This will be fun," Sofia insisted.

Debi sighed and reached for the last Butterfinger.

"This isn't a vacation," Ben said. "I'm running for my life. I have to keep reminding myself of that."

Half amused, Sofia glanced up from the latest issue of *Elle*. "Yes, it's just like *The Fugitive*."

They had been stuck on the runway for at least thirty minutes. Typical for LaGuardia. Flying commercial was such a bore these days. It used to be the way to go. Now it was just bus travel by air. Secretly, Sofia yearned for a wealthy friend with a private plane. How divinely decadent it would be.

Ben's tall frame was folded into his window seat like a collapsed lawn chair. "How long is this flight?"

She could barely tear herself away from the fascinating article about a revolutionary new eye cream. "We have to take off first," she murmured. "After that, about seven hours, I guess."

"Jesus Christ Almighty!" Ben exclaimed.

Sofia stopped reading to regard his empty lap and free hands. "You need a book."

He shrugged diffidently. "Reading's not my bag."

She returned a look of pure astonishment. "How did you make it through law school?"

"With great difficulty. But I had no choice then. Now I have an option."

"Well, you have to do something."

"What are you reading?"

As if put out, she displayed the cover of *Elle*. It was graced by a tanned and toned supermodel. Bold cover copy promised FASHION FIRSTS, SKIN CARE BREAK-THROUGHS, and THE NEXT JAMES DEAN, among other female interests.

Ben nodded with intrigue. "Do you have another one of those?"

"Why can't you do what most men do in these situations?"

"What's that?"

"Hold a Tom Clancy or John Grisham novel and just pretend."

He thought about it. Then he leaned back and closed his eyes. "I'll take a nap, instead."

Finally, the plane raced down the tarmac and flew into the sky. She flipped through *Elle* (for the articles),

Vogue (for the pictures), *US Weekly* (for the gossip), and *O The Oprah Magazine* (for the inspiration).

The flight attendants scooted down the aisle to take beverage orders and pass out snacks. She drank her apple juice and munched on the granola mix, thinking about Mr. Pickles. He was zonked out on a tranquilizer and caged inside his regulation pet carrier, braving the trip from the cargo hull. *Sweet angel.*

Ben had been serious about that nap. He was sleeping with his mouth slightly agape, breathing hard, almost producing a soft snore, but not quite. *Very cute.*

Sofia was bored now and wanted him to wake up. She tapped his shoulder. No response. She pushed him a little. Nothing. Finally, she shook his body—violently. He opened his eyes.

"Did you sleep with Charli Grant?"

He closed his eyes. "No."

"Why should I believe you?"

"What kind of man would lie about *not* sleeping with a famous sex symbol?"

"Maybe the kind looking to get lucky on a free trip to Carmel."

A long second of silence. He opened his eyes again. "I shared a kiss with her—that's all. And not even a real one. It was the kind of kiss a nephew might give an aunt. A quick peck on the lips. Anyway, why are you bringing up Charli? I thought we settled that."

Sofia raised a curious brow, betraying nothing. "She stuck around after you left yesterday. I learned some interesting things."

"This should be good. Like what?"

"You never want to get married."

"False," Ben said easily. "What I said was this— I'd never get married *unless it was for keeps.*"

"Oh." Deep down she believed him.

Ben smirked. "Charli had a lot to drink the night we went out." He paused. "So what else did she say?"

Sofia debated whether or not to spill the rest. In all honesty, she felt a bit silly. Maybe Charli Grant was crazy. Oh, well, she reasoned, better to get everything out in the open.

"Charli said that you're like Warren Beatty before Annette Bening—lots of women, no commitment. A real playboy."

He seemed amused by this most of all. "Not true. The last woman I slept with was my ex-girlfriend, CZ."

"The woman who left you for the hockey player who can't read?"

"That would be her. He *can* read, by the way. I don't want to disparage the guy. But he's no Evelyn Wood. That's for sure."

Sofia leaned in closer. "Why would Charli make up such wild stories?"

Ben met her gaze and held it with a smoldering intensity. "I have no idea."

"Maybe she's trying to discourage me from getting involved with you."

"Is it working?"

"I'd say just the opposite."

"So you're encouraged."

"Very."

He moved in, close enough to breathe her breath. "It's good that we're both enthusiastic. Playing hard to get is for Harveys."

"What's a Harvey?"

"A square—the kind of person who walks out of a restaurant because the appetizers are too expensive."

She smiled, hoping a kiss was imminent. "I adore appetizers that cost too much. By the way, you talk funny."

He laughed. "You think so?"

"Sometimes I feel like I could use a Ben Estes to English dictionary."

"You don't need one of those. I'll tutor you privately."

"What if I'm a slow learner?"

"Not a problem. I take my time with everything."

Sofia sucked in a tiny breath.

And then Ben claimed her mouth with his, gently at first, but the hunger was there. She could feel it, taste it. Yet he held it in. It was passion in slow motion.

Closing her eyes, she thought it was the greatest thing ever. This idea of holding back opened up a delicious yearning. What would happen if they lost control? And it was bound to happen soon. After all, the attraction they shared was so obviously of the I-want-to-tear-your-clothes-off variety.

"Are you finished?" It was a flight attendant—the youngest, prettiest one to be exact.

Sofia pulled herself away and faced the tray table. Her plastic cup sat there empty, save for the tiny granola bag, which was crumpled into a wad and placed neatly inside. The subtext was quite clear. If this woman could wave a magic wand, then Sofia would be collecting beverage/snack debris, and she would be kissing Ben.

"I'm finished with *that,*" Sofia said pointedly.

Being with a guy whom every girl seemed to want was a new experience. Hints were dropped like cluster bombs even in the face of lip lock. Imagine what moves were made when she wasn't around! It could send a true jealous type to the brink of insanity.

The flight attendant soldiered on, and Sofia regarded her companion carefully. She understood all the fuss. He was tall, devastatingly handsome, impeccably dressed, charming beyond compare, and funny in a very refreshing, self-deprecating way.

"Women go ape for you," she announced.

"Are you swinging from the vine, too?"

Sofia felt the pink of a blush. "Not really. But I'm close to beating my chest and making loud noises."

Ben grinned. "It's true—women dig me. Only up to a point, though. Once they figure out that I don't have a job and that I run out the door not to get somewhere on time but to avoid my landlord because last month's rent is late, the swooning stops. Trust me. For most girls, I make a great two-week boyfriend. After that, the accountant with the stomach paunch begins to look pretty damn good."

Suddenly, he took her hand, threading his fingers through hers and grasping tight. That unseen moment was *it*. The touch caught her off guard. Sofia sensed a slight jump in her heartbeat.

"That's why you're such a kick," he continued. "You see beyond my bad credit report."

"There are worse things," she said silkily.

"Such as?"

She mulled it over. "Not noticing what's important. I love the way you spent time with my sister yesterday. It took her mind off those dreadful teenagers. You made her feel special, and that means a great deal to me."

Ben's playful expression turned thoughtful.

"Did I mention that I signed her up for Speed-Dating tonight?"

He gave a knowing nod. "You announced it last night and then again as we were boarding. Does Debi really want to do this?"

"Debi never really wants to do *anything*. That's why I push her."

"One blind date can be bad enough. How many does this gig cram into a night?"

"At least eight."

"Jesus. I'd rather have a root canal."

"Come on; it's a great idea."

"Would you do it?"

"Oh, never in a million years. Seven minutes with a stranger I'm either not attracted to or ambivalent about is way too long."

Ben laughed. "So why force your sister into it?"

Sofia turned serious. "Because I think she's lonely, and it breaks my heart. This might be a total waste of time. I'm not expecting her to meet a man and get married next month. But maybe she'll make a new friend. What's wrong with that?"

Still holding her hand, Ben raised it to his lips and kissed her thumb. "Not a thing."

"Debi just needs to be pushed a bit, that's all," Sofia went on. "We've always been each other's best friend. She's only two years older, you see. But it's always been hard for her to make friends of her own. Growing up, I always included her, so she learned to rely on mine. I thought college would bring her out. All she did was study, though. Now she's working for Papa and *living* with him, too. Well, we both do that. But at least I work in New York and move out for a few days every month."

"The answer might not be a date," Ben offered with philosophical directness. "Maybe Debi just needs to do something for herself."

Sofia pondered this but couldn't help thinking of her *own* life. What had *she* done for herself lately? Dropped out of college. Charged up enough credit card bills to cover the national debt of Costa Rica. Coasted in a dead-end job. Where was her life head-

ing? The question stirred up major angst. She
checked her watch. Oh, God! This plane wouldn't
be landing for *hours*. How could she sit still for that
long?

She needed fresh air.

She needed a cigarette.

She needed . . . *a life.*

None of which seemed immediately available. Something had to give. Turning to Ben, she said, "A drink
would do me good right now. You're the expert. What
does one order at thirty thousand feet?"

He grinned, nodding with approval. "Let's think
this one out. Jilly's not here. I only trust martinis in
his hands. The ice cubes are too small to make a
good Jack Daniel's and water. But I think we could
make a Bloody Mary work."

Another flight attendant passed by, one who didn't
seem to want to make it into the Mile-High Club with
Ben. Sofia ordered the drinks and, taking a deep
breath, leaned back in her seat.

"You're worried about Debi, aren't you?" Ben
asked sympathetically.

Sofia waved off the question. "Oh, please. Debi will
be fine. She's got a college degree, and the right man
will come along eventually. It's *me* that I'm worried
about."

A quizzical look skated across Ben's face. "I don't
get it."

Abruptly, she turned to him. "You better catch on
quick." Then she bit down on her lower lip. "Wait—
I forgot about your law degree. You'll be fine, too.
It's just *me!*"

Ben merely stared.

The Bloody Marys arrived, and Sofia gulped hers
like a marathon runner chugs Gatorade. Could one

of the flight attendants score her a Xanax? Even a
Tylenol PM would do.

Remain calm. Take slow, deep breaths.

Winning this trip was truly serendipitous. Being
away from all the chaos of home would be good medi-
cine. Plenty of time to meditate, get into her own
head, and figure out a way to chart a better course
in life, to empower herself. That's what the Oprah
magazine advocated. *Empowerment.*

She glanced over at Ben. Why did he have to be
so damn irresistible? Crawling into bed with him
would only create more smoke. And she definitely
needed to clear the air. *Don't fool around with the hot
guy sleeping in the same room,* she told herself. That was
vacation rule number one.

"Are you feeling OK?" Ben asked.

"Promise me something."

"Name it."

"I need some space. There's a lot to figure out.
Don't touch me or kiss me anymore on this trip."

"This is a joke, right?"

"I'm totally serious."

The flight attendant passed by again.

"Another round please," Ben called.

Chapter Eight

"Gorgeous," Ricky trilled, applying the final coat of gloss to Debi's exotically dark lips.

She checked the work, pleased with the results, never one to deal in unrealistic expectations. A make-up artist could enhance and conceal, but saying bye-bye-bye to a double chin required so much more.

"What do you know about the Zone Diet?" Debi asked.

"You eat a lot of yellowfin tuna and string beans, I think," Ricky said. He leaned in, sniffing her decolletage. "Are you wearing perfume? I can't tell."

She shook her head. "I'm out of White Diamonds and need to pick up some more. Do they sell it here?"

"*White Diamonds!*" Ricky shrieked. "Honey, that is *so* over. You're young; you're with it. The last thing you want to smell like is a blue-hair from the Midwest. Here's a quick test. Do you play slot machines, love to hear Kathie Lee sing, and vacation by tour bus?"

"No, no, and no."

Ricky breathed an exasperated sigh. "OK, then." He darted to the other side of the counter and fetched the Honesty tester. "This is a great fragrance, and I'm not just saying that because I work for Aspen," he said, spritzing the inside of her wrist.

She sniffed. There were hints of mint, vanilla, cotton candy, and rosewater. It reminded her of the fact that all the anxiety over this SpeedDating business had curbed her appetite and caused her to skip lunch.

"You like?"

She brought her wrist under her nose a second time. "I'm not sure. It makes me hungry."

Ricky smiled. "It will make men hungry, too—*for you*. Focus groups loved this fragrance. They took it to college campuses and sports bars. Something about the smell of food does it for guys. I don't think that works for gay men, though. At least not for me. But if someone bottled a pot roast and mashed potatoes perfume, I believe it could make a fortune. You'd be fighting off straight men with a bat."

Debi grabbed the bottle and sprayed her pulse points. Then she checked her watch. No more stalling. It was time to head for Starbucks.

Ricky seemed to pick up on her inner turmoil. "Just be yourself," he said gently. "Show them a little of that personality, and they'll want to see more."

She made a wry face. "You sound like a mother in one of those after-school specials."

Ricky returned a half smile. "I wish I could go with you, but a certain lying bitch who was supposed to close tonight called in sick. I know she's going to the Macy Gray concert. I heard her talking about it yesterday."

"How evil," Debi remarked. Then she just stood there, lingering.

"You better get going. If you're late, all the men with good jobs and a full head of hair will be taken."

She still hesitated. "Why does it feel like I'm going stag to the prom? Maybe it's because no one wanted to dance with the fat girl, and what was true then is still true now."

"Sweetie," Ricky started, only to be distracted by Debi's handbag, a sleek black number with an enormous buckle bearing the letters CD. "That purse is fabulous. Christian Dior, right?"

Debi nodded. "It's Sofia's."

He tilted his head to one side. "Of course." Then his expression did a quick change to stern and focused. "Now, I want you to keep this in mind. The men who are going to be there tonight are showing up for the same reasons you are."

"Because their sister signed them up and pressured them into saying yes?"

"No!" Ricky rolled his eyes. "Because they're interested in meeting new people and finding a potential mate. Believe me, honey, nobody's expecting Elizabeth Hurley to walk through the door. Besides, if you don't go, your sister will kill both of us."

Debi stewed for a moment. The irony was not lost on her. Even though Sofia was on the opposite coast, she still managed to call all the shots. It was a rare talent.

Taking a deep breath, Debi tried to psych herself up. Eight dates at seven minutes a piece. That's fifty-six minutes. Just under an hour. In the time it takes the cast of *Law and Order* to solve a case and try it in court, this whole ordeal would be over. It seemed less frightening now.

"Call me later," Ricky insisted. "I want to hear *everything*."

As if in a daze, she ventured out of Berrenger's, down the busy street, and into Starbucks at seven-thirty on the dot. There were at least forty people milling around, ranging in age from twentysomething to fiftysomething.

She approached what appeared to be a registration table and announced her name. Then she was handed a date card, informed that women sit on the east side of the table, advised not to talk about where she lived or what she did for a living, and instructed to shift down a seat when the cowbell rang.

It was surreal. Suddenly the clock was ticking, and she was sitting across from Mark, a public school teacher who lived with his mother. This guy wasted no time in breaking the taboo conversation rules. He ate up the seven minutes with a passionate rant about Manhattan housing costs, so she never got the chance to tell him that she was a bookkeeper who lived with her father. Maybe they were meant for each other.

Jeff was next. A short bald man in his early fifties who boasted about his confidential job with the federal government. Translation—postal carrier. He openly admired Debi's "childbearing hips" and announced his desire to have more kids (he already had three from two previous marriages) while his "stuff was still potent."

And then came Sean. A rumpled writer for a Republican-themed Web site. He railed about social programs that encourage poor people to stay that way, expressed an unabashed love for the National Rifle Association, revealed his hope that *Roe v. Wade* be overturned, and blasted gays for tearing away at the moral fiber of the country. She wondered if he really knew this was a date. Maybe he got lost on his way to *Meet the Press* and thought she was Tim Russert in drag. Finally, the bell rang.

Debi shifted down. "Oh, my God!" she gasped at the sight of the man who would be her date for the next seven minutes. She could hardly believe her eyes. It was Vincent Scalia! Her sister's perpetual fiancé. Her father's dream son-in-law. Her own lifelong crush. In his three-piece suit and pomade-slicked hair, he was trying too hard. But in the world according to Debi, he was Mel Gibson personified.

Vincent's eyes got big, his face reddened, and his hands couldn't find enough to do. "Debi! What are you doing here?"

"Trying to find a date that I wouldn't push in front of a bus. So far, no luck."

He laughed a little. "You're funny." Then he looked around nervously, avoiding eye contact. "This is embarrassing."

She didn't agree. This was more than she'd ever dreamed. Every ghastly minute with the last three undesirables suddenly seemed worth it now. It was only a *seven-minute* date with Vincent. But it was a date nonetheless.

"What do you think of SpeedDating so far?" Debi asked.

"The women I've met seem nice . . . but none of them . . . . There's only one Sofia," he said glumly.

Now they were down to six minutes. In the interest of time, she decided to just come out with it. "My sister's not going to marry you, Vincent." It was kind but firm.

He simply sat there, stunned and hurt.

This reaction worried her. "Certainly this doesn't come as a surprise."

"It's tough to hear out loud."

"Tougher than being stranded at the altar three times in a row?"

"Your dad was always there to pump me up and keep me focused on the next wedding."

Talk about the blind leading the blind! "But obviously your way of thinking has changed," she began, attempting to lead him to higher intellectual ground. "I mean, you're *here*. Looking for a date."

"Do you think Sofia will be jealous?" And he was serious.

Debi's idiot alarm began ringing like mad. She still had hope, though. Perhaps all this man needed was honesty—the sledgehammer kind. "No." It was simple, to the point, and most important—*true*.

He was instantly crestfallen. "My last three dates said the same thing."

Every bit of Debi's hope was fading—fast. Did Vincent have a degree from the Fat Larry and Little Bo University? Maybe. *With honors*. No matter, the flame for him burned on. "Let me take a stab in the dark here. It's my belief that talking about another woman you want to marry can kill a first date."

Vincent looked fuzzy. "I thought women liked sensitive guys."

"Sensitive with *them*, yes. Sensitive about other women—not quite as useful."

His brow furrowed. "I see."

Debi wasn't certain that he did.

Suddenly he brightened. "Maybe you could help me."

She experienced a surge of excitement. Her heart moved. Yes! He wanted her to help him get over Sofia. It was a job she was born to fill. "I'll do my best."

"You're the closest person to Sofia. You know what she likes, what she doesn't like. With your help I know I could win her over."

As the words ricocheted in her mind, Debi fought like hell to conceal the disappointment. All she could muster was a frozen, half smile. Her throat felt parched. Tears threatened to burst, but she bravely held them at bay. She felt ridiculous. Who was she kidding? Vincent didn't want her. No man did.

"Will you do it?" Vincent asked.

"Sure," Debi heard herself say. It was the wrong kind of attention from the man she wanted to be with, but it was attention just the same. There was something to be said for proximity on any terms.

"Never count your orchids before they grow out of your bird," Ben whispered conspiratorially.

The stranger in the car-rental line stared back at him as if he were insane.

"Thought I was going to have some *fun* on this vacation. Know what I mean, Charley?"

"My name's Ted," the man said, somewhat testily. He was a clean-cut, button-down type. The kind of guy who was probably president of his senior class and deep into student government during his college days.

"Hey, I meant no offense," Ben replied easily. "Everybody's a Charley. I have a friend back in New York, Taz. He writes screenplays. I call him Charley Hollywood." He paused a beat. "What kind of car are you asking for?"

"I don't know. Maybe a Taurus."

Ben smiled. "Guess I'll call you Charley Four-Door Sedan."

The man looked around suspiciously. "Are you part of some hidden-camera stunt?"

Ben laughed, rubbing his eyes. "Relax, pal. By the way, you're Charley Paranoid now. I just thought we could relate since we're stuck in this line together. Besides, I don't think the lady behind me speaks English."

The man bounced a glance beyond Ben to the Asian woman beside him. He gave up a half smile and seemed to thaw out a bit. "So, you're here on vacation?"

Ben shifted his feet. He felt like taking a nap. Cross-country jet lag was no joke. "Sort of. See that girl over there?" He pointed to Sofia in the waiting area. She was bent over and making goo-goo sounds at a groggy Mr. Pickles.

The man nodded approvingly. "You're a lucky man."

"The verdict's still out. This chick started having some kind of pre-midlife crisis on the way here. She thinks she needs to figure out the rest of her life *right now*. Doesn't want to fool around, either. That's a real bunter, believe me." Ben nudged his new friend, man-to-man style. "I've seen the coming attractions, Charley."

Charley Paranoid stared blankly.

"We've canoodled, hooked up, run a few bases," Ben explained. Briefly he considered a third and final name—Charley Not So Bright.

But he was nodding knowingly now.

"The dog's a kick in the ass, too. Do you like little dogs that yap and wear ribbons?" Ben didn't wait for an answer. "I can't handle them. Too much fuss. My kind of dog is Old Yeller. Now, there's a dog."

"Old Yeller got shot in the end," Ted pointed out.

"Before that part," Ben said. "Benji was cool, too." He stood there silently for a moment. "I take it you're on vacation."

"Oh, yes. We love the wine country."

"Ah," Ben said enthusiastically. "Sounds romantic. You must be here with your wife."

"Sort of. My lifetime partner."

Ben didn't get the distinction between wife and lifetime partner, but he pretended to. Maybe it was a newer, more optimistic term in response to the 50 percent divorce rate. He smiled and bobbed his head. "Charley Positive." Then he looked around. "Where is she?"

Charley Positive metamorphosed into Charley Annoyed. "*He* is seeing about a lost piece of luggage."

Ben got the lifetime partner reference now. *Charley Gay.* It'd been a long flight from New York to San Francisco. "That's great," Ben said. "Not the missing luggage, of course. That sucks. But the fact that you found someone to share the rest of your life with. That's great."

Ted nodded proudly. "Thanks for saying so."

"How does it feel to be gay these days? Is it as much a gas as it seems to be? I mean, it's almost trendy now. In fact, I feel like a bit of a Harvey because I'm straight. Rupert Everett's a great ambassador for you guys."

The line advanced. It was Ted's turn with one of the rental agents. He moved ahead and seemed relieved on multiple levels.

Ben approached the counter next. A minor controversy ensued because their car had been reserved in Sofia's name. The fact that she had no driver's license further complicated the matter.

"I've always taken the train or a cab," Sofia explained to the sullen agent whose Alamo Car Rental name badge proclaimed her Emily H. "I imagine finding a decent parking spot could eat up half a day in New York, so why bother driving? And if I don't drive, why waste time at the DMV? I hear it's quite dreadful there."

"Ma'am," Emily H. began in a terse tone, "it is Alamo policy that in order to drive one of our automobiles, you must have a valid license to operate one."

Sofia turned to Ben. "This is too much trouble. Let's just ride one of those cable cars. I hear people adore them."

Ben cracked a reluctant smile. This girl was self-possessed in the most delightful way. "People do adore them," he said patiently. "But those people are going from Union Square to Fisherman's Wharf. We're going to Carmel, which is at least two hours away." He glanced to Emily H. for confirmation.

"At least," she said.

"We can take a taxi," Sofia offered brightly.

"That would eat up more cash than I have," Ben said.

Emily H. was almost to the point of full-tilt exasperation. She zeroed in on Ben. "Do *you* have a driver's license?"

"Yes, but it's from Mississippi."

Sofia gazed at him in astonishment.

"I have an aunt in Jackson," he explained. "The family spends Christmas there every other year. My uncle taught me how to drive." He zipped open his carry-on bag and began to search.

Emily H. started to click away on her keyboard.

"You can drive in California with a Mississippi license?" Sofia asked, with the most innocent incredulity.

"Yes, ma'am," Emily H. responded crisply.

Wide-eyed, Sofia turned to Ben. "Did your uncle teach you how to drive on roads?"

The question managed to freeze him in place. He wondered if she had ever ventured beyond the East Coast.

Before he could answer, she fired off with, "And did you learn to drive using a car or a tractor?"

Yes! His license was safely tucked in one of the interior pockets. He checked the date, saw that it was valid for another year, and proudly presented it to Emily H.

"What about all the alligators?" Sofia went on.

He silenced her with a hand on either shoulder, leaning in to gaze directly into her eyes. "There are busy cities and streets in Mississippi, just like in New Jersey."

"But not long ago I saw an episode of *ER* where Dr. Benton—he's the handsome black doctor who never smiles—helped out at a clinic in Mississippi. He had to travel through swamps by boat."

Ben wanted to smother her with kisses. She was *that* cute. "This is commonly referred to as *bad television*. Look at *Friends*. They never go to work, yet they have spacious apartments in Manhattan."

"What about the movie *A Time to Kill* with Matthew McConaughey and Ashley Judd? That was set in Mississippi and nobody had an air conditioner."

Ben nodded as if to say he understood her confusion. "Again, don't trust what you see on the screen. Would it be sexy if Ashley Judd had said, 'Honey, I'm cold. *Go get me* a sweater.' No. More tickets are sold if she's perspiring in a *tight T-shirt*. Trust me. There are air conditioners in Mississippi. In fact, my aunt and uncle keep theirs at sixty-five degrees."

Sofia looked alarmed.

"They claim to be warm-natured," Ben said.

Satisfied, she eagerly addressed Emily H. "This car rental is part of a vacation that I won. Everything is first class. Will we be driving away in a Mercedes?"

Emily H. retrieved a set of papers from the printer. "Your arrangements indicate economy class. You can upgrade to luxury for an additional charge."

Sofia's lips compressed into a pout.

"We'll take what's provided," Ben chimed in quickly. Every dollar counted. He was, after all, missing several days of not working.

And then with her bored countenance and officious tone, Emily H. gave voice to the million-dollar question: "Chevrolet Cavalier or Ford Escort?"

They chose the former. It came in red, and Sofia maintained that a red car gave off stronger vacation vibes than a green one. Ben didn't argue. Minutes later he was exiting onto the US-101 South ramp toward San Jose.

"I just realized that I haven't had a cigarette all day!" Sofia announced with great exuberance. "Do you know what this means?"

Ben shook his head. He had no idea. With this girl, it could mean anything.

"I allow myself six a day, so right now I could smoke three in a row without stopping. How deliciously decadent."

"Or you could keep going and maybe kick the habit."

"That's a terrible idea," Sofia said, lighting up. She took a deep drag. "I do some of my best thinking when I smoke."

"So what's on your mind?"

"Our sleeping arrangements. Temptation could get the best of us. We should ask for separate rooms."

"You know, you should really quit. Have you read the side of the pack lately?"

Sofia giggled. "Ben, I'm serious."

"So am I. This is some of the worst thinking I've heard in years."

"What is jumping into bed going to do for us?"

"Make us very, very happy."

"For fifteen minutes."

"Twenty. You forgot to add in foreplay."

"You're being ridiculous."

"OK, twenty-five. I'll hum a song afterward. Girls love that."

Sofia released a heavy sigh. "My life is in a shambles, Ben. Sex with you won't do anything but complicate it more. This is the first time that I've ever been away from my family. I need to take this opportunity to think for myself and decide what I'm going to do."

He grew quiet. It made profound sense. Maybe he should do the same. All this running from landlords, chasing after low-paying singing gigs. Sure, it was fun now. But soon it would be pathetic. And then what? His stomach grumbled. "I'm starving. How about stopping for a bite to eat?"

Sofia twisted around to check on Mr. Pickles in the backseat. Then she looked at Ben pleadingly. "Can you wait until we get to Carmel? Mr. Pickles has endured such a stressful day of travel, and I want to get him settled at the hotel as soon as possible."

He glanced back at the dog resentfully. "That's two hours away."

Sofia stared at the road ahead. "Have a cigarette," she said stubbornly.

Chapter Nine

It took more than three hours to get there. Sofia insisted upon stopping several times along the Pacific Coast Highway. They took crazy pictures of themselves standing atop rocks on the beach. Even Mr. Pickles joined the action.

"Oh, God! It's *so* beautiful," Sofia squealed gleefully, dancing around until she fell to the sand in a dizzying heap.

All Ben could do was clap delightedly, as if he'd just witnessed a performance by Sandy Duncan. There was such lightness in her display, something so pure, simple, and hopeful. If ever there had been a moment when he could pinpoint the first sign of falling in love, then it was that one.

He watched her wade ankle deep into the ocean, then turn back flirtatiously. "I dare you to take off all your clothes and swim out to there," she challenged, pointing to some vague location in the middle of the sea.

Ben stepped forward. "I will . . . if you will." And then he loosened his tie and began undoing the top buttons of his Oxford shirt.

Sofia laughed, equal parts fear and titillation, watching him in almost amazement.

He finished with his shirt and started to unhook his trousers.

"Feel how cold this water is!" she insisted, pink-checked with embarrassment.

"I don't care," Ben said recklessly, thumb and index finger poised on his zipper. "A dare's a dare. And a skinny-dip's a skinny-dip." His gaze threw down the first gauntlet. *"No undies."*

Sofia stared back in awe, then looked around the deserted beach and up to the highway. "What if someone catches us? We could be arrested." In the face of danger, a practical conservatism had taken over.

But Ben paid it no mind. The zipper was all the way down, revealing Hugo Boss boxers. "It's risky, baby. That's why they call it a dare."

"You go first." There was a teasing quality to her voice, calculated laughter in her eyes.

He gave her a shrewd little smile, and the zipper went back up. "Did the boys in Jersey fall for that back in the day?"

"What do you mean?"

It was the most incompetent attempt at guiltlessness Ben had ever heard. And yet he was captivated by it. Briefly, he wondered—with a certain regret—about the other guys who'd known her before him. A vital part of him longed for her to have no history. He wanted to be the only one. "We strip together and swim together. On the count of three. . . . One thousand one . . ."

"OK!" she screamed. "I'm chicken. I can't do it.

The water's too cold. Plus I'm terrified of sharks and killer whales."

"Killer whales?"

"Didn't you see *Orca?"*

He laughed, then gazed at her triumphantly. "You bailed out on the dare, so I guess it's going to be *truth."* Provocatively, he raised his brow. "I get one question. I can ask you anything."

Sofia covered her mouth and turned away playfully. "Oh, my God! Maybe I'm better off just braving the water." And then she faced him, obviously intrigued, eyes sparkling. "OK, but please don't ask me one of those goofy Barbara Walters questions like what kind of tree I would like to be."

Ben gave her a penetrating stare to prolong the drama, to search her gorgeous face.

"Come on!" Sofia whined, unable to endure the pressure. "Don't take so long, or I'm going to lie."

"If you could have one wish granted, what would it be?"

The question tripped her into a faraway place. Pensively, she looked out at the endless ocean, stared down at her feet in the sand. "Our mother died when I was thirteen. I would want more time with her. For me and Debi. Maybe we wouldn't be so lost." Her voice had taken on a rare timbre. When a tear formed, she killed it with her knuckle and smiled weakly. "That's my truth."

Without thinking, he wrapped her in his arms and held her. They said nothing, and it felt so right, so natural.

When they finally arrived at the hotel, it was everything Sofia had said it would be. The Cypress Inn, a

stately Spanish Colonial co-owned by the legendary
Doris Day, exuded old-fashioned charm. There were
exposed rafters, overstuffed couches, and an intimate
library bar.

The staff doted on Mr. Pickles as if *he* were the
most important guest. Right away, the front-desk clerk
offered him a little biscuit, which the dog greedily
accepted.

Ben was less than enamored by the ritual, but he
put forth what he thought was a reasonably sincere
smile, even petting (awkwardly) Mr. Pickles's furry
head. But the effort only earned him a low growl.

The bellboy ushered them to the tower room,
named for the spiral staircase that led up to a snug
little bedroom, complete with skylights, book nooks,
beautiful tile work, and an incredible view of Carmel.

"Mr. Pickles and I will sleep up here," Sofia
announced. "Do you mind taking the couch downstairs? Then we won't need separate rooms."

Ben gave her a look. Since a growth spurt at fourteen, his days of sleeping comfortably on couches
had ceased to exist. And what about that moment on
the beach? Wasn't he in with a chance to *share* the
bed? Finally, he turned to the bellboy. "Is there a
chiropractor on staff?"

Sofia waved off the concern and flung herself onto
the mattress, rolling around, giggling. Mr. Pickles
jumped up to lick her face. She appeared to enjoy
this. The pleasure of pets had always been lost on
Ben. Dogs and cats were useless. They couldn't talk,
make money, or flush the toilet.

"There's so much to do!" Sofia wailed with impatient glee. "Tip the nice young man so we can start
our vacation."

And so he did, in exchange for the inside scoop

on the best pizza in town. They headed straight for A Little Pizza Heaven on Dolores Street and shared a Valley Garden Pie with broccoli, spinach, zucchini, squash, artichoke hearts, and shredded Parmesan. Then they strolled through downtown Carmel, ducking in and out of art galleries, coveting lots of things they liked but nothing they could afford.

It was dark, and the long flight had taken its toll, but they agreed to kick back a few drinks on the patio of the famous Hog's Breath Inn before calling it a night. In an unconscious move, Ben reached for her hand as they sat there in silence, people-watching, relishing the fact that they were far away from New York.

"This is nice," Sofia said quietly.

"And just think, if your father wasn't trying to kill me, we wouldn't be here together."

"I've never been so fond of attempted murder."

"Do you mean that?"

"Absolutely."

"Baby, you say the sweetest things."

The plan seemed to be working against her now. Like she could get to sleep with Ben down there, only a spiral staircase away. *Not* sleeping with him had become a distraction all its own. She hadn't thought squat about her future all day. Just him. And how great he was. And how fantastic he must be.

This would only happen to me, Sofia thought. Most girls dreamed of a big wedding. She'd had three and boycotted every single one. Now here she lay, alone in the dark, getting all hot and bothered about not getting hot and heavy.

But neatly tucked away in her beauty case was a

pharmacological solution to this problem. *Xanax*.
One little pill could help her deal with the fact that
she wanted to shag Ben as much as she wanted a
revolving house credit at Bergdorf Goodman. Hell,
after the drug did its work, she could probably handle
the Middle East peace crisis, too. And throw in the
whole East Coast/West Coast rapper feud. Piece of
cake.

God, it was *so* tempting. Specifically the Xanax, now,
not sex with Ben. Of course, that still held appeal. But
the prospect of a pill made her wonder. Wasn't it
incongruous to seek chemical relief over a guy you
hadn't slept with? Yes, Sofia decided, it definitely was.

Vowing to stay strong, she sat up and dialed the
only person who could tell her anything she needed
to know about men and sex. Ricky Lopez. Her life
was so *Will and Grace*.

He answered groggily on the second ring.

"I think I'm horny," she announced without pre-
amble. "Tell me something sad or gross to snap me
out of it."

"It's three o'clock in the morning."

Sofia glanced at her travel alarm situated on the
nightstand. "It's just midnight here."

"Hello? Time difference."

"This is an emergency. Besides, I never took geology. You can't expect me to memorize every time
zone in the world."

"You mean geography," Ricky corrected.

"That's what I said."

"No, you said *geology*, which is the study of the
earth's crust."

"Thank you, Mr. Science. Can we get back to my
problem now? God, I need a cigarette. How many
have I had today?" She conducted a silent rundown.

"Just five. I'm OK. I can have one." Lighting up, she took a long, deliberate puff. "I've had the most incredible day with the most incredible guy."

"But you're still horny."

"Yes."

"There's your sad story. Can I go back to sleep now?"

"Don't tease." She paused a beat. "I'm trying to keep things . . . you know . . . uncomplicated."

Ricky sighed. "Then sleep with him. Sex clears the air. If he's great in bed, you keep him and see where it goes. If he's lousy, you run a credit check and stick around only if he's rich. But I think you're missing out. I've heard that he's an amazing lover. *Amazing.*"

Sofia sat statue still. Her body temperature shot up several degrees. The hunger to know every detail, no matter how minute, became overwhelming. "Where did you hear that?"

"A friend of mine is friends with his ex-girlfriend's old roommate."

She tried to visualize the trail in her mind and got lost.

"You know how women can be," Ricky went on. "They can't keep a great lover a secret any more than they can a great hairstylist. That lounge lizard rocks in the bedroom. The story is, women actually *beg* him for sex. The only man who could get me to beg is Dean Cain. And he would have to be wearing the Superman costume."

Sofia could barely breathe. Finally, she managed to say, "That's just gossip. And it's not even firsthand. It's like third or fourthhand. You know how talk gets switched around."

"No woman screws up a story about a man who's great in bed. She stores that information verbatim. I bet you she even knows what she was wearing when she heard it.''

Sofia surveyed her attire. "Pajamas by Nick & Nora.'' Then she felt her forehead. It was warm. Did she have a fever? Yes. Of the Peggy Lee variety.

"You owe it to yourself to find out," Ricky said.

Sofia thought this over. There was an ex-girlfriend of Ben's she didn't know, but apparently trusted. Considering the fact that she was close to marching down the spiral staircase and demanding that he prove his reputation, this person's lovemaking review wielded as much credibility as a thumbs-up from Roger Ebert. "This feels like sex by referral.''

"What's wrong with that?''

"It's tacky!''

"Honey, it's public service!'' Ricky roared. "There are too many men walking around who should only get into a bed if they're tired and need a nap. Where's Ralph Nader when you need him?''

"Am I actually having this conversation?'' Sofia asked.

"If a guy is good enough in bed, you can never feel burned. Case in point—me and Robert. The son of a bitch stole my DVD player. But he was dynamite between the sheets. I still smile when I think of him.''

"Yes, I am having this conversation.''

"What can you lose?''

"Control, for starters.'' She sighed, exasperated. "I love you, but you're a bad influence.''

"I think I'm onto something with this Ralph Nader business. *Consumer Reports* puts new toasters through all sorts of tests, yet guys are free to roam the streets. Where's the watchdog group to stop them from boring us at dinner or disappointing us in the bedroom?

Is this something I could call my congressman about?"

"I'm hanging up." And then Sofia replaced the receiver, obliterating Ricky from her life. Until tomorrow at least. They would probably talk again before noon.

Suddenly Sofia was dying of thirst. Massaging her throat, she obsessed over the inevitable. Going down there. Where he was sleeping. The thought filled her with a crazy mixture of dread and illicit excitement. What if everything Ricky had said was right on the money? Wouldn't she be insane not to find out if this rumored five-star lover was worth the hype?

Before she made up her mind, Sofia was moving down the stairs to fetch a glass, scoop up some ice, and take a quick peek. Did he sleep in the nude?

But Ben was on his way up the stairs. They met halfway. The answer was no. Over boxers he wore a weathered gray T-shirt emblazoned with LATIN FUNK XXL. She nearly yelped at the sight of him, freezing in place. "What are you doing?"

"I couldn't get to sleep and heard you talking. Thought you might want to do something."

She took an indignant step backward. *"Such as?"*

He gave her a strange look. "Go out for another drink. It's only midnight. That's early. I'm usually just getting started about now."

The suggestion does have merit, Sofia admitted to herself. It was certainly a safer choice than staying here, wide-awake, half dressed, and unable to get his alleged sexual prowess out of her mind. "I'm game."

"Good. There's a place called the Sunset Lounge about four miles south of here. A jazz combo usually plays on the weekends."

She nodded agreeably. "Sounds like fun."

"Great," Ben said. His gaze lingered a moment. "Then I guess I'll get dressed." He turned to head back downstairs, waiting until he reached the last step to add, "Oh, and by the way, the talk about me being a great lover is true."

"What?" Sofia gripped the banister.

Casually, Ben spun to face her. "The information Ricky passed on was accurate."

She experienced a blinding wave of outrage and humiliation. "You were eavesdropping! You bastard!"

Ben raised his hands as if to calm her down. "It wasn't by design. I promise. I picked up the receiver to call Taz and there was Ricky telling you to sleep with me. How can you expect me to hang up on a conversation like that?"

With no words at her disposal, Sofia merely stared.

Ben started up the stairs toward her. "I bet you'd like nothing better than to give me a whirl, share a cigarette afterward, and say something like, 'I've had better.'" He pointed at her teasingly and laughed a little. "Tell me that isn't true."

The nerve! Especially since it *was* true. Damn him! "I can't be manipulated that easily. Besides, hype doesn't work with me. I never saw the last *Star Wars* movie, for example."

He was directly in front of her now. "Really? It wasn't bad."

She tried for a nasty look. "What you did was rude."

"Allow me to properly apologize, then." And he leaned in for a kiss, his mouth assertive, claiming hers hungrily, exploring like he had all the time in the world.

Sofia stood there, paralyzed with desire, experiencing an almost drugged-out sensation. It was no wonder. His tongue affected her like a narcotic, and she felt like a girl in serious need of rehab.

The kiss went on for what seemed like forever, until, regretfully, Ben drew back. "Let's go upstairs."

"What about the Sunset Lounge?" Sofia murmured. She was grasping. She knew that. The last thing she cared about was some stupid bar. But it sounded better than, "Shut up and take me right here you son of a bitch," which, in all honesty, is what crossed her mind to say.

He smiled that devastating smile. "Why bother? We've got the Sun*rise* Lounge right here."

It was a line, but it worked. Sofia felt like she could run forever on the superleaded fuel of this man's allure. Those gorgeous eyes. That devilish charm. Adding the rumored reputation of sensual skill to the mix was just too much. Oh, God! She didn't want him now. She wanted him five minutes ago.

"There's nobody here but me and you," Ben said. "You have nothing to hide. You can go wild with me. You can really let go."

Sofia felt her lips part slightly. This was called blissful erotic wonder. His hands cradled her waist as she walked backward up the stairs, facing him, kinetically aware that a bed and several lost hours were just a few steps away.

"I'm going to make you come," he said matter-of-factly. "And when you do, I want to hear you scream. Don't hold anything back. It's just us."

She watched him, mesmerized, as he piloted her into the sanctuary of the cozy bedroom. Suddenly, she was against the wall, pinned there, ever so gently, with her arms over her head.

"You're my pleasure prisoner," he announced with playful arrogance, tenderly nipping her earlobe. As one hand held her wrists, the other moved down to the top button of her pajama top. "These look cute on you."

Sofia felt his warm, plundering tongue slip into her ear, and the sensation triggered instant arousal.

His nimble fingers undid the first button. "But they'd look just as cute off of you." And then the second button was history . . . and the third . . . and the fourth. In a single breathless moment, he slipped her top off and whispered, "Your skin is so soft," as he kissed her neck and shoulders.

"Aspen makes a great body lotion," she murmured. "It's rich in alpha-hydroxy acids." And then the realization of her own words hit her. Oh, God! How unsexy was *that*?

Ben didn't miss a beat. He just laughed and said, "I get turned on when you talk cosmetics to me."

Sofia giggled. "I use an oil-free moisture gel with an SPF of fifteen," she said in a raspy voice.

Ben gripped her passionately, kissed her more urgently. "Yeah, baby, yeah."

Playing along, she ran her fingers through Ben's hair and moaned out, "The main ingredient in my toner is purified rosewater."

"You're making me so hot," Ben said thickly. His tongue grazed the underside of her breast, just where it met her rib cage.

Sofia took in a quick breath. It was so sensual that she wanted to prolong the moment, freeze the feeling.

He outlined her lips with his fingertips and gazed into her eyes. "This could get out of hand. Maybe I should head back downstairs and just go to sleep."

"No!" Sofia protested.

Ben laughed at her, not mockingly, but with empathetic joy. He pulled off his shirt, revealing the sculpted chest, cut arms, and chiseled abdominals that his tasteful wardrobe usually kept hidden. "I suppose I can stick around. You seem pretty desperate for me." There was a teasing glint in his eye, a tiny smirk on his lips.

Boldly, Sofia reached down and stroked him. He was fully aroused, and there was no hiding his erection in those boxers. "Don't do me any favors," she said.

His grin widened. He reached around and slipped his hands into the back of her little pajama shorts, sliding under her thin cotton panties to cup her bare bottom. And then he squeezed. Leaning in, he whispered into her ear, "Are you sure about that?"

Sofia could barely concentrate. She had no idea what was coming next, yet she had never anticipated an event with such intense desire. "About what?" she finally asked.

"About me not doing you any favors."

"Yes," she lied. "I am."

"So you don't want me to go down on you?"

"No, thanks."

He laughed a little.

Sofia smiled, loving the game, the sensation of his breath in her ear.

"I'd get a pillow and make myself comfortable. I like to spend a lot of time there."

"Not interested."

They were both laughing now, drunk on the build-up of a tension about to explode. Sofia bought into the hype now. Ben was incredible. He knew how to have fun, and he knew that you could be having sex before intercourse. *This* was sex—the silly banter, the yearning to do more but the discipline to hold back, the touches that strategically avoided the hot spots.

"I guess you don't want me to make love to you, either."

"Not really."

"Can I tell you what I'm dying to do to you?"

"If you want to. I really don't care."

Gently, he pressed into her so she could feel the increased intensity of his hardness. "When I get all the way inside you, I want to stop and take a rest. Then I want to look into your eyes and let all the sensations rush over us. Does that sound nice?"

Sofia couldn't play this game of ambivalence another second. She wanted him to do everything he mentioned and more. His creativity amazed her. Most men were so predictable in bed, as if they memorized their moves from one of those late-night Cinemax movies that her father loved so much. A French kiss. Nibble on the neck. Slobber on the breasts. A couple licks down there. Several uncomfortable thrusts. Roll over and fall asleep. Ben had a whole new approach. He kept things *very* interesting.

"Can't you feel how excited I am?"

Sofia merely nodded. The heat of his arousal was burning into her. Ben was a tall man with large hands and big feet. The rest of him was *definitely* in proportion. She brought her hands down his smooth chest, let them rest on his hips a moment, and then slowly began to pull down his underwear.

"That's not the move of a girl who's not interested."

"I changed my mind."

The boxers were at his feet now. He was naked. Completely. *Impressively.* Nothing but that incredible smile. "You know, on second thought, I'm really not in the mood."

She giggled, staring down at him. "Well, a close friend of yours didn't get the memo."

Ben shrugged diffidently, stealthily removing her pajama bottoms and panties, then picking her up. "He never listens."

Sofia straddled his hips and cupped his face in her hands, staring at him intently. "What does this mean, Ben? I'm being serious now. I don't have sex just because there's nothing good on television, like your friend Kitty."

He laughed. "It means we'll wake up smiling. The rest we can figure out later." And then he placed her onto the bed. . . .

Chapter Ten

Joseph Cardinella signed every check for his legitimate businesses and filled every cash envelope for his not-so-legitimate ones. That way, he could keep a watchful eye on his concerns.

Staring at the financial reports Debi had prepared, he put one hand on his belly and used his other hand to reach for a Tums. His daughter had a habit of pointing out problems by highlighting them with a fluorescent marker. Once again, Vegas Records was colored shocking pink.

Annoyed, Joseph glanced up from his desk.

Fat Larry had just stuck a pencil in his ear and was now staring at the eraser tip, fascinated. Little Bo was studying *Soap Opera Digest* with more than passing interest.

That's all it took to pull the pin on Joseph's hot temper grenade. "Why the fuck do I pay you nut jobs?"

Fat Larry broke into an immediate flop sweat.

Little Bo stuffed his magazine under one of the sofa cushions.

"I want you to find out why Vegas Records is burning a hole in my pocket! Who's running that outfit, anyway?"

"Oh, you got real nice people working there, boss. Real nice," Fat Larry said.

"Yeah, real nice, boss," Little Bo added earnestly.

"What the fuck is *nice?*" Joseph demanded.

"They always got a smile for us," Fat Larry said.

Little Bo nodded. "And pleasant conversation."

Joseph popped another Tums. *Jesus Christ,* he thought. *I've got Wacky and Cracky here.* "That's great if I'm having a fucking tea party! But I'm trying to run a fucking business!"

"You know, boss," Fat Larry began, concentrating hard, "I don't think many people are buying record albums these days. The cassette tape seems to be catching on, though. Maybe we should make more of those."

"Yeah, I like the cassette tape," Little Bo echoed. "It's easy to carry around."

"Just get over there!" Joseph barked. "I want to see business plans, marketing reports, and product samples before I shut that loser down!"

"You got it, boss," Fat Larry said, shuffling toward the door.

"You want us to rough up the joint, show 'em we mean to settle up right?" Little Bo asked.

"Don't think! Just do what I tell you! And what about that fake Sinatra creep? Has he sunk to the bottom of the Hudson yet?"

"No sign of him, boss," Fat Larry reported.

Little Bo nodded. "Yeah, it's like he disappeared."

Joseph grunted. At least there was *some* good news. Fuhgeddaboudit.

The lunkheads started out.

"And don't drag your asses taking care of this Vegas Records errand!" Once alone, he stared back at the reports, pleased to see that his bingo parlors were performing well. They were like little cash factories. Nothing wrong with that. Besides, it gave the old-timers something to do and didn't bust their bank accounts. QVC should be so responsible! Those sell-evangelists hypnotized people into spending money they didn't have.

He pushed the papers away and sat there in the silence, ruminating over the Sofia situation. Maybe this vacation in crazy California would calm her down, make her see the world sensibly for a change. All this moving in and moving out business had to stop. He glanced up, as if to heaven. Joseph knew that his beloved Jacqueline hated to see all this conflict.

But what choice did he have? Sofia displayed no signs of self-directed ambition. She needed a secure future, and the Cardinella interests were just limping along. Enter Vincent Scalia, first son of a fine Mafia family. That kind of merger would put a treat in everybody's bag.

Thinking of the Scalia clan's hold on movie piracy made Joseph's mouth water. Their outfit made the profits from the bingo parlors look like loose change. Sure, it was illegal, but going to the multiplex could break a family budget. Why not let the public buy the latest Harrison Ford flick from a street vendor? Plus, once Sofia and Vincent got married, the Cardinellas could snuggle up to some of the action.

Joseph paused. The house was too quiet. Thoughts of Debi crept into mind. Last night she'd stayed out late. Earlier today she'd left a message, something about getting her hair and nails done, then plans for dinner. What the hell was going on? He could always count on her to be home.

The idea of a frozen pizza stirred up feelings of loneliness. On impulse, he decided to head into Manhattan, grab a bite to eat, and pick up some presents for his girls. He got a kick out of surprising them like that.

He arrived at Berrenger's one hour before closing time, just long enough to browse and pick out the perfect gifts. Approaching the cosmetics department, he saw Ricky Lopez standing behind the Aspen counter and did a double take.

When Ricky made eye contact, he mouthed an unmistakable, "Oh, shit!" Then he ducked down to avoid detection. But it was too late.

Joseph stomped over and knocked hard on the glass to get Ricky's attention.

Sheepishly, Ricky rose to a standing position and attempted to act surprised. "Mr. Cardinella! What brings you out tonight?"

Joseph squinted his eyes suspiciously. "You're supposed to be in California with Sofia. At least that's what she told me."

"Yes . . . I know . . . I am . . . I mean . . . I was . . . something . . ."

He stared daggers at the stammering fairy. "Who went with her?"

Ricky averted his gaze. "Debi? I think. . . . I'm really not sure."

"Debi's here," Joseph said flatly.

"Well, there you go," Ricky said, laughing nervously. "You obviously know more than I do." He shook his head in a display of zaniness. "Wow. It's been a crazy week. Am I here? Listen to me. I'm starting to sound like Shirley MacLaine. Did you know that in a previous life I was a Mayan princess."

Joseph didn't crack a smile. "Give me the number where she's staying."

Ricky blanched. "The number?"

"I know you've got it," Joseph snapped. "You talk to each other every day."

Ricky stepped over to the register, scratched the number onto the back of a business card, and reluctantly handed it over.

Joseph pulled out his cell phone and punched in the digits.

"Good afternoon, Cypress Inn."

"I'm looking for my daughter, Sofia Cardinella."

"Yes," the operator chirped sweetly. "But I'm afraid she's asked the front desk to hold her calls. I'll be happy to take a message."

Joseph stalled, putting his crafty mind to work. "Actually, I need to get a message to her traveling companion."

"Mr. Pickles?"

"Not him," Joseph chuckled, playing along. "The other guy."

"Of course," the desk clerk said, amused. "And what note can I leave for Mr. Estes?"

Joseph gripped the cell phone tighter. A rush of anger went straight to his head. "Tell that lowlife bastard to drop dead!"

"Is that bastard with all caps or is lowercase fine?"

"All caps!"

"Alrighty, then."

He shut off the phone and turned back to Ricky, who was nowhere in sight. Still enraged, he called Fat Larry's cellular. "Where the hell are you?"

"Is that you, boss?"

"No, it's fucking Donald Trump."

"We're still at Vegas Records."

"Drop that. I want you two on the next plane to San Francisco."

"You got it, boss."

"Listen carefully. I want you to rent a car, drive to Carmel, find the Cypress Inn, and kill that sleazy Sinatra wannabe once and for all! He's shacking up with my daughter!"

"Should we fly to San Francisco first, boss?

It felt like a montage from some romantic movie. The part where the two beautiful stars do all sorts of fun things while the love theme plays. Celine Dion usually sings it.

Sofia and Ben were lounging naked in bed, eating fruit and laughing as he tried to polish her fingernails. "You're terrible at this," she teased.

He looked up at her with mock hurt. "I am not. Hold still."

"You're getting polish on my skin!"

"Hold still!"

"Can I do yours next?"

He looked up again, serious this time. "Absolutely not."

"Let me paint one or two of them black. A lot of men do it now. Look at Carson Daly."

"The MTV guy?"

"Yes. Isn't he cute?"

Ben grinned. "Adorable. But I don't take my fashion cues from junior Dick Clarks."

"Just let me try it on one nail."

"No."

"Pleeeeease . . . I'll let you make love to me," she purred.

He finished her right hand and blew softly on it. "I've already made love to you. Several times last night and twice this morning. Which reminds me. An afternoon quickie is definitely in order, but we can wait until your nails dry."

She watched him start on her left hand and experienced a surge of delight. Ben Estes *defined* the concept of a Fun Guy. Suddenly, a thought occurred to her. "What's the longest time you've stayed in bed with a girl?"

"Two days." He didn't look up. Polishing nails was serious business. "How about you?"

"Just one. His name was Karl. He married a girl from Queens and moved to Newark to sell vacuum cleaners."

"Sounds like a dream."

"Not really. He was too quiet in bed. I could never tell when he . . . you know . . . *reached a climax.*" The last three words were delivered in a faint whisper. "He didn't sigh. . . . He didn't shudder. . . . *Nothing.* Sometimes I wondered why I was there."

Ben polished off the pinkie and blew once more. "I like to keep a girl informed. Sort of my own sexual wire service."

Sofia patted his head with her free hand. "Which is very useful, especially for girls—such as myself— who like to stay up on current events."

He gestured toward his work. "You like?"

"Very much, except for the ghastly smear on my right index finger." She sighed, adoring being pampered by a man. "Do you know how to give facials?"

He raised a lewd eyebrow. "Yes, and I use *all-natural* ingredients."

Sofia felt the warmth of a slight blush on her cheeks. "If I hadn't cut off all my hair recently, I would let you braid it."

Ben leaned back and studied her intently. "I'm trying to picture you with long hair. I bet you were sexy."

"And with short hair?"

"Off-the-charts sexy."

"As in beyond number one or didn't make the list?"

He climbed on top of her, kissing her deeply. "What do you think?"

Sofia kept her hands in the air to protect her wet nails. "I think you have a future as a manicurist."

Ben let out a satisfied moan and scooted down to lay his head on her stomach, just below her breasts.

"I told you about my record holder for days in bed. Tell me about yours," she said.

"It was CZ."

"The significant ex?"

"Ba-da-bing. We had a pretty good time. Never could agree on food, though. She hated Chinese."

The telephone jangled.

Sofia gave it a strange look. "It must be the front desk. I told them to hold all our calls."

"What calls?"

"Any calls we might get."

"I'm not expecting any."

"Everyone should be expecting a call from somebody." She carefully grabbed the receiver, thinking of her nails, after the third ring. "Hello?"

"You've got big trouble." It was Ricky.

She didn't skip a beat. "Honey, I'm in bed with it!"

"You didn't!"

"*I did.* Five times already. And counting. By the way, how did get you through?"

"I told the front desk it was a family emergency, *which it is.* Your father knows."

"Knows what?"

"That I'm not in California with you. I'm calling from Berrenger's. He just left the store."

"What did you tell him?"

"As little as possible, and then I hid in the break room."

"Really?" Sofia managed absently, stifling a moan as Ben ran a lazy tongue across her navel.

"Are you listening to me?" Ricky asked.

"Of course," she trilled, marveling at Ben's sculpted arm as he stretched to reach a condom off the nightstand.

"Buying designer is a waste of money. Knockoffs are better."

"I agree," Sofia muttered, her gaze glued on Ben as he tore open the mylar wrapping. She leaned forward to help him slip it on.

"I knew you weren't listening!"

"Of course I am."

"You would never buy Louis Vuitton from the trunk of a Buick."

"Yes, I would. In a minute." Caressingly, she guided Ben inside her with both hands.

"Liar," Ricky hissed.

Ben took the phone away from her. "Who's this?"

Shocked, Sofia covered her mouth.

"Ricky."

"Hi, Ricky. Call us back in about five minutes. We're in the middle of something. It won't take long." And then he hung up.

She roared with laughter. "I can't believe you just did that!"

Ben broke up, too, tracing the outline of her breasts with his fingertips, driving her crazy. "What could be more important than this, anyway?"

She pretended to mull over the question. "Shopping."

"Oh, yeah?" He gave her a gentle, corkscrew motion thrust. This man really knew how to use his hips.

"Well, it's at least a close second," Sofia whispered, almost breathless.

Ben nodded confidently. "That's what I thought." He planted his hands opposite her shoulders and straightened his elbows.

Sofia embraced him with her legs, brought her feet onto his buttocks, and pushed down her heels to drive him deeper inside. The angle was delicious. She could actually feel him against her G spot.

"I lied," Ben confessed.

"About what?"

"I told Ricky five minutes. It's only been two, and my rocket's ready to launch. Oh, baby!"

"Say my name."

"Betty."

She laughed and bit down on his arm.

"Ouch! OK I'll be serious. Patrick, you feel so good!"

She bit him again, laughing harder now. It was amazing how his quick arousal and silly humor could increase her own pleasure. Every moment in bed with him sparkled with surprise.

Suddenly Ben dropped to his elbows. Just so he could kiss her on the mouth and engage in a delicate tongue dance. "I'm about to come. Can you go there with me?"

She pressed her heels into his buttocks once more, harder this time. Then she arched her back. And the sensations knocked the breath from her body. Now he was inside her as deep as he could go, his rock-hard penis was playing her G spot like a mandolin, and the smell of hours of sexual abandon hung in the air around them, humid with lusty indulgence.

The combination of it all offered intense rapture, though not enough to make her climax. But Ben had taken her to great heights last night and even earlier this morning. The earth didn't have to move every time. And this unspoken reciprocity made her feel like she was on some kind of sexual whirligig ride.

Last night Ben had performed oral sex for what seemed like forever. Oh, boy, did this man ever know how to *get down* when he *went down!* He actually came just from giving her head. Sofia never knew such a man existed, one who could ejaculate just over the sheer joy of satisfying a woman that way.

Now he was gripping her shoulders tightly, breathing harder, letting out a series of long sighs and loud moans that could probably be heard on the busy streets of Carmel below.

Sofia reveled in it, loving the fact that she could help him arrive at such fast and intense ecstasy. *This* was sex. Her experiences with other men could now be filed under *unfortunate body collisions*.

Spent, Ben kissed her deeply and disconnected, rolling off to one side. He grabbed a cigarette from her pack on the nightstand and lit one, offering her the first puff. A gentleman to the end.

She accepted it with a smile. "This is a nonsmoking room, you know."

"Then you shouldn't do the little trick with your feet, baby. Talk about hot. That's a real fire hazard." He took the bad habit back and dragged deep, closing his eyes.

"What are you thinking about?"

"You."

"What about me?"

Ben opened his eyes and gave her a sexy look. "Your pussy must be lined with mink. That's how good it feels."

Sofia felt a moment's pure shock. "That's so *dirty*." She started to laugh.

"Are you offended?"

"No," she said simply, emboldened by the erotic adventure of it all. "It makes me feel . . . I don't know . . . powerful."

"Why don't you try it, then?"

She rolled over onto her stomach, briefly hiding her face with her hands.

Ben grinned, stroking her bare bottom. "Come on. Tell me something dirty."

"I can't."

"You've got it in you."

Sofia stalled for time by taking her turn with the cigarette. "What makes you so sure?"

Ben waited for her to finish a puff and took it back. "Because I've been making love to you since midnight." He glanced at the clock. "And we're heading into late afternoon. I know what you're capable of."

She hesitated. "I've never said anything dirty."

"It's just us here. This is a safe place to liberate yourself."

"You have a magnificent cock."

Ben nodded, taking another deep drag. "Now that

is some sexy talk.'' He watched his smoke curl up to the ceiling. ''I'd like to hear you say that again.''

''What man wouldn't?'' She smirked, took the cigarette, and snuffed it out in an empty water glass. ''Why don't they have any ashtrays?''

''It's a nonsmoking room.''

''That's no excuse.'' She remembered the decanter downstairs. ''They have sherry. Who drinks sherry?''

''People like my parents,'' Ben said.

Sofia rested her chin on his chest. ''Why did you have to bring up the subject of parents?''

He kissed her nose. ''I like to think of myself as versatile in the ways of dirty talk.''

''My father knows that I'm not here with Ricky.''

''Does he know that you're here with me?''

''I don't think so. Not yet, anyway.''

''What's the worst that can happen?''

''You could be killed.''

''That's pretty bad.''

''Do you have to sing Sinatra songs? I don't think he'd hate you near as much if you sang the music of, say, Pat Boone.''

''That wouldn't solve the problem.''

''Why?''

''Pat Boone? I'd kill *myself.*''

Chapter Eleven

Sofia and Ben had matched his record with CZ and stayed in bed for two days. Not content to merely tie with an ex-girlfriend, Sofia wanted to smash that statistic like a guitar. Her mission—to go for three.

Right now they were horizontally content, gloriously exhausted, basking in the afterglow of another sexual marathon, limbs intimately interlocked, sheets rumpled and twisted around them.

"I'm hungry," Ben said. "Let's have breakfast in the garden courtyard." He kissed the top of her head. "Some fresh air would feel great."

"We can't do that," Sofia said. Her incredulous tone implied that Ben had just suggested they do something foolish, like hitchhike to Alabama.

"We're on vacation," Ben said lazily. "We can do anything we want."

She rose up in protest, pinching his nipple. "I thought we were going to set a new bed record! If we go eat in the courtyard, we'll have to stop counting at two days.''

Ben regarded her with puzzled amusement. "You're serious."

Sofia straddled him, pinning his arms over his head. *"Very."*

"As much as I love being in bed with you, baby, I'm starting to get cabin fever."

"Did you get *cabin fever* with CZ?"

"Yes," Ben insisted. "I still have nightmares about it. I was broke and couldn't afford to take her out to a nice restaurant. So the whole us-against-the-world lovers bit was actually just a clever gimmick."

"You can't afford to take me out, either," Sofia said.

"But this vacation is paid for," Ben pointed out. "We're cheating ourselves by not taking advantage of that."

Looking uncertain, she let go of his arms and steadied herself by placing her hands on his shoulders.

He cradled her hips and swept an appreciative gaze up and down her body. "Do you realize that you've already passed CZ in an area far more important?"

Sofia brightened immediately. "What?"

"With you, my spunk gun has fired twelve times in two days."

She played with his hair. "I thought only high school seniors could do that."

"Twelve times," Ben said, reaching up to claim her breasts and gently tweak her nipples. "And that's without Viagra."

"You," she said, pressing a finger into his sheet-of-steel stomach for emphasis, *"are a stud."*

"With CZ, I think it only happened seven times in two days, and I'm being generous."

That was all Sofia needed to hear. CZ had nothing on her. She was up by five. Climbing off Ben, she started to head downstairs.

"Where are you going?" he complained.

"To take a shower, put on makeup, and dress up in something pretty."

Ben swung out of bed and onto his feet. "Want some company for the first part?"

Sofia stared at him with faux coolness. "To be honest, I'm sick of you."

He moved toward her, confident as hell. "Not me."

She broke into a grin, unable to hold the pose. No man had a right to look that good naked. It was uncanny. "You are so sexy," she told him.

"I know."

"It's much sexier to be unaware of it. Or at least to pretend to be."

"OK, how's this?" He slouched his shoulders and made a pathetic face. "You wouldn't want to make love, would you?"

"Now, that's sexy."

He pulled her close and ravaged her mouth with his own. Against her thigh, Sofia could feel his growing excitement. She looked down. He was almost fully erect. *Again.* "That thing between your legs should take up stamp collecting or something. I need a break."

"But we haven't done it on the stairs yet," Ben said.

"We haven't done it on the top bookshelf, either."

He pretended to like the idea. "How's your balance?"

Downstairs, three assertive knocks hit the door.

"It's probably someone from the hotel making sure we're still alive," Sofia joked.

Ben moved swiftly past to begin his descent. "I'll take care of it."

"Like that?"

"What's wrong?"

"You're naked. Not to mention hard. You could get arrested."

"It's perfectly legal to *answer* a door when you're naked and hard. Now *knocking* on a door in this state is another matter entirely."

Sofia watched him go down the stairs, sure that he was bluffing, certain that he would come running back to say, "Gotcha!" But in the name of exhibitionists everywhere, Ben stayed true to the cause of nudity in all its splendor. *The Full Monty*, indeed.

She listened to him open the door. Just as quickly, she heard it slam shut. Then he came bounding up the stairs—two and three at a time—still in the buff but considerably less aroused. He was all panic now. "Your father's goons are here!"

Sofia could scarcely believe it. "Fat Larry and Little Bo?"

Ben nodded, looking around desperately. "Shit, all my clothes are downstairs." His gaze fell on a messy lump at the foot of the bed. "These will have to do."

She watched him slip on the same boxers and T-shirt he'd been wearing just before their self-imposed exile. Suddenly it occurred to her that neither one of them had worn a stitch of fabric for two days. There'd just been an endless cycle of sex, showers, room service, and tips to the bellboy to walk Mr. Pickles. Now her eyes became fixated on the design emblazoned across Ben's chest. "What does LATIN FUNK XXL mean?"

He looked annoyed. "It means get the hell away from the two mob rejects at the door!"

Sofia gathered up her pajamas and started to put them on. "Did they recognize you?"

"I don't know. They spent more time looking at my dick than my face."

"I've always wondered about them," Sofia mused, buttoning her top. "They never married, you know."

"I'd say they have limited options, no matter which way they go. Not many women—or gay men—are hot for the John-Gotti-gone-retarded type."

"Maybe you could take them shopping one day. I've always hated the way they dress."

Ben flitted toward her, taking firm hold of her upper arms. "This is *serious,* Sofia. Do you understand? Those guys came to my apartment building with designs on *shooting* me. Now they've followed me across the goddamn country, and I'm pretty sure it's not for tips on getting that *GQ* look!"

She witnessed the fear in his eyes. She felt it in his touch. Papa had gone too far. This was way over the line, even for him. Invitations, caterers, and ugly bridesmaid dresses were one thing. But sending his two flunkies to inflict bodily harm—or worse—was quite another.

"What the hell is it going to take for your father to leave me alone?" Ben asked.

An answer fell out of the sky. Such a solution would be shocking. But very effective. Sofia decided to give voice to it. "Family is sacred to Papa. He would never kill my husband, no matter how much he hated him."

Ben furrowed his brow. "What are you saying?"

"I'm saying we should get married."

"I've heard that you don't show up for your weddings."

She tugged at his shirt. "I'll show up for this one." A pause. "Let's not even have a wedding! Why spend a fortune on bad organists and a reception for relatives we wish we didn't have?"

Ben merely stared.

"I don't love you—"

"It's beginning to sound like a marriage already."

She tugged at his shirt again, more fiercely this time. *"Let me finish.* I don't love you all the way . . . but I'm halfway there."

"You're slightly ahead. I'm only about three-eighths."

"Our sex life is fantastic—"

"It *is* our life," Ben put in. "At least it has been for the last two days."

She pressed a finger to his lips. "Stop interrupting. The thing couples fight about the most is money. We don't have any, so we can't fight about that."

"It's the having-no-money part that is usually the root of those arguments," Ben said.

Sofia waved off his comment. "My father hates you. I know how unfair that is, so to make things even, I'll do something to make your mother not like me."

"That's easy. Just breathe."

She straightened her spine defensively. "What's that supposed to mean?"

"You don't stand a chance with her. She's still furious about me breaking up with my high school girlfriend, Mary Beth Cooper."

"What happened?"

"She came out as a lesbian—on our prom date."

"So why was your mother furious?"

"Denial. She's still convinced that Mary Beth simply has an odd habit of moving in with her best friends." He stopped. "You have this amazing ability to take me off point. The subject is—"

Three more knocks rapped the door.

Mr. Pickles stirred slightly this time but remained curled up in the corner.

"That," Ben said. He began to pace.

"What do you think of my idea?"

"About getting married?"

She nodded.

"It's insane."

"By what standard? You sing out of a karaoke machine for a living."

"It's really not a living—just occasional earnings when I'm lucky."

Boom! Boom! Boom! The knocking could be officially upgraded to pounding now.

Mr. Pickles bolted from his corner, barking as he began a mad dash down the stairs to scratch the door.

Ben posed the question swarming all around them. "Marriage?"

"It doesn't have to mean forever," Sofia tried to assure him. "Think of me as your future ex-wife. It's trendy now to have a divorce under your belt before you're thirty. We're both twenty-nine. There isn't much time."

Ben gave up a so obviously smitten smile. "Forget what I said about three-eighths. I'm halfway there, too."

She felt her heart move. "Really?"

"Maybe even three-quarters. Let's get married."

"Are you sure?"

"This way I won't get shot, right?"

Sofia nodded dreamily.

"Then let's do it."

"OK, I'm going down there to stall Fat Larry and Little Bo. You call the front desk and find out where we go to get married in a hurry. And be sure to tell them that I'm not pregnant. I don't want anyone jumping to conclusions.''

As expected, she stood face-to-face with her father's sycophants when she opened the door.

Mr. Pickles attacked Fat Larry's ankle.

Sofia picked up her dog and did her best to calm him. Stressful situations triggered his acne problem. Had she thought to bring along his special medication? Pretending to act surprised, she quickly embraced the guys as Mr. Pickles snapped and snarled.

''Sofia, your father sent us to have a talk with your friend,'' Little Bo explained.

She returned a blank look. ''Who?''

Fat Larry and Little Bo traded confused glances. ''That singer,'' Fat Larry said.

''You mean Ben Estes?''

They nodded.

''You're in the wrong state, fellas. Ben's in New York.''

''We know that he's here, Sofia,'' Little Bo said.

''Yeah,'' Fat Larry put in. ''A few minutes ago he came to the door buck naked.''

Sofia stared back as if they shared the head of Medusa. ''This door?''

''That's right,'' Little Bo confirmed.

''You two are seeing things and could obviously use a good nap! And I resent the implication that I would have anything to do with a *naked man!* Honestly!''

Fat Larry became agitated. ''As sure as my ankle's bleeding from a dog bite, a naked man opened this door!''

''Are you calling me a slut?'' Sofia asked sharply.

Fat Larry got nervous and broke out in a flop sweat.

''We know what we saw,'' Little Bo said.

''You *are* calling me a slut!''

"Nobody said nothing about anybody being a slut," Fat Larry said.

"The last I heard, women who cavort around in hotel rooms with naked men are sluts, and that's exactly what you're accusing me of doing."

"Sofia—" Fat Larry began.

She raised a hand to stop him. "I'm too upset to talk about this." Now she fought against fake tears. "I don't know if I'm going to tell my father about this or not. I'll have to think about that." And then she closed the door.

Ben crept down the stairs and into view.

"What did you find out?"

"How would you like to get married on the beach?"

Sofia twirled around once, stopping suddenly to put Mr. Pickles down. "It doesn't take much to make him dizzy. I don't want him to throw up," she explained, then continued twirling. "I love the idea!"

"There's a guy here who used to run one of those twenty-four-hour chapels in Las Vegas. He did all the ceremonies dressed up like Elvis."

"Call him!"

"He's already on his way. Lucky for us, business is slow."

"This is fabulous." She sighed. "A beach wedding with Elvis."

"The King was his old shtick. He dresses up like Jay Leno now."

Sofia was crestfallen.

"He has a prosthetic chin and even opens the ceremony with a five minute monologue."

She shook her head. "We should get dressed and leave the hotel before Fat Larry and Little Bo come back."

Ben leaned over to fetch some clothes out of his open suitcase. "Oh, Christ!" he shouted.

Sofia was startled.

He glared contemptuously at Mr. Pickles. "That little shit pissed in my luggage!"

Sofia dashed to the scene—and the smell—of the crime. "It's my fault," she said quickly. "I haven't been giving him enough attention, and he's jealous. Mr. Pickles is very sensitive."

"So am I!" Ben raged. "About smelling like dog urine!"

She surveyed the damage, lifting a few articles to see how much had soaked through. *Oh, God.* Working hard to conceal her surprise, she wondered when Mr. Pickles had started this destructive campaign. This was much more than a single whiz. But Ben didn't have to know that. At the bottom, she discovered a pair of unsoiled khakis. Everything else needed to be washed. Handing off the pants to Ben, she said, "Wear these for now. We'll have to find a laundromat later."

He snatched the khakis ungratefully. "What about a shirt?"

Sofia shook her head. "You're holding the only survivor. I suppose you'll have to keep on that T-shirt."

Ben pulled the fabric out from his chest. *"This?"* His tone was sour.

"What *does* LATIN FUNK XXL mean? I should know if you're going to get married in it."

He shoved one leg at a time into the pants, tucked in the T-shirt, and proceeded to finger comb his bed-head hair. "It means I hate little rat dogs that piss on my clothes."

"Ben!" Sofia admonished, moving fast to coddle

Mr. Pickles. She covered his ears and kissed his head. "Dogs understand hostility."

"Really? That's good to know." He took a menacing step toward his nemesis. "DON'T PISS ON MY CLOTHES!"

Mr. Pickles cowered momentarily. Then he growled.

"You're just making things worse," Sofia hissed. "You have to combat negative behaviors with positive energy."

"I have to get married in clothes that make me look like I'm going to a flea market. Don't ask me to do a happy dance."

She stared down at the floor. Maybe Mr. Pickles needed to see a pet therapist. Oprah had one on her show a few weeks ago. "This won't happen again," she promised.

Ben grabbed his toiletries bag. "I'm going to brush my teeth and shave."

Sofia waited until she heard the water running, then went upstairs to change. She chose some hot pants by Jose Enrique Ona Selfa, a luxurious Preen top that revealed more than it covered, a delicate Chanel belt with oversized pearls, and a pair of strappy, stiletto heel Versace sandals. The whole ensemble had scorched one of her Visa cards. It was not typical bridal wear. But this was no typical wedding. *Jay Leno?* What's up with that?

She tottered down the stairs, and the moment Ben saw her, she knew that all was forgiven. His jaw hitting the floor gave it away.

"I can't stay mad at anyone who looks that hot."

"Apology accepted."

"That wasn't an apology."

"Of course it was."

"What do I have to apologize about?"

Sofia felt an overwhelming need to smoke. Prewedding jitters? She lit a cigarette and gave Ben a don't-go-there look. "You yelled at Mr. Pickles."

"Because he pissed all over my clothes."

She shrugged diffidently. "He's just a sweet little dog. He can't tell us why he's upset about something, so he communicates his feelings in other ways."

"What about my feelings about wearing clothes that make me smell like a kennel?"

"That's my point. You just aired your issues verbally. It's out in the open now." Sofia stubbed out the cigarette. She really needed to quit. Maybe that patch thing would help. But then she wouldn't be able to wear anything sleeveless. People would think she was some kind of nicotine addict.

Ben shook his head, took her hand, and started for the door. "Let's just get married."

Sofia felt an incredible tingling sensation. She was beaming inside and out. "At least you know that I'm not marrying you for your money."

"Even if you were, it wouldn't bother me. I'm happy to share the few hundred dollars I have in the bank."

"Jay Leno is waiting for us."

"I never imagined that someone would actually say those words to me." He stopped at the door, gazing into her eyes. "This marriage will be full of surprises."

Chapter Twelve

In the hotel lobby, they were spotted by Fat Larry and Little Bo.

"Hey, you!" Fat Larry yelled.

Sofia and Ben broke out into a dead run.

Fat Larry and Little Bo followed in hot pursuit.

It was tough going on the high heels, but Sofia managed to keep up. She glanced behind to see they had a comfortable lead. "For two smokers, we run pretty fast."

"Motivation helps. Two stupid men with guns are chasing us," Ben said.

But maintaining a decent speed proved impossible. There were traffic jams, merchants wall-to-wall, and poke-along tourists. Ben held her hand tightly, pulling her, practically dragging her through the crowd.

"I feel like Pamela Anderson in *V.I.P.*," Sofia cracked. "She never wears sensible shoes on that show."

And on they ran down Seventh Avenue, Fat Larry and Little Bo still lurching past pedestrians, far behind but steady on the chase. If nothing else, the guys had tenacity.

Sofia struggled to remain in vertical motion and go through her tiny beaded bag at the same time. She pushed past two shades of Aspen lipstick, a cream concealer, a half-empty pack of Virginia Slims, matches from Swifty Morgan's, and a Visa so close to the credit limit that it seemed to give off radioactive vibrations. Finally, her fingers wrapped around the cell phone. She snatched it out. Thank God Debi's mobile number was on speed dial.

"Hello?"

"It's me!" Sofia shouted, almost out of breath. Oh, these shoes were killing her. The price a girl pays to be sexy.

"Why are you screaming?" Debi asked.

"Fat Larry and Little Bo are gaining on us. Papa sent them here to kill Ben."

"I can't believe it."

"It's true! Our father is deranged!"

"No, I believe that. I can't believe those two made it to Carmel. They get lost in parking garages."

"Well, they're here, and by the time we stop running, I'll have blisters on top of my blisters."

"I told you to pack sneakers. Papa's gone too far this time."

"That's *exactly* what I was thinking."

"He should get his own life, maybe start dating a retired stripper. That's what men like him do in Jackie Collins novels," Debi said.

"Brilliant!"

"I'll find a woman named Bubbles and set it up."

"Are you sitting down?"

"I'm walking in Central Park."

"Find a bench."

"The news is that big?"

"Bigger. Ben and I are getting married."

Debi indulged in a moment of shocked silence. "When?"

"Right now."

"But you hardly know him."

"We just spent two days in bed together."

"Did he fart or belch?"

Sofia pulled a face. "No!"

"You don't really know each other until he's comfortable enough to do that in bed."

"May he always be a stranger, then!"

Curious, Ben turned back.

"Don't ever fart in bed," Sofia told him.

"I'm obviously getting that out of context," he said, charging ahead. They were on Ocean Avenue, moving away from the town and toward the Pacific.

"When I become Mrs. Ben Estes, Papa will have no choice but to call off this nonsense."

"Ironically, he's still forcing you into marriage," Debi observed.

Sofia thought about this. "You're right! And this time it isn't costing him any money!"

"But that doesn't mean he won't pay. I want to be there when Ben calls him Dad for the first time."

"I can just picture it." Sofia laughed a little. "Have you talked to Ricky today?"

"He called earlier in an uproar. Something about you becoming a sex-crazed woman who believes in designer knockoffs."

"Why doesn't he just call me a girl from Queens!"

"I think he did."

"Well, it's a lie! I'd never buy anything fake!"

"So, there's truth to the sex-crazed part?"

"Like Ricky can talk," Sofia shot back. "He knows the body measurements of every guy on *Dawson's Creek.*"

"I still don't understand the whole James Van Der Beek thing."

"You know what I just thought of? All the dedicated people who showed up to my last three weddings. Will they be mad that I got married without them?"

"They're *still* mad. You kept all the gifts."

Sofia felt a sudden twinge of sadness. Whenever she daydreamed about her wedding, Debi was always right there as her maid of honor. "I wish you could be here."

"Maybe I can. Keep your cellular near all the action. People have phone sex and seem to enjoy it. Why not a phone wedding?"

"I love that idea!" Sofia squealed. "You're my maid of honor."

"Phone weddings are great. I don't have to wear that awful satin dress or stop Aunt Rebecca from turning her head upside down in the champagne fountain."

Sofia paused to pay attention to her surroundings. She gasped. They were on Carmel Beach, a snowy-sanded stretch of heaven shadowed by cypress trees.

Ben spun to face her, squeezing her hand. "Are we really going to do this?"

"What choice do we have? I can't run another step in these heels." She held the phone up to his ear. "Say hi to Debi, your future sister-in-law."

"Hi, Debi. . . . Thank you. . . . No, I don't love her. . . . She doesn't love me, either. . . . We'll get there eventually. . . . I see Jay Leno. . . . He's doing the ceremony. . . . I'm serious. . . . Have to go. . . . Oh,

Debi, I'm an only child, so it feels great to have a sister. Here's yours."

Sofia cradled the phone to her ear again. "I'm back."

"What's this about Jay Leno?" Debi asked.

"It's not the *real* Jay Leno. It's a man who dresses up like him." Sofia squinted to capture a good look from where she stood in the sand. "He's got on a fake chin and a nice suit . . . and Ben's laughing. He must be funny, too." She sighed rapturously. "Debi, the beach is gorgeous."

"How can you get married when the two of you openly admit that you're not in love?"

"Most couples fall *out* of love after they marry," Sofia pointed out. "We're going to fall *in* love. It's a much better way. I think everyone should get married to someone they don't love."

"Only you could make a logical case for that."

"Oh, no!" Sofia erupted, hand going over mouth. "I've been so self-involved that I forgot to ask. How was SpeedDating?"

"It was everything I didn't want it to be. I prefer one long bad date to eight short ones."

"It couldn't have been that awful."

"One guy was older than me and still lived with his mother. Another guy was almost as old as Papa and boasted about his sperm count."

"*Yuck.* Was there at least one normal guy?"

"Vincent was the closest thing."

"*My* Vincent?"

"Is he yours?" Debi asked. "You've never claimed him before."

The sharp tone caught Sofia off guard. "I didn't mean *mine* in the literal sense. Just the Vincent that I know. What was he doing there?"

"He thought finding a new girlfriend would make you jealous."

"How pathetic."

"It gets worse. Now he takes me out to dinner for tips on how to change into the kind of man you want."

"Oh, Debi, that's a terrible way to spend your time!"

"It beats the old guy who's into sperm worship."

"These are your options?"

"Welcome to Planet Fat Girl."

Sofia shut her eyes a moment. "Don't talk about yourself that way. I won't stand for it."

"Welcome to Planet of the Plus-Size Girls?"

"Debi!"

"Sofia!" It was Ben calling her.

"Hold on," she instructed her sister, scooting over to husband-to-be and Jay Leno look-alike.

"There's a problem," Ben said.

She held out her bare hand. "You bet there is. No ring!"

Ben fixed a stern gaze on her. "We don't have a witness."

"I usually bring someone dressed up like David Letterman," the Jay Leno impostor explained. "But he's got diarrhea."

Sofia leaned in to whisper, "Too much information." Then she thought of Debi. "My sister!"

"We need a *live* witness," Ben said. "Oh, shit." He swallowed hard. The blood drained from his face.

Sofia spun around.

Fat Larry and Little Bo had finally caught up with them.

* * *

Ricky Lopez stared at the check from his mother. He could count on it to arrive every two weeks. It was hard to accept the fact that she afforded it only by taking extra shifts at the hotel and doing alterations and light sewing on the side. No matter its origin, Ricky needed the money. It kept him afloat. At least part of the sum did. He lived frugally and put whatever remained in the bank.

Sending a check was Cynthia Lopez's way of expressing love and apologizing for her inability to stand up to her husband, also Ricky's father, also a bigot who would rather ignore his son than admit he had a gay one.

Despite the rift, Ricky and his mother remained close. They arranged secret meetings in Manhattan regularly. These get-togethers were always subject to quick cancellation because she lived in fear of Juan finding out about their visits. Long ago his father had banned Ricky from their lives and often warned Cynthia that if ever that stance was defied, she would rue the day.

This evening they had a date for coffee at Dean & Deluca. She loved the place because you could see the *Today Show* studio from there. His mother had a mad crush on Matt Lauer. *Come to think of it, so do I*, Ricky thought. He decided to call and make sure they were still on.

The housekeeping manager at the Charade was a sweetheart. He paged Cynthia to find out which room she was cleaning, then transferred Ricky to that extension.

"Hi, Mama."

"Did you get your check?"

"Yes," Ricky answered, somewhat guiltily. "Thanks."

"The city is expensive. It makes me feel good to help."

Ricky managed an ambivalent smile. He knew that sending the checks provided his mother with a great deal of comfort. But the reason behind them—his son-of-a-bitch father—never made the assistance easy to accept.

"How's work?" she asked.

"OK, I guess. The department manager of cosmetics is a fuckhead."

"Ricky!"

"I'm not the only one who thinks so."

"You've got a good job. Show the proper respect."

"Yes, Mama," Ricky said. But he wouldn't. Authority wasn't something he regarded with any degree of respect. They were worlds apart that way. "Are we still going for coffee?"

"I think so." She released a heavy sigh. "The hotel is booked. We've been cleaning nonstop. I hope we won't have to work late."

"Me, too. I've got a big surprise for you."

"What kind of surprise?"

"You'll see." Ricky was purposefully cagey.

"No presents. I don't need anything. Save your money."

He had been. Lots of it. Ricky grinned, pleased with himself. A statement from the bank regarding his investment account had just arrived. He was sitting on a *serious* nest egg.

His plan from the beginning had been to sock away as much as he could so that one day he could take his mother on the finest European vacation money could buy. England, France, Germany, Italy. The finest hotels, the best restaurants, the most fashionable shops.

All her life, Cynthia had worked hard at labor jobs that hurt her feet, strained her back, and kept her in a certain place—the bottom of the barrel. Ricky wanted to show his mother—even for just a few weeks—that she deserved to live like the people she cleaned up for. He wanted to treat her like a star. And after all these years, the money was finally there. They just had to set the dates now.

"I love you, Mama," he said. "Call me at the store if something comes up. Otherwise, I'll see you at six. Don't work too hard."

"I just do my job. The guests like a clean room."

" 'Bye, Mama." He hung up and checked his watch. His break was supposed to have ended over ten minutes ago. Whatever. Without Sofia, shifts at Berrenger's just dragged on. He decided to call Debi again. What's another five minutes?

The entire hello-it's-me-how-are-you bit wasted time, so he just launched right into things whenever someone answered the phone. "I'm *so* over the beauty industry. I need a career change. Maybe I could model for Tommy Hilfiger."

"You're too old. You should've thought of that ten years ago."

"I'm twenty-seven!"

"Pick up a magazine. None of his models look old enough to vote. Maybe you could get catalog work with JC Penney. Can you pretend to be a straight father of three?"

"I said I wanted to be a model, not an actor."

"I can't talk right now. I'm at a wedding."

"Who's getting married?"

"*My* sister. *Your* best friend."

"What?"

Howard Berrenger popped his head into the break room. "Mr. Lopez—"

"My break just started," Ricky cut in. He declared the lie with such conviction that Howard seemed to buy it.

"Sorry," Ricky said, back to Debi now. "Fuckhead is walking around with his stopwatch. Start over."

"Sofia's getting married."

"GET OUT!"

"She's on Carmel Beach right now with Ben and Jay Leno."

"How did you get there so fast?"

"I'm in Central Park. This is a phone wedding."

"Like phone sex?"

"Yes, only without the shame after it's over."

"What's this about Jay Leno?"

"Long story."

Ricky paused as the hurt arrowed down. "Why didn't she call me?"

"Longer story."

He tried to shrug it off, knowing that Sofia would never intentionally leave him out. "I've heard talk that he's great in bed, but this is ridiculous."

"I have to click back over. I don't want to miss the ceremony. I'm maid of honor, you know."

"Call me with *details*," Ricky implored. He replaced the receiver, still a bit stunned. Sofia Cardinella. *Married.* To a man she barely knew. It was so Angelina Jolie and Billy Bob Thornton.

"I do," Ben said.

Behind him, Fat Larry fought back tears.

Sofia had convinced them—without much effort—

that Joseph wanted Fat Larry to give her away and Little Bo to be the witness. They were so touched to be asked that it never occurred to them to question anything.

Fat Larry was officially crying now, even dabbing at his eyes with a handkerchief.

"He's the emotional one," Sofia whispered. "It took him a week to get over the movie *Beaches*. You know, the one with Bette Midler?"

Ben nodded, amused.

Jay Leno cut in to deliver the traditional vows.

On her "I do" cue, Sofia turned to the costumed officiant, raising her hand slightly. "Can we add a few things?"

Ben and Jay shared a quizzical look.

"Feel free," Jay said.

Sofia took both of Ben's hands in hers and gave him direct, mischievous eye contact.

"What are you doing?" he asked.

"I swear to make you my favorite banana milkshake every Sunday afternoon," she said.

Ben caught on instantly. "And I swear to drink at least half of it even though I hate bananas."

Sofia giggled. "I swear to learn more about Frank Sinatra and better appreciate your passion for his talent."

"I swear to remain steadfast in my disapproval of Michael Bolton."

Sofia broke up, her entire body shaking with laughter. "Your turn, silly."

Ben felt a surge of emotion that took him by surprise. "I swear to give this marriage my best shot, and I mean that right here." He made a loose fist and put it over his heart. "Ever since we met I've had nothing but problems. That's usually what happens when you get hung up on a girl. But with you, I don't mind so much. It's all worth it. You make me feel alive in a way I only used to feel when I sing."

Sofia opened her mouth to speak but said nothing. His words had obviously made a profound impact. Finally, she asked, "Do you swear to love Mr. Pickles?"

He saw the glint in her eyes and gave her a shrewd grin. "I swear to make an honest attempt to tolerate him." Then he turned to Jay. "Doesn't she look radiant? Have you ever married a prettier woman?"

"I do," Sofia said softly.

Jay widened his eyes. "Then I now pronounce you husband and wife."

Ben felt his stomach take a dive as the last statement resonated in his brain. They'd actually gone through with it. They were married. Sofia was his wife. He was her husband.

"You may kiss the bride," Jay said.

He didn't mind that part. Pulling her close, he gave her a deep soul kiss that took the edge off his anxiety. When they came up for air, he stared down on her. "Mrs. Estes, I presume?"

She clung to his body. "That's me."

"Yes, they're a lovely couple. . . . They look very happy. . . . She's right here," Jay Leno said, offering Sofia her phone. "It's your sister."

With great glee, Sofia accepted it. "Did you hear everything? I'm so happy. We owe it all to Jay. He held up the phone throughout the ceremony. I'm sure his arm is fatigued. Talk to your new brother-in-law."

Ben took custody of the cellular now. "Mind if I call you sis?"

"I insist," Debi said. "Do you realize what kind of family you just married into?"

Ben laughed, glancing at Fat Larry and Little Bo. "I have a pretty good idea."

"Treat my sister right, or you'll answer to me. And I'm far more dangerous than our father."

"Then that would make you what, a terrorist?"

"Don't fuck around with a Cardinella," Debi teased.

Ben watched Sofia. "Too late for that." She really didn't have on clothes, just strategically placed swatches of fabric. Yet she pulled it off, coming across as a daring seductress, not a hooker in search of a public defender. And that body. *Shazam!* He loved thin dames. And Sofia could stroll through an Oreo without disturbing the filling.

"When are you coming back?" Debi's delivery was more demand than question.

"Darling," Ben began, addressing his wife, "your sister wants to know when we're going back. Here, I'll let you tell her." He passed the phone.

"Not for two more days," Sofia said. "The rest of the trip is our honeymoon. . . . A reception? . . . Of course . . . That would be fabulous. . . . Book Swifty Morgan's. . . . It's Ben's favorite haunt. . . . It'll be too much fun. . . . Call Ricky and tell him I love him. . . . A kiss to Papa . . . 'Bye!" And she signed off.

Ben stood there, taking a moment to consider the ramifications of what he'd just done. Marriage. How would it change the dynamic among him, Kitty, and Taz? Would he have to get serious all of a sudden and go back to practicing law? Life as he knew it had just changed dramatically.

"Debi's going to start planning a reception for us at Swifty Morgan's."

"I heard," Ben said stiffly. *Oh, Charley.* He'd better place a call himself to announce the deed before his sister-in-law showed up to make party plans. If the cats at Swifty's didn't hear it straight from him, they'd think him a big fink. He gestured to her phone. "Mind if I borrow that?"

"Sure, but I think the battery's about to go," Sofia warned, handing it over.

Ben dialed one of the few numbers he knew by heart.

"Swifty Morgan's," Jilly answered.

"I can't find a decent martini in California."

"Ben!" came Jilly's rejoinder. "It's not the same here without you, man."

This made Ben feel special. He was genuinely homesick for the place. "Who's holding down the joint?"

"Kitty's right here. She just lost a big client, and everybody's paying for it."

Ben got the picture right away, feeling sorry for poor Jilly. "Put her or the phone. I'll give her some sunshine."

A moment later. "I hate California men," Kitty said.

"You hate New York men, too."

"That's right. It's down to guys from the Carolinas. How's Carmel?"

"From what I've seen—very nice."

"How's the mattress?"

"Oh," Ben replied, taking his voice down an octave. "Very comfortable."

"I figured as much."

"Jilly said you lost a client."

"Some nineteen-year-old bitch on the Upper West Side fired me because I couldn't promise Nick from 98 Degrees at her birthday party. I explained that the group is on tour. She's obviously on crack. And it was a big job. I needed it to pay my American Express bill this month."

"Something else will come up."

"I know. I just need a day to feel sorry for myself."

"Where's Taz?"

"He's in a meeting about his screenplay."

Ben perked up with interest. "That's great."

"I know the producer," Kitty said. Already her tone had dumped ice water on the subject. "He's a nobody. Jilly's got more connections than this loser. I tried to tell him, but Taz doesn't want to hear the truth. He'd rather get happy talk from a bum."

"Maybe this guy has his act together now."

Kitty scoffed. "This crumb couldn't green light a student film, much less a feature."

Ben took a breath. "I have to tell you something."

"So tell."

"Sofia and I got married."

Kitty's silence stretched on and on.

He knew that telling her wasn't going to be easy, but he thought she'd have *something* to offer. "This is the part where you say, 'Congratulations.' "

"If you want me to read lines, you should send a script in advance," Kitty said coldly.

"I know this comes as a shock."

"I don't get it, Ben. You've only known this girl for a few weeks. Is she pregnant already?"

"No."

"Then you could've just moved in together until this ran its course. Why get married?"

Ben turned to Sofia, who'd stepped several feet away in an effort to give him some privacy. She carried her impossible heels in one hand as her lovely little feet worked to form big letters in the sand that would spell his name. At this moment, it didn't seem like their impulsive act had anything to do with Joseph Cardinella's threats. No longer was it three-eighths, halves, or three-quarters. He realized that he felt this all the way. "I love her."

"How sweet," Kitty snarled.

"I mean it. It's crazy. Really coo-coo. It didn't hit me until just now." He shielded the phone and bellowed to his wife, "Hey, baby! I love you!"

Sofia turned, her mouth agape. Never had she looked more beautiful. Jesus Christ Almighty. He felt like the luckiest bastard in the whole world.

"I give it six weeks," Kitty said.

Chapter Thirteen

Ricky sipped his latte, wondering when to break the big news.

"How's your friend? What's her name . . . Sonya?" Cynthia asked. She broke off a piece of chocolate-orange biscotti and began to crunch.

"Sofia," Ricky corrected. "As a matter of fact, she got married today."

"That's nice. Maybe you'll find a wife soon."

He just looked at her, as if waiting for the rest of the joke. "That's a tall order, especially since I'm in the market for a husband."

Cynthia said nothing, eyes cast downward. She drank deeply on her regular coffee.

The joy of seeing his mother rarely lived up to his anticipation of the event. There was a way he wanted her to be—excited, interested, full of love—that she almost never was. No matter, Ricky couldn't wait to spill the fantastic news. Once she heard *this,* it would be like a brand-new morning.

"When's the last time you had a vacation, Mama?"

"A vacation?" She shrugged. "Those are for rich people."

"What if you could go anywhere in the world?"

"Stop talking crazy. You fantasize too much."

"I'm serious."

Cynthia sighed, exasperated. "I don't know. I've always wanted to see Europe."

There was no hope in her response, no sense that what she desired could ever be achieved, as if her wish might as well have been to find a million-dollar check in a cereal box.

"You must have a lot of vacation time built up at the hotel," Ricky said.

"Oh, lots of it." Glumly, she added more cream to her coffee. "I just take a day here or there to go see your Aunt Christina in Newark."

Under the table, his toe tapped something wild. He was ready to burst. The words just had to get out of him. "We're going to Europe."

Cynthia gave him an indulgent smile. "Maybe one day."

"I mean right now." His tone was matter-of-fact.

She returned a funny look.

"You know that money you've been sending me every month for all these years? Well, I've been saving as much as I can, and every dollar adds up. Not to mention I found a smart investor." He leaned in to emphasize his next point. "Mama, we can go anywhere in the world. *First class.*"

She appeared more worried than excited.

Maybe she's in shock, Ricky thought.

Then Cynthia regarded him as if he were crazy.

But Ricky pressed on. "Think how much fun it will be. *Europe!* And not the budget tour, either. We'll vacation just like the stars do."

Now her look was one of intrigue. "How much money do you have?"

"Thirty thousand."

Cynthia's head jerked backward.

He nodded severely. "It's true."

"You can't blow all that on a stupid vacation."

"Well, maybe half or two-thirds. Whatever it costs for us to travel like celebrities." He smiled. "Mama, I've been dreaming about this—planning for it—since I was seventeen."

She shifted uncomfortably. "I could never leave your father."

"You're not *moving* to Europe," Ricky protested. "We're talking about a few weeks."

"Still," Cynthia said. "It wouldn't be right."

Ricky could hardly believe it. He'd played this moment over and over again in his mind. In that version, there were tears of joy, extended hugs, squeals of delight, and praise/awe for his crafty financial maneuvering. Yet here, in the real world, there was barely a blip on the screen.

"I shouldn't have coffee this late," Cynthia said, as if the subject were over. "I'll have trouble getting to sleep."

Ricky just sat there. "Mama, are you listening? You act like I'm asking you to join me on a bus tour to Branson."

"It does sound exciting," she admitted. "But I could never get away for that long."

"You just said that you had weeks of vacation built up."

Cynthia hesitated. "How would I explain a trip like that to your father?"

"You must mean Juan, the sperm donor," Ricky said tightly.

"Don't talk that way."

"I could say the same to you. Calling him a father is obscene."

"He's a good man," Cynthia argued. Then she shook her head. "If he ever found out that I've been sending you money . . . I don't even want to think about it."

Ricky could feel the heat of anger rising up. He rarely got mad at his mother. But weak-minded people tested his tolerance, and he knew she was much stronger than this pathetic script let on. "You sound like a battered woman."

Cynthia ignored the comment, gazing out the window to take in the *Today Show* set.

"You don't have to live in fear. Didn't you see *The Burning Bed?*"

She turned to face him, instantly red-faced. "That's not funny."

Ricky regretted the words right away. His real target was Juan. Firing point-blank at his mother only hurt her. "I'm sorry. That wasn't fair."

"I've been in love with him since I was fourteen years old. I don't expect you to understand that. It's not your business to, anyway." She reached out and took Ricky's hands in hers. "I wish I could change him where you're concerned. But he's proud and stubborn . . . and . . . he's just not open-minded." A pained, conflicted look skated across her face. "I really wish I could go with you . . . but I can't."

Ricky pulled his hands away. "I've watched you

work hard my whole life and never do anything special
for yourself.''

"Don't worry about me. I'm fine. Start putting all
that energy back into *you*.'' She glanced at her watch
and grimaced.

"I should give you back the money.''

"No!'' Cynthia said sharply. "Every dollar of that
is yours. I won't take a dime. Keep it for your future.''

"Thirty grand isn't a future, Mama.''

"Well, at least it's an opportunity,'' she argued.
"Go to Europe if you want. But be sensible. Don't
spend like a rock star and come back with nothing.''

Ricky sighed. "I have no burning desire to go to
Europe. I thought that was your dream.''

"That was just talk. My real dream has always been
to see you happy and successful.''

"Reconsider Europe. That dream I can guarantee
in your lifetime.''

When his mother left to catch the train, Ricky felt
like there'd been a death in the family. How would
he get over this? For ten years his motor of purpose
had been to save money, to sweep her away from
work and Juan, to show her an extravagant time in
an exotic locale.

He hailed a cab to his apartment, grabbed his work-
out bag, and took off for the gym. Negative energy
consumed him. Better to burn it off with crunches
and weights than with fattening food or alcohol.
Besides, he did his most productive thinking during
intense exercise. Now that he suddenly needed something else to live for, he hoped the answer would
come sweating out of him.

* * *

Susan Lucci was singing badly and dancing clumsily. But her hair looked *great*. Debi observed this from a very expensive orchestra seat in the Marriott Marquis Theatre.

She looked around. The audience was positively beaming. Bernadette Peters, who'd originated the title role in this revival, was on vacation. No one cared. They were enchanted by this spirited production of *Annie Get Your Gun* starring Erica Kane.

Debi wanted to make a run for it. Unfortunately, the second act of the ridiculous jamboree had just cranked up. An early exit from the center of the row would cause a major disruption. Future point to remember—always insist on aisle seating.

She tried to enjoy the show—the cute songs, the silly banter, the corny special effects. Was there anything that pushed the edge of reality more than a *musical?* Her head was just not there tonight. Debi simply couldn't make the required leap of faith. Too much on her mind.

Next to her, Vincent sat there, stiff and miserable, as if someone had handcuffed him to a chair and sentenced him to watch Lifetime Television for Women—on Super Bowl Sunday.

Who could she blame for this dreadful experience? Oh, that's right. *Herself.* Debi had grown tired of just sitting at coffee shops with the lovelorn Vincent and being hit with a barrage of questions about her younger, thinner, prettier sister.

Favorite color? Whatever's in season.

Favorite food? Halloween cupcakes.

Favorite television show? *Entertainment Tonight.*

Favorite song? "Physical" by Olivia Newton-John.

Debi wondered where he was going with these interviews. It sounded like a Q&A for *Tiger Beat.* Shallow or not, playing nursemaid to a man's obsession for another did little for her own self-esteem. She'd considered calling Dr. Laura, then decided her confidence had suffered enough. The radio shrink would only finish her off for good.

On the stage, feet were clomping and Indians were breaking into song. Oh, God! Why had she left such an important task in Vincent's hands? A Broadway show like *Annie Get Your Gun* was hermetically sealed for tourists. Real city dwellers didn't shell out eighty dollars a ticket to see Susan Lucci. They watched her for free on *All My Children* and paid good money for the likes of Betty Buckley.

Debi's mind wandered. For some inexplicable reason, an illicit thought regarding Prince William popped in and out of her head. An immediate fear registered. Did that make her a pedophile? No, he was at least eighteen now, much taller, and heir to a fortune, not to mention a throne. Instant relief. Clearance for future erotic thoughts of the young prince.

In the darkness, she struggled to read the program. But she could make out this much—several numbers still remained. Damn Annie Oakley! A fierce restlessness settled in. Nails looked gorgeous, however. Gazing at them provided a moment's pure calm. Cerebral journal entry: weight a nightmare but manicure a dream. This was progress. After all, a girl had to start somewhere.

Vincent scratched his crotch. What should have been a discreet touch became a full-scale adjustment. He was itching, moving items around. How did men walk around with those things?

Debi tried her best to focus on the show, but this

remodeling of his private parts seemed to go on forever. When would it stop? She began to panic quietly.

Now the woman to his right glanced over, if only to see what all the commotion was about. What an embarrassment! This event had actually distracted a well-heeled patron from the talent on the stage.

Finally, the madness ended. *Thank you, God. For your mercy, I'll stop eating frosting straight from the can.* Debi breathed a sigh of relief. Suddenly it dawned on her. Could she be with a man who engaged in public war with his nether region?

When the answer came, it crashed down on her head. As if she had a choice in the matter! The second Vincent discovered that Sofia had married Ben would be the very second he put an end to these *meetings*. That's what he called them. She much preferred the term *dates*. Hence, her insistence that he take her out to the theater and then to a nice dinner. It seemed a very *datelike* thing to do. Only then would she agree to indulge him with more banal Sofia secrets along the lines of Favorite Sweater or Favorite Julia Roberts Movie.

After the final curtain call, they joined the rest of the crowd in the slow-crawling line that led out to the street. Vincent kept a proprietary hand on Debi's arm, a move not lost on her. *Wildly romantic,* she thought. *And very chivalrous as the body crush of big-event exiting can be dangerous.*

Vincent competed successfully for a taxi right outside the theater.

Debi was impressed. Not many men could do that. Most guys had to walk a few blocks to a less congested area, convince you the subway's a good idea, or even settle for a gypsy cab. As a rule, Debi strictly avoided the latter, as the driver could be a serial killer and therefore not worth the few extra dollars in fare savings.

Traffic was in gridlock. But this time she didn't mind at all. They were cozily esconced in the taxi's rear cabin. In one word, *heaven*. "What did you think of the play?" Debi asked.

Vincent shrugged. "Too much singing if you ask me."

OK, semiheaven. Cultural IQ needs improvement. "Well, it was a *musical.*"

"I don't remember them singing that much in *Grease.*"

Frustration. *New subject,* she told herself. "Maybe we can go to a movie next time." She smiled at her own quick thinking. How smart to make future plans *before* the tragic announcement. "Is there anything out that you want to see?"

"I like movies where they blow up stuff."

"In that case, I'm sure there's something at the multiplex starring Nicholas Cage."

"What kind of movies does Sofia like?"

Debi looked away to hide her disappointment. "Old ones, mostly," she managed. "Anything with Audrey Hepburn."

"Is that the old lady from *On Golden Pond?*"

"No, that's Katharine Hepburn."

Vincent nodded with mild interest.

Debi had planned to break the news after dinner, but she no longer saw the point to prolonging the inevitable. Why not tell him now and watch him run like hell? Then she could go home and eat like Shamu.

The cab lurched forward. They were moving briskly now.

She shifted in her seat to face him. "There's something you should know. . . . It impacts your future plans quite significantly.''

Vincent gave her a blank stare. "What?"

She decided to drop it like a water balloon. "Sofia got married today."

"Your sister, Sofia?"

"Yes, the only other one I know is Sophia Loren."

"I don't get it. Where?"

"California."

"What time?"

Debi tried to recall. "Maybe midmorning. I'm really not sure."

"Does your father know about this?"

Debi could hardly believe it. Four questions. None of them concerning *who* Sofia married. Obviously, he never watched *Matlock*. "I'm not sure if Papa knows yet or not. That all depends on Fat Larry and Little Bo."

Vincent's brow furrowed.

"They were at the wedding. Fat Larry gave her away."

Briefly, he buried his face in his hands. "I never counted on her marrying someone else."

This was driving Debi crazy. "Don't you want to know *who* she married?"

"I don't need to ask. She's always with that guy who works with her at Berrenger's . . . Ricky. I always thought something was going on between those two."

"Ricky Lopez?"

Vincent shook his head, oblivious to her incredulous tone. "Sofia Lopez," he murmured. "That doesn't even sound right. Sofia Scalia has a better ring to it."

"Hello? Ricky's gay. She didn't marry him. Ben Estes is her husband."

The name failed to register.

"The singer from Villa," Debi said impatiently, gesturing with both hands.

"That Sinatra impersonator in the monkey suit?"

Finally. Debi bobbed her head. "I think he prefers tribute artist and tuxedo, though."

"Your father told me he wished that bum was dead."

"Well, as of today, that bum is his son-in-law."

"What the hell does she see in that guy?" Vincent demanded.

"The short list is that he's tall, handsome, charming, and reportedly excellent in bed."

"But I'm all of those things!"

Debi just stared. He really believed that. It was sweet. But also delusional. She touched his arm. "You're only tall to grade-schoolers." Her voice was soft. "Handsome and charming? I agree. Excellent in bed? I guess I'll have to take you at your word."

The cab pulled up to Lola and jerked to a stop.

Vincent sat there, almost catatonic.

"We're here," Debi said.

"You go ahead. I think I'll take the train back home."

Whatever hope remained spiraled down fast. This was happening just as Debi had thought it would. With Sofia officially unavailable, Vincent had zero interest. Her mind raced. Maybe she could get him drunk and take advantage of him. Just for tonight. Definitely worth a try. Two years of celibacy would end and a lifelong crush would be consummated. That was making the best of a bad situation.

"Let's go in and at least have a drink," she urged him gently, trying not to sound desperate. "You shouldn't be alone right now."

"Don't worry. My plan is to round up some friends and go to a strip club."

Debi fought against elbowing him in the stomach. "That's so college boy breaks up with girl from back home. You're a sophisticated man." *Pause to collect self after absurdity of last statement.* "Let's talk this out over drinks and a good dinner at Lola's."

Vincent wavered a moment. "OK," he agreed, leaning forward to pay the driver. "I'm wearing boxers, anyway. I'd rather have briefs on when I'm getting a lap dance."

"Too much information," Debi said tightly. And then she swung out of the cab and strutted into Lola's, hell-bent to make this man forget about her sister, if only for one night.

Sofia called it honey cock. It was, without a doubt, the most scrumptious dish she'd ever tasted. How to make? Take one man that you love, add his very hard penis, slather with Grade A clover honey, and eat him up. No fat grams! Only one hundred twenty calories!

Yum. She kissed, licked, and sucked on her craving, attention focused, passion never wandering, intensity sky-high, doing it all with the smoothest, most continuous, lustful movements.

"Stop, baby. *Please.* I can't take it," Ben moaned, sprawled out on the mattress, so amazingly tall that his legs hung over the foot of the bed just past his calves.

Sofia was crouched between his thighs, massaging his firm-as-concrete stomach, taking her task as seriously as global warming. "You're such a liar," she trilled devilishly. "You *can* take it, and you *don't* want me to stop."

"I know," he whispered, tenderly caressing her head as she probed her tongue into the slit on the top to retrieve a luscious dribble of hidden honey. "But it would sound too greedy to say what I'm really thinking, which is . . . can you do this in twelve-hour shifts?"

She laughed a little, covered her teeth with her lips, and slid him slowly into her mouth, gradually increasing her speed as she moved her head up and down excitedly. What a delicious meal!

Ben was going crazy, lost in ego-gratifying, supreme-commander, slave-to-the-feeling ecstacy. "Oh, baby . . . This is the hottest ever . . . Damn . . ."

He was almost there. The magic moment. Sofia could tell by the pattern of his breathing, the tightness of his testicles. Potential for a pretty mess was high, especially with the sticky, ooey-gooey honey in the equation. So she simply wrapped her lips tightly around him, swallowed his sacred essence in one greedy gulp, and gazed back at him with a look on her face that told him she thought it better than a scoop of French Vanilla from Baskin Robbins.

His expression was total satisfaction and inspired awe. "I can't believe you love to swallow."

"It's mainly protein and sugar." She grinned. "Besides, it's your *intimate gift*." A brief giggle. He didn't have to know that she was quite adept at taking it in and bypassing her taste buds.

Ben pulled her close. "It makes me feel special," he said softly.

She snuggled as tightly as possible, amazed at how beautiful and reciprocal their sexual relationship was.

"Do you know what a turn-on it is to watch you do that?"

She breathed in deep, loving his masculine scent. "I have a pretty good idea."

Wrapped in each other's arms, they relaxed in an easy silence. After a few minutes, Ben said, "I should take a shower. There's honey in my pubic hair."

Sofia laughed. "My chin is all sticky."

"I don't feel like getting up now, though. Too comfortable."

"Same here."

"We sure are some nasty, funky, and lazy newly-weds."

She let out a blissful sigh. "Totally." A thoughtful pause. "What do you think will happen when we go back to New York?"

Ben didn't answer.

"There's my father to deal with. You mentioned that Kitty is bent out of shape. I love it right now— just the two of us. All we have to think about is fun and pleasure. What will happen when we have to let the rest of the world in?"

Ben still didn't answer.

Chapter Fourteen

When the plane touched down in New York, Sofia experienced an anxiousness that bordered on psychosis. Even her breathing seemed off.

"What's with the death grip, baby? You trying to break my hand?"

"Oh," she murmured, realizing that instead of holding Ben's hand, she was crushing it with all her strength. "Sorry."

He smiled and hooked an arm around her waist as they moved through the gate toward the terminal. "Man, I can't wait to sit down at Swifty Morgan's for a real drink. Nothing against the West Coast, but Jilly's in a class by himself."

Barely listening, she ran her nails softly down the small of his back.

"We can drop our luggage at my apartment and head over there."

The meaning of his words suddenly hit her, followed by a mild alarm. "I'd feel better if we dealt with Papa first."

"Won't we need a drink for that?"

She grinned wryly as they stepped into the terminal. Welcome to New York. Wall-to-wall-people graffiti. Everybody in a rush. *Doris, we're not in Carmel anymore.* A bank of pay phones beckoned. "I'll meet you at baggage claim," she said quickly, making a beeline for it.

Debi picked up on the second ring.

"I'm back."

"You sound like you're in a tunnel."

"Worse. LaGuardia. On a pay phone."

"Did you wipe off the receiver with a moist towelette?"

"Of course. One of Mother's most useful lessons."

"What's wrong with your mobile?"

"I forgot to charge the battery last night. I'm calling about Papa. How is he?"

"Very quiet." Debi's voice dropped an octave. This was grave.

"We're on our way home to face him."

"Tonight?"

"I want to get this over with."

"Maybe you should wait until morning."

"Why? I'll never get to sleep, and it's not like he'll go to bed and wake up a sensible person." Unconsciously, Sofia had twisted the strap of her Kate Spade purse so tightly around her finger that the tip was purple. "God, Debi, I feel like I'm still in high school and got caught staying out all night with Luke Romano. I'm almost thirty. This is supposed to be *my* life!"

"At least your taste has improved," Debi pointed out. "Ben is actually worth the trouble."

Sofia felt herself growing bored with her current plight. She could never stay wigged out over an issue for very long. Pensively, she put a finger to her lips. Was there a possibility of ADD? That would explain quite a bit. Perhaps she should be taking the occasional Ritalin instead of Xanax. *Must check science articles in* Glamour *and* Marie Claire *for the answer.*

"I don't know," Sofia mused, thinking back on Luke now. "If I had the chance to do it all over again, I'd still hook up with him. He was my bad boy. Every girl needs a hoodlum in her past. It builds character."

"OK, fast forward seventeen years. Your teenage daughter has a mad crush on Luke's illegitimate son. What then?"

Sofia was truly stumped. "I hate hypnotic questions."

"You mean hypothetical."

"Those are worse." Her brain went to work. "First, I would sit her down and share the best object lesson I know."

"Which is?"

"The Lana Turner and Johnny Stompanato story. Armed with that, I know she could make responsible and appropriate choices for herself." She nodded proudly, pleased with her answer. "How's everyone else?"

"Ricky's depressed but won't fess up why."

"Justin from 'N Sync probably hasn't answered his fan letter yet."

"I think it's deeper than that."

"Deeper than Justin Timberlake? This sounds serious. I'll see him at work tomorrow."

"Let me ask you something. What is it about the Cardinella girls and alcohol?"

Sofia giggled. "Where did *you* throw up?"

"All over Vincent in the cab coming back from Lola's. He took that harder than the news of your marriage. Maybe that means he's getting over you."

"Good. Then we'll *both* be rid of him. Listen, I better run. Mr. Pickles is probably off the plane by now. I'll be home as soon as I can. Brace yourself for the reunion."

At baggage claim, Ben had corralled all their luggage plus Mr. Pickles, who was still out of it from the tranquilizer. "So, what's the plan?"

Sofia took a deep breath. "Luggage to your place. Train to Papa's. Family squabble. Train back into city. Cab to Swifty Morgan's. Bitchy comments from Kitty. Martinis by the dozen."

Ben grinned. "Better not forget our sunglasses." Then he stared down at Mr. Pickles. "There's one problem, though. My building has a strict no-pets policy."

Sofia stared back in shock. "What are you saying?"

"The dog will have to live at your house."

"Then so will you."

"I'm not moving to *New Jersey.*" He spat it out like milk way past the expiration date.

Indignantly, she put a hand on her hip. "Well, I'm not moving to Manhattan without Mr. Pickles. It's settled, then.

Ben looked confused. "What is?"

"We need to find a new apartment in Manhattan that accepts pets."

He started to laugh. "Do you have any idea how impossible that is? We'll never find anything affordable in today's market. Thanks to a friend's mother I used to shag during my first year of college, I've got a killer lease. It can't be beat."

"The rent or shagging your friend's mom?"

"Both, actually. She looked like Kathleen Turner, the *Body Heat* years."

Sofia grabbed the pet carrier and started off, leaving Ben to contend with everything else. "Then we'll just have to sneak Mr. Pickles in and out of your building. I can dress him up in baby clothes. No one will ever know."

He struggled to keep up. "Baby, are you coo-coo? One glance at him and our number's up. It'll be scramsville."

She scooted past a businessman and cab-jacked him. "Family emergency," she explained without apology.

He opened his mouth to protest.

"You're a dear to catch the next one," she said, cutting him off before he got started. "Big hugs." Then she tumbled inside.

Ben piled the luggage into the trunk and got in next, just as the taxi took off like a bullet.

"I can't deal with the train. Getting on, getting off." Sofia sighed. "I told the driver to take us straight to Papa's after we drop off the luggage."

"That's expensive," Ben complained.

"But think of all the money we'll save by not moving into a more expensive apartment."

He gazed back in disbelief.

She tapped his thigh. "Don't worry. I have savings."

"How much?"

Sofia thought about it. "Scratch that. I cleaned it out for my spring wardrobe. I do have a Visa that's never been used, though. If things get tight, we can live on that."

"You've never lived on your own, have you?"

"Does summer camp count?"

Ben put a hand on her knee and leaned back,

closing his eyes. "I need a quick nap. Wake me when it's time to carry all that luggage again."

She watched him sleep most of the way, feeling lucky to have met him. *Sofia Estes*. The name turned over and over in her mind, triggering absolute glee. Everything would need to be changed—credit cards, checking account, time card at work, Blockbuster membership, etc. Now was the perfect opportunity to reinvent herself. She could wow the world with a new image to go along with her new name.

When they arrived at Ben's building, she remained in the cab with Mr. Pickles while he unloaded the bags and secured them inside the apartment. Minutes later he was back. And off they went.

"Think how much fun it will be to redecorate our new place," Sofia said.

Ben looked at her. "*Our* place?"

She nodded. "I adore Pottery Barn. Ricky can help us, too. He has a great eye for interior design."

"My apartment is fine just the way it is. And it's only six hundred square feet. Clearing things out to give you a drawer and some closet space will be renovation enough."

"But it's your bachelor pad. We have to transform it to represent the *married* Ben Estes. What are your thoughts on beige?"

"*Beige?*"

She put a comforting hand on his forearm. "Don't worry. I'm not opposed to color. For instance, I can see one wall in the bedroom painted a rich plum."

They rode in silence for several seconds.

"I should also mention my Hello Kitty lamp," Sofia said. "It reminds me of my mother. We'll have to incorporate it somehow. Maybe the living room. It can be the kind of offbeat decorative piece that gets the conversation started at our cocktail parties."

"Baby, I—"

"Book club!" Sofia broke in excitedly. "I can start my own. Girls only, though. That can be your night to hang out at Swifty Morgan's. Let's see, there's me, Debi, Ricky—"

"You're counting Ricky as a girl?"

Sofia nodded earnestly. "Some people say that if you want *honest* talk from a woman, find a gay man." She paused a beat as an idea came to mind. "Do you think Kitty would join my book club?"

"I don't think that's her bag. She's not a big reader."

"Oh, we'll probably never get around to reading the books. Well, maybe the latest Jackie Collins. Or something revolutionary in the self-help field, like *How To Never Feel Inadequate Again.*"

"Is that actually a book?"

"No, but someone should write it. I'd definitely pick it up. Anyway, Kitty would only be reading two books a year, tops. And skimming counts. I know a girl on the Upper West Side who just scans the dust jackets. She's very busy."

"So why call it a book club?" Ben asked.

"Because. I can't very well call it the Come Taste My Great Recipe for Artichoke Dip, Drink Some Wine, and Let's Gab Club. Besides, book club is trendy, and it has an intellectual ring to it."

"By the way, you mentioned cocktail parties a minute ago," Ben said. "Not a fan. That's what bars are for."

Sofia frowned. "And you mentioned *closet space*. I'm fully utilizing three closets now and could easily expand to a fourth."

"Six hundred square feet." He gestured to the taxi's backseat. "This represents about half of that. I have a twin bed. Not because I want to pretend like I'm twelve, but so I can fit other furniture into my bedroom."

"Calm down. I'll find the right person. There are designers who work exclusively with small spaces."

He took her hand, squeezed it gently, and kissed her palm. "We can't afford that, baby."

"I want it to be perfect."

"Then help me pay the rent on time. That's a good start."

"One day we'll have lots of money. You're going to make it as a singer, and my beauty company will take off."

"Where are you with that?"

Sofia hesitated. "Predevelopment."

"Good answer."

"Doesn't that sound impressive?"

"It does."

She cozied up, resting her head on his chest as he wrapped his arms around her. "I don't want to struggle. That's so boring. And it doesn't suit us. You need money to tip too much, and I need it for great shoes."

Ben kissed her left temple. "Two very noble causes."

"I'm serious," she half whined, half moaned.

"I don't doubt that for a second."

"There's nothing wrong with people who buy shoes at Payless. It's just not for me."

"And in my book, leaving fifteen percent makes you a crumb."

Sofia peered up at him. "Yeah," she whispered.

When he kissed her, it was tender, wet, and quietly passionate. "I love you, Mrs. Estes."

"Right back at you, Charley." And then she settled back against his chest and drifted into a light, peaceful sleep.

By the time he nudged her awake, they had arrived at the house. Instantly alert and suddenly nervous, Sofia felt a burning need for a cigarette but pushed aside the craving.

She used her own key at the front door. It only got her so far. The security chain had been attached. *Strange*, Sofia thought. *We never use that.*

Suddenly Papa appeared, facing her through the narrow opening, his eyes hard and unyielding.

Sofia swallowed hard. "Papa, why is the chain on?"

Joseph looked past her to Ben, saying nothing.

She laughed a little, all nervous energy. "Are you going to let me in?"

"Not with him. He's not welcome in this house."

A hot anger ignited within her. "Papa, open the door," she snapped. "Ben is my husband. The three of us need to talk."

Joseph shut the door in her face. She heard the clatter of the chain. Then it opened all the way. Light from the interior of the house poured onto the steps, illuminating Ben like a star of the stage.

Sofia stepped inside.

Ben, with the pet carrier clutched in his right hand, moved to follow, but Joseph blocked his path. "Not a chance, creep."

"Papa!" Sofia wailed.

"My guess is that it's too soon to call you Dad," Ben said.

"You catch on quick."

"Enough, Papa! I'm a grown woman, and it's high

time you started treating me like one. I married this man. He's my *husband,* not some boy down the street I'm asking permission to date. You have to respect my choice.''

"All I have to do is die!" Joseph roared.

"Could you pick up the pace on that?" Ben cracked. "There's a Jack Daniel's and water with my name on it at Swifty Morgan's."

Sofia silenced Ben with a look.

Joseph shook a disapproving head at his daughter. "Your mother is turning over in her grave."

This totally enraged her. Blood rushed. "Don't you *dare* try to use that on me! My mother would ask me one question. 'Are you happy?' And that would be the end of it. She would accept Ben as a member of this family."

Sofia sensed movement. She glanced up to see Debi at the top of the stairs.

Joseph pointed a finger at Ben. "The lowlife you call a husband is nothing to me. And if he sets foot in my house, he'll die in it. That's a Cardinella promise."

Sofia felt the tears well up and cascade down. She could sense a seismic shift in the planets. A whole new life was beginning. Part of it wonderful . . . part of it painful.

"Well, here's another promise, Papa," she began quietly. "I'm an Estes, now. And if the man I married is nothing to you, then the same goes for me." With that, she walked out of the house, refusing to look back, tears streaming.

"Sofia!" It was Debi this time.

She didn't stop.

The front door slammed shut.

Sofia looked up and down the dark suburban street. "Shit. We let the cab go." Feeling like she truly deserved a cigarette now, she lit one, smoking it between crying jags.

Ben placed a comforting arm around her. "Maybe you should go talk to him, Sofia. I can take the train into the city. I don't want to be the one standing between you and your family."

Debi came rushing out of the house.

Sofia extricated herself from Ben to embrace her sister. "He's such an ass!" she cried, careful to hold the cigarette far enough from Debi's head so as not to set her hair on fire.

"I've never seen him act this way. Maybe he has a tumor," Debi said.

Sofia drew back and took a drag. "This is insane."

Debi stepped over to hug Ben. "If it's any consolation, I don't think you're a creep."

He gave her a half smile. "I'm trying to convince your sister to stay here and talk to your dad."

"I meant what I said," Sofia announced stubbornly. "He's impossible. Who has time for it? I've got a job, a husband, a beauty products company—"

"You've got a company?" Debi cut in.

Sofia shrugged. "It's in predevelopment. But once it's up and running, I'll have less time to deal with him than I have now, which is no time at all. That's, like, negative time. I'll have to cut back on work, I guess, to make things balance out."

Debi looked confused.

Sofia turned to Ben. "I'll come back to get my stuff when I know he's not here. Let's go home." And then she started toward the road, flagging down what looked to be a gypsy cab. It was. She cut a deal with the driver and shouted back, "He'll take us to the train station for five dollars."

Ben hesitated.

"Come on!" She flicked her cigarette into the street, got into the car, and rolled down the window, frustrated by the childproof glass that stopped halfway. "I'll call you later!" she yelled to Debi.

Reluctantly, Ben slid into the seat beside her.

The raggedy sedan took off.

Debi remained in the yard, just standing there, watching the scene unfold.

Sofia tried to focus on her next steps. Papa would see to it that she felt this independence where it hurt the most. Financially. Whatever credit cards he'd cosigned—most of them, unfortunately—would probably be canceled tomorrow. That left her with a Discover Card and her Berrenger's account.

"Remember that unused credit card I mentioned?" Ben nodded.

"Well, don't count on that."

"Did you see the look on your sister's face back there?" Ben asked.

"Yes," Sofia answered quietly, knowing how much Debi hated it when she made occasional escapes to Ricky's apartment. This new move was a permanent one. It wouldn't be easy for her. "What do you want me to do about it?"

"Slow down," Ben said. "Think about what you're doing. We have something special, but it can't take the place of your family. That's too intense. We'll be finished before we get started."

"I can't take care of Debi," Sofia argued. "Anyway, I'm not abandoning her. I'm just getting on with my life. This isn't *Dallas*. How long are we supposed to live together at Southfork?"

The car jerked to a stop in front of the train station. "Five dollar plus tip," the driver barked.

Ben lifted up the pet taxi to peer through the grate

at a still-sleeping Mr. Pickles. "What kind of drug did you give this little guy?"

"He has to be totally sedated during travel, or he'll itch like mad and create bald spots." Feeling tired and suddenly drained, she leaned on Ben's arm and let out an exhausted sigh. "Fourteen hours ago we were in San Francisco waiting on a plane. Now we're in New Jersey waiting on a train."

Ben cupped one of her cheeks with his hand and gazed thoughtfully into her eyes. "Are you OK?"

"This deal with my father has been coming for a long time. If it hadn't been you, it would've been my continued refusal to marry Vincent. Or something else entirely."

His gaze stayed on her like a laser. "You don't have to play tough with me."

She started to cry.

Ben held her tightly, assuring her that everything would turn out fine.

The train screeched into the station, and they boarded right away.

Sofia tried to shake off this sudden penchant for tears. "Enough family drama. That's not sexy."

Ben put on a hurt face. "What about a sensitive husband who tries to comfort you?"

She smiled. "Now that's *very* sexy. But don't be *too* sensitive. I mean, I don't want you to start reciting poetry or discussing the Brontë sisters."

He reached out to take her leg; then he slipped off her shoe and began to massage her foot, his strong fingers concentrating on the arch. "What about this?"

"Sexy."

"What about us soaping each other up in the shower when we get back to the apartment?"

"Sexy."

Though longing to get home to his last suggestion, she agreed to stop in at Swifty Morgan's for a quick drink. The moment Ben hit the door, a surge of excitement jolted the bar. Whoops and hollers all around. In the span of seconds, the jukebox was piping out Sinatra's classic version of "New York, New York."

Kitty dashed over to embrace her pal. Over his shoulder, she fixed an icy glare on Sofia. "Look who's back," she told Ben, leading his eyes with a pointed finger to a stunning blonde at the bar. "It's CZ."

Ben was speechless.

Sofia wanted to blink and find herself anywhere but here. Across the room, her new husband's beautifully groomed, impeccably dressed former lover appeared to be delighting his friends with great aplomb. Meanwhile, she'd been in the same clothes for fifteen hours, her makeup was a mess, and in her hand was a pet taxi containing a drugged out Yorkie.

Not sexy.

Chapter Fifteen

Mr. Pickles paced back and forth across the same tiny patch of grass for twenty minutes before squatting to make bookie.

"Good boy, honey!" Sofia praised.

The Yorkie danced around in response.

She checked her watch. Ten minutes ago her shift had started at Berrenger's. With her mind racing about being late for work, her beauty company, Papa, Debi, and CZ, she thought nothing of reentering Ben's building and proceeding up the stairs, Mr. Pickles in full view.

A few prolonged looks from passersby tickled her curiosity, but she paid them little attention. The real conundrum was CZ Rogers. Why was she back in New York? Sofia could still hear her voice and the way it sliced into the smoky den of Swifty Morgan's.

"You must be pregnant," CZ had accused. "The

Ben Estes I know couldn't commit to flossing every night, much less marriage."

"I'm not expecting, but thank you for your concern," Sofia had told her "As for Ben's decision to commit, it's amazing what the right woman can do."

In the great American pecking order of pithy comebacks, that had been right up there with some of Alexis Carrington's best work. Even Kitty had thought so. Sofia had seen a glimmer of respect in her eyes after the last syllable dropped.

"What a precious little dog!" The exclamation came from a sweet old lady leaving her apartment on Ben's floor.

Last night's highlight footage got pushed out of mind. Sofia beamed proudly. "Thank you. His name is Mr. Pickles."

"How darling." The woman gave Sofia a studied glance. "I don't believe I've seen you around."

"I'm moving in with Ben Estes. He lives down the hall. We just got married."

"Congratulations! Ben's a very nice young man."

Sofia extended her hand to formally introduce herself. She learned that Mrs. Townsend had lived in the building for seventy-one years!

Suddenly her new friend glanced up and down the hall, as if worried. "You know, dear, they have a strict rule against pets in this building."

"I know," Sofia whispered. "We're trying to keep him a secret."

"Be careful," Mrs. Townsend cautioned. "I'd hate for the super to find out. That could mean trouble for you."

"Thanks for the warning." They promised to share a pot of tea and visit soon; then Sofia ambled off, appreciating her new home already. What a delightful neighbor.

"Honey, are you awake?" she called out as she entered the apartment.

"Barely. Need coffee." The reply came back weak and groggy.

Freeing Mr. Pickles from his leash, she smiled. "I'll make you a fresh cup." This gave her goose bumps. She was making coffee for her husband! Could anything be *more* fun?

"I just met the nicest lady in the hall," Sofia bellowed as she fooled around with Ben's cheap little machine, making a mental note to grab the new coffeemaker from the stash of wedding gifts piled up in Papa's garage.

"No nice ladies exist on this floor," Ben said, a little stronger this time. "The ones I know are either crazy or evil."

"Don't be silly. Mrs. Townsend's a doll."

His bare feet hit the floor with a resounding thud. A nanosecond later, Ben stood in the cramped kitchen, buck naked, hair sticking up in unfortunate ways, face drained of color. "She's crazy *and* evil."

"Oh, stop," Sofia sang, kissing his cheek. "You really *do* need some coffee." She went back to searching the cabinets. "Where do you keep the filters?"

"Mrs. Townsend hates me. She wants her granddaughter to move into the building and would do anything to get me evicted."

Sofia froze.

Ben seemed to pick up on this. "Exactly what did you say to her?"

She continued staring into the cabinet. There was peanut butter (not her favorite brand—they'd have to talk), honey (erotic memories of Carmel—add to grocery list), and big marshmallows (was he a Girl Scout?).

"Sooofeeeaaaa," he said, stringing out the sound of each vowel like Ricky Ricardo on *I Love Lucy*.

She faced him, biting down on her lower lip. "I might have mentioned that we were trying to keep Mr. Pickles a secret."

"You told Mrs. Townsend this."

"I think you're wrong about her. She's an angel."

"Yeah—*of death*." Ben groaned. "I'm sure the super knows by now. And the landlord. And the *New York Post*."

"So, where are the filters?" Sofia asked, hoping to get back on task and drop this subject of the two Mrs. Townsends.

"I'm out. Use a paper towel."

"You're out of those, too."

"This must be why I go to Starbucks."

Sofia frowned. "I wanted to make coffee for you."

"Did you want to get me evicted, too?"

"I'll stop by Mrs. Townsend's apartment on my way to work and straighten this out. We really clicked. Don't worry." She stepped over to offer him a slow, seductive, juicy kiss.

At first, he tried to resist, but then he gave in, moaning softly.

She felt him wake up where it counted. "You know, we haven't made love in our new home yet."

He reached for the top button of her blouse. "Well, baby, that's just plain laziness."

She made a halfhearted attempt to try to stop him. "I'm already late for work."

"I'll write you a note," Ben said, pulling her into the bedroom. Gently, he pushed her onto the bed and climbed on top of her, feasting on her neck and removing her panties at the same time. "Dear Mr. Berrenger," he began, as if dictating to a dutiful secretary. "Please excuse Sofia's tardiness today. She was making love with her husband."

Sofia laughed uproariously. And proceeded to do exactly that, driving him crazy with the strength of her vagina. Contract. Release. Fast. Slow. The sensuous power of her inner muscles rippled over his big, beautiful cock, undulating like mad, sending them both to the moon and back. The kissing, licking, stroking, and caressing never stopped. It went on and on.

Afterward, completely spent, they lay side by side, sharing a cigarette.

"You know," Ben said, his hand delicately placed on the inside of her thigh, "if this marriage is going to survive, we really need to do something about our sex life."

Sofia kept her eyes on the ceiling that desperately needed a fresh coat of paint. "As in improving it?"

"Yeah. It really sucks."

She took a drag, stubbed out the cigarette, and put on her best effort to mimic Kitty. "Honey, you don't know from sucks. You're so bad in bed I bet you can't even pleasure yourself. What chance does a woman have?"

Ben hit his forehead with both hands. "That was scary!" He started laughing. "Baby, you do Kitty better than Kitty does Kitty."

Sofia got out of bed and began to search for her clothes. "You think so?" She found her panties on the floor and her blouse under the sheet. As for her skirt, it was rucked up around her waist and wrinkled as hell. What a way to treat vintage Chanel. She smoothed it out the best she could.

Ben arched his back and craned his neck to gaze at her upside down. "You look so hot."

She slipped on her underwear. "I look like a girl who just got through shagging."

"My point."

Grinning, she buttoned up her blouse. "I'm *so* late."

"But you've got that glow."

Sofia loved that she was going to work this way, slightly disheveled, with his scent all over her, the memory of their erotic waterfall fresh in her mind. It was undeniably sexy. She bent down to kiss him on the forehead. "I have to go. I'll miss you."

Ben grabbed her hand and pretended to pull her back onto the bed.

"Don't tempt me," she whispered, twisting away.

"What am I going to do without you for a whole day?"

"I don't know. Go out and get a record deal or a string of concert dates at Radio City Music Hall. We need the money."

He flipped over onto his stomach and propped himself up on his elbows to give her a thoughtful stare. "Maybe I will. You inspire me. I haven't had true inspiration for a long time."

Sofia blew him a kiss, grabbed her lab coat embroidered with the Aspen Cosmetics logo, sang the bye-bye song to Mr. Pickles, and headed straight for Mrs. Townsend's apartment.

When the door opened, the sweet person that Sofia had met just minutes earlier was replaced by a scowling, hostile creature. *"What?"*

Sofia was taken aback. *Will the real Mrs. Townsend please stand up?* "Hi, I just wanted to clarify—"

"Too late, missy. I've already informed the super,

the landlord, and started a petition in the building. I suggest that you unpack *slowly.*"

Sofia just stood there, stunned. "I don't understand."

"Good apartments are hard to find. My grandchild deserves it more than that bum you married."

This battle-ax had gone too far. "Now, wait a minute. My husband is not a bum!"

Mrs. Townsend squinted to study Sofia's hands. "I see the asshole didn't buy you a ring."

Sofia was speechless. Everything had been going full tilt. She'd completely forgotten about a ring. The quick fire of anger was lit and flaming. But first there was the matter of this hag insulting Ben. Only his wife could do that. "He may be broke, but he's *not* an asshole!"

"In my day, a man did whatever he could to put a ring on a woman's finger."

"That was a different time. People traveled by stagecoach." Sofia held up her hand. "Speaking of fingers, why don't you pick one."

Mrs. Townsend seethed. "This used to be a respectable building."

"Until you turned into Bette Davis from *Whatever Happened to Baby Jane?*"

"Bitch!"

"Old bitch!"

"Tramp!"

"Fossil!"

Mrs. Townsend readied herself to slam the door in Sofia's face.

"Wait!" Sofia cried.

"What?"

Sofia hesitated. She knew this was hotheaded thinking, but she needed to put forth some sort of official protest on the issue of her diamond-free hand. "Where's that petition? I'm pissed about the ring, so I'll sign it anyway."

After scratching her name onto Mrs. Townsend's clipboard, Sofia stalked back to the apartment. "Hey!" she shouted from the entryway. "How's this for inspiration? Your wife still doesn't have a wedding ring!" Then she slammed the door and left for work.

Oh, shit. Ben lay there, motionless. *The ring.* How much were diamonds these days? Probably more than he could scrape up before Sofia got home tonight. Princes got away with murder on this score. Royalty never antes up for big stones. They just pass down family jewels and call them heirlooms.

He reached for the phone and punched in Kitty's office number.

"Kitty Bishop."

"It's Ben. Have breakfast with me."

"You must still be on California time. Everyone else in the city is thinking about lunch."

"Oh," he remarked, glancing at the alarm. It was past eleven.

"My lunch meeting just got bumped, so you're in luck. How does the Four Seasons sound?"

"Expensive."

"My treat."

"Generous. I accept."

"I'm doing PR for a new disco singer, and I use that term loosely. The music blows, and her vocals are so enhanced, processed, and synthesized that it could be a record for Alvin and the Chipmunks. Anyway, her father's loaded. Tell me what you think of her new promotional photos, and I'll expense account the meal."

Ben smoothed a hand down his cheek. He needed to shave, shower, and put on the Ritz. The Four Seasons required a million-dollar look. "I take it she's just a bored and beautiful rich girl."

"That would be an easier sell. She's actually average with crooked teeth. Daddy should've sent her to an orthodontist instead of a record producer."

"I bet you're still pushing her as the next Madonna anyway."

"It's called PR, honey. My job is to spin it, not believe it. How's married life?"

"Sofia's estranged from her father, and there's a strong chance I'll be evicted for harboring a dog that pees on my clothes." One beat. "But the sex is great."

"Sounds better than most marriages I know. There goes my other line. I'll see you in an hour." Click.

For a guy out of work, Ben really knew how to power lunch. The Four Seasons teemed with major players. Barbara Walters occupied a center booth. Rock star Bono from U2 sat at another table, opposite Timothy Shriver, the brother of Maria Shriver and the director of the Special Olympics. Nearby, Hugh Hefner held court with three giggling Playmates—identical blond twins and a voluptuous brunette. One of the sisters made noises about taking a "skinny-dip" in the four-hundred-foot pool, which beckoned with its white marble fountain.

He tracked the scene until he spotted Kitty.

She raised her martini glass to signal that he'd kept her waiting too long.

Ben had to give Kitty her due. Inside this famous

restaurant, with its imported wood paneling and twenty-foot ceilings, with its forty-plus years of social history and elegant ambiance, his best pallie from the wrong side of the tracks didn't act lucky to be here. She gave off the unmistakable countenance of a woman who belonged.

He grinned. "You know how to live, Kitty."

A waiter materialized to inquire about his drink wishes just as his butt made contact with the chair.

"Two fingers of Jack Daniel's, four ice cubes, the rest water," Ben said.

"Would you prefer that in a traditional rock glass, sir?"

Ben smiled at Kitty. "I like this guy." He turned to the impassive waiter. "You must know Jilly."

The waiter returned a blank look. *"Jilly,* sir?"

"Never mind. Put a rush on that drink. This lady's already ahead of me."

"What's on your mind?" Kitty started in as soon as the waiter disappeared. "We never see each other in the daylight unless there's a particular issue."

"I'm broke."

"You're the only man I know who dukes a twenty to the guy who hands you a towel in the bathroom. Stop tipping so much. Next problem."

"I'm serious. I have to make something happen soon. This singing career is going nowhere, and I need . . . *stuff*. A wedding ring for my wife, for instance. Maybe even a place to live by the end of the day."

His drink arrived. But he didn't touch it. Better to let the ice settle.

"Honey, you passed the New York bar exam."

"After three attempts."

"Doesn't matter. You've got options. With your looks, you could get on with any firm in Manhattan."

"What do looks have to do with it?"

"Hot men are good for business. It's an edge. Use it."

The thought of going back to that life gave him a sick feeling. "I can't do an eighty hour week of proofing contracts and writing briefs."

Kitty eyed him suspiciously. "Is this your way of asking me for a loan? You know my policy on that."

"No," Ben said, holding up both hands to drive the point home. "That never even crossed my mind."

She raised her martini glass and drank up in relief. "Good. Because Taz still owes me five hundred bucks. The two of you need to stop dreaming and start working."

On that note, now seemed as good a time as any to start on his own drink. He took a healthy sip. It was perfect. Jilly had some real competition out there. "Is this your way of calling me a loser?"

"Permission to speak honestly."

"As opposed to the sweet-talk you usually offer?"

Kitty rolled her eyes and launched in with, "You want to be a successful singer, but you don't really work at it. For years, I busted my ass doing grunt work at PR firms. I slept with supervisors and clients, stole Rolodexes, eavesdropped on confidential meetings— whatever it took to get ahead."

"I hope you edit this speech for career day at your old school."

Kitty tilted her head. "I tell the kids not to eaves-drop. That's rude." She pounded the table with her fist just hard enough to make the silverware clink. "No one is going to tap you on the shoulder at Swifty Morgan's and say, 'You sir, are the next Harry Connick Jr.' If you want this, you're going to have to sweat for it. And you haven't even put forth enough effort to get winded.''

Ben couldn't deflect a single word. Kitty had a rare talent for truth at its coldest and hardest. But sometimes a man needed to hear it. This was one of those times. He drank deep on the Jack Daniel's.

The waiter returned to talk about the menu.

Kitty sent him away.

Something inside Ben erupted, an internal button that made him want to kick his own ass. "I need to stop fucking around."

"Now you're talking," Kitty said, smiling as she finished her martini.

"You're the idea girl," Ben said. "If I were your client, what would you suggest?"

Kitty smirked. "That you pay me a deposit on a three-month retainer."

"After that."

She gave him a critical stare. "Lose the karaoke machine. That's for beauty contestants who show up at state fairs to destroy 'The Wind Beneath My Wings.' You need real musicians backing you up."

"OK. How about the New York Philharmonic?"

"Don't be glib. People pay good money for my image advice." She kept on with the assessing stare. "You've got the voice, the looks, the easy charm. What you need is a spectacular, a showcase in the right venue with a few well-placed VIPs and press people to create a buzz."

Ben nodded, liking the sound of it.

Deep in thought, Kitty pursed her lips. "I'm not sure if the Ol' Blue Eyes tribute is the way to go. There's a kid who sang at the Brad Pitt and Jennifer Aniston wedding. He does Sinatra."

"So?"

"It's been done. Only better. A little boy Sinatra is a slam dunk in terms of PR. Personally, I hate kids. But most people love them and find them entertaining." She shook her head. "America has no taste."

"But that's my whole act," Ben argued.

Kitty leaned across the table. "And, honey, it's not working."

Ben felt like the sky was falling. "Why didn't you tell me this before?"

Kitty thought about it. "Because you're one of my best friends, and I've never really looked at you with my PR hat on until you asked me to."

"How do I stage one of these spectaculars?"

"Lots of training and rehearsals. Right now you're strictly amateur hour."

Ben blanched. He was swallowing bitter pills by the handful. "Did I do something to piss you off?"

"This is how I work. Clients get the real shit. The press gets happy talk." She cast a glance up and down his body. "Are you a good dancer?"

He returned a cocky grin, remembering his recent night grooving to salsa beats at Copacabana with a certain television icon from yesteryear. "Ask Charli Grant."

Kitty pulled a face. "No thanks. I'll take your word for it. But you still need solid training. I know an awesome choreographer I can set you up with. Plus a voice coach. And a producer to flesh out the concept for the spectacular."

Ben looked at her as if she'd just announced that little people live in salt-and-pepper shakers. "Let me ask you something. In your estimation, do I have *any* talent?"

"Oh, please," Kitty said, waving off his insecurity.

She searched the restaurant, shot a disgusted look to Hugh Hefner and his girls, then asked, "Where the hell is our waiter? I'm starving."

"You sent him away."

"For a few minutes, not for life." She focused on Ben once more. "How badly do you want this?"

He searched his heart. An image of Sofia flashed in his mind. His wife. Man, that was a new one. But he liked the sound of it, the way it made him feel. And he wanted to make her proud, to find success at something he loved, to share his passion for music and entertainment with as many people as possible. Kitty knew what she was talking about. It wouldn't be the easiest road, but a gut thing told him it would be paved with yellow brick.

"It's in my blood," Ben said.

"I know it is." Kitty smiled. "Give me a couple days to pull the right people together. I'll make them cut you a good deal."

"I'm broke, remember?"

"I have an idea for that, too. A short-term solution for your cash crisis. How would you like to make two hundred fifty dollars an hour?"

His eyebrows shot up with interest. "I'm listening."

"Come with me." Kitty rose from her chair with the grace of a bullfighter and blazed a trail through the Four Seasons as if she'd designed the floor plan.

The power lunchers hit the pause button on mega deals to notice.

Strut. Pout. Put it out. Kitty Bishop rocked with YES I CAN attitude.

He followed her until she passed through the door of the ladies room; then he stayed back, confused.

A few seconds later she reappeared, gave him a look of annoyance, and yanked him inside with her. "Take off your shirt."

"What?"

"I want to see your chest and abs."

Ben's mouth fell open in shock. Could it be?

"Honey, don't go there," Kitty said, obviously reading his mind. "That happened one night. Years ago. To this day I still feel like I slept with my brother." She shook off the thought. "Take it off."

Ben peeled off his jacket, tie, and dress shirt. "What's this all about?"

Kitty gestured to the last item—his undershirt.

Reluctantly, he pulled it over his head, if only to find out where this was going.

Kitty walked back and forth in a small semicircle, surveying him like cattle. "How many crunches a day do you get in?"

"A hundred," Ben said.

Kitty poked him in the stomach. "Liar. Start doing three hundred before bed every night." She eyed his crotch. "How big is your dick? I can't remember. That was three years and probably sixty men ago."

"I've never measured," Ben said.

"Every man measures. And adds two inches. Let me see your bulge."

"No!" Ben shrieked, feeling suddenly prudish.

"Honey, come on," Kitty snapped impatiently, moving in to pull down his trousers herself. "Not bad. A little padding wouldn't hurt, though. It's all about fantasy, you know."

Just then two women—sleek fashion-executive types—entered the ladies room, stopping short with alarm.

"Oh, great," Kitty chirped. "An informal poll." She addressed the newcomers now. "What do you think of him? On a scale from one to ten, ten being the hottest. Imagine a wild birthday party for one of your good friends. He shows up to strip."

Ben couldn't believe it.

Both women raked him up and down with lustful glances.

"Ten," said one. "Very tall, nice body, in great shape but not a gym freak, face like a movie star. I'd hire him in a second. My friend Jen is getting married next month. He'd be great for the bachelorette party."

Her colleague nodded in almost agreement. "I give him a nine. He loses a point for not having a tan."

"Thanks," Kitty said easily, as if she'd just borrowed a tampon from one of these women.

"No problem," the first one said, moving on to one of the stalls.

"Get dressed," Kitty told Ben.

He did. Quickly. Then he raced out to catch up with her.

She arrived back at the table first.

"A stripper?"

"It's only temporary. You'll make gobs of cash. How else are you going to be able to pay your rent and foot the bill for these industry pros who will help you put together the spectacular?" Her eyes got big. "I just came up with the best slogan: the only man who does it *your* way."

Ben wondered if this was his cue to throw up.

"Wear your tux. Do a slow strip to 'Strangers in the Night.' Women will go wild." She paused. "You'll have to shave to look good in your thong, of course."

"This is not going to happen." He tried to sound resolute.

"I can easily get you eight parties a week. That's two thousand dollars."

Now he was intrigued. "Is there a dental plan?"

Chapter Sixteen

Aspen Cosmetics had started a new free-gift-with-purchase promotion. If ever there was a worst day to show up late, then this was it.

Sofia had been scheduled to open the counter at ten o'clock and fly solo until noon. *Yikes.* Shoppers were swarming the area like locusts. Free gifts in the beauty industry were a pain. Some women went mad for the cheap zip closure bag that usually contained a lipstick, a perfume sample, a few squirts of moisturizer (barely enough for Barbie's face), and maybe one application of the latest eye-shadow color.

To get this treasure, they were required to spend at least fifteen dollars on product. Most picked out the cheapest item—a deodorant stick with hints of the Honesty fragrance. The truly audacious would return it for a refund the next day, keep the gift, and walk away thinking they possessed the financial savvy of Alan Greenspan.

As Sofia approached, she got a hope-you-die-soon look from Claire, who'd left her Clinique turf to handle the Aspen crisis. In the demimonde of cosmetic sales, this was akin to carrying another woman's child to term. The real kicker—Claire could be a bitch even in her best mood. The long day just got longer.

"Welcome back," Claire snapped, stalking out of the Aspen island and back to her own.

Suddenly Sofia noticed hostile glances being lobbed in her direction from all the girls. Had winning the vacation triggered this much envy? Then she quickly surmised that Ricky must have passed the word about the impromptu marriage. Many of her coworkers were miserably single. Oh, God! They must hate her now. But these lipstick commandos didn't know the half of it.

No ring.

An incorrigible father.

Possible homelessness.

So her life was hardly The Cindy Crawford Story. She tried to ignore the chilly reception and concentrate on the free-gift frenzy, which continued nonstop until Ricky arrived at noon.

He raced to scoop her up in his arms, then halted, sniffing her hair. "I smell morning sex."

The warmth of a blush rose faster than a new Britney Spears single. Sofia shushed him, not wanting the others to hear. "Ricky, I've never had so much sex—morning, afternoon, evening, middle of the night."

"Stop. You're making me sick. In the last week I've only had cybersex."

"How does that work exactly?"

"You learn to type with one hand."

Sofia leaned against the counter. It felt great to be

back with Ricky but dreadful to be back at Berrenger's. She was nothing more than a glorified shop girl. This bothered her now more than ever.

"How's your father dealing with the news?"

"We're not speaking." Suddenly she remembered her sister's talk about Ricky's depression and moved quickly to change the subject. "What about you? Debi mentioned that you've been down."

His face took on an inscrutable sadness. "It's my mom. I've been saving money for us to take a vacation together. She's always wanted to go to Europe."

Sofia placed hand over heart. "That's so touching. I had no idea."

"Mama won't go. It's just the thought that counts, I guess. She refuses to leave . . . *him.*"

Sofia glanced down. When it came to Ricky's family, she never quite knew what to say. It was such a tragedy. "Not having a good mother when you're an adult is awful. Sometimes you just want to be babied and looked after. But I've heard that having a good one can be just as aggravating. Parents are so complicated. For adult children, I think it's always a mess, no matter how perfect they seem or disastrous they really are."

"Yeah," Ricky agreed. "I have a friend whose mother sends him pamphlets on HIV prevention at least once a week. She calls it a demonstration of love. I'd rather get past-due notices from American Express."

Sofia perked up with pride, pleased that she had uttered something useful to her best friend.

"I can't expect her to choose me over her husband." Ricky smacked his forehead with his palm. "I keep having to remind myself that this is the same woman who let him kick me out on the street on my seventeenth birthday."

She hooked an arm through his and scooted closer, catching a whiff of Creed's Silver Mountain Water. He always smelled so damn good. "And now you want to take her on vacation. Another example of how it's only a matter of time before we become parents to our parents."

A customer lingered. Not the typical Berrenger's type. More like Wal-Mart. Nothing against the retail giant. After all, it was a great place to buy household supplies.

"May I answer any questions about Aspen?" Sofia inquired.

"Is this where you get the free gift?"

Ricky let out a barely audible groan.

"Yes," Sofia answered patiently, "but it does require a minimum fifteen-dollar purchase."

"That's not free! Forget it!" And the woman left to wreak more havoc on the world with her unfortunate taste and ghastly manners.

"There has to be a better life," Ricky said.

"Ben gets up at the crack of noon. Maybe that's the answer."

Ricky turned and fixed an earnest look on her. "Are you serious about this idea of starting a beauty company? I mean, really serious. Not like the time you wanted to be a backup dancer for Paula Abdul."

"Funny you should mention that. It's been on my mind quite a bit lately." One beat. "The beauty company," she clarified.

"Then let's do it. You've got the style, Debi's got the brains, and I've got the money. This could be huge."

Sofia regarded him carefully. "You want to be an investor?"

"Without an influx of big cash to get things rolling, this is all talk. I'm sitting on thirty thousand."

"Dollars?"

"Let me check on that. It could be pesos."

She clutched him fiercely. *"Thirty thousand dollars?"*

He smiled.

"How did you save that kind of money?"

Ricky shot a look down to her feet. "For starters, I don't wear four-hundred-dollar shoes. And I don't drink. I socked away a lot from Thursday to Sunday on that alone."

"This is amazing. You must feel so powerful."

"Are we on the same page? I said thirty *thousand,* not thirty *million.*"

"Still, it's an enormous amount of money to have at one's disposal, especially for someone your age." She paused to let the shock wear off. "You'd be willing to risk it on my beauty company?"

"Why not? Our idea of ambition has always been to ride the clock for an extra half hour or to take a longer break without Howard Berrenger finding out. We'll never get ahead that way."

Sofia wanted to squeal with delight. "We are *so* on the same wavelength." Her stomach did a flip. Fate had intervened. This was her chance.

"There's a show on CNN called *Movers*—"

"With Jan Hopkins," Sofia interjected. "I watch it, too!"

Ricky's face lit up. "Oh, my God! I thought it was just me."

"No, I love it."

"My secret dream is to be profiled on that show."

"Shut up!" Her heartbeat took off. "That's totally *my* secret dream!"

They held hands and started jumping up and down. All of a sudden, Sofia stopped. Her feet were killing her. "I'm in heels," she explained, pulling herself together. "Did you see the one where they interviewed the woman who runs the Bliss spa corporation?"

"*Love* her hair," Ricky said.

Sofia nodded excitedly. "I want to *be* her." She searched her memory. "What's her name?"

Ricky thought about it. "I can't remember. I know she married a Frenchman, though."

"It doesn't matter. We want to be just like Bliss Girl. That's our mantra."

"Works for me," Ricky said. "I used to worship Marlo Thomas in reruns of *That Girl*. The series ended in 1971, so it only makes sense in the new millennium to worship Bliss Girl now."

Sofia clapped her hands. "I'm calling an emergency board meeting. Oh, that was fun. I love saying that." She stepped over to the register and called Debi. "How would you like to live the life of your dreams?"

"The last person who asked me that was an Amway salesman," Debi said.

"The board of my new corporation is meeting tonight, and you're on it."

"What corporation?"

Sofia considered the question. Leave it to Debi to be a stickler for details. Inspiration seized her. The mission of the company was beauty. Why not name it after the most beautiful woman she'd ever known? She put a hand to her throat, feeling an emotional tickle. "The corporation is called Jacqueline," Sofia said grandly. "Named after our mother.

* * *

"Honey, the man is *hot*," Kitty was saying into her cellular. "And did I mention *straight*? Most male strippers are gay. That makes the fantasy too much work. . . . Carolyn deserves to whoop it up with a real guy at her bachelorette party. . . . Trust me; I slept with her fiancé a few years ago, and she needs to see a big dick before taking those vows. . . . He'll be there."

Kitty clicked off the tiny phone and slipped it into her purse. "Where the hell is Dino?"

Ben could only smile as he caught the disapproving glances from other shoppers inside the intimate showroom of jewelry designer Dino Angiello. Kitty had the uncanny ability to offend someone about every thirty seconds.

"Your first gig is tonight." She reached for one of Dino's business cards and scribbled an address on the back.

"Tonight?"

"Honey, when I talked about training and rehearsals, I was referring to the spectacular. Stripping is easy. Just smile, move your hips, and try to maintain an erection."

Ben didn't want Sofia to find out about this part of his life. Way too embarrassing. The plan was to just make the money he needed and get the hell out.

"Remember this—every booking can make or break you. If you're lousy, word travels fast. If you're a hit, you stay busy."

"This means Sofia will be alone tonight," Ben lamented. "I'd planned to have dinner ready when she got home from work."

"You sound like a Connecticut housewife."

He ignored the comment. "I hope the two of you can be friends."

Kitty pulled a face. "I haven't had a girlfriend since third grade. I date like a man and do business like one, too. Most women can't relate to that."

"Sofia wants you to join her new book club."

"*Book* club? You know I only read the columns."

"I have it on good authority that skimming the dust jacket counts. Her sister and best friend are in it."

"That's not a selling point." Kitty stared into the display case that featured Dino's sterling silver cuff bracelets.

"She's not going away, you know. This isn't a pretend marriage."

"Just one that won't last."

His first instinct was to walk out and leave her there. But Kitty stopped him. "Ben . . . wait." She took a deep breath. "I'm happy that you're happy, but this is still hard. It used to be just you, me, and Taz. The whole dynamic has changed. I need some time to get used to the idea. Isn't it enough that I'm here helping you pick out her ring? I'm not a total bitch."

"Of course you are." Ben grinned, returning to the counter. How could he stay angry? This girl was the closest thing to a sister he'd ever known. But there was that isolated incident of incest. Close cousin? Better.

Just then Dino appeared. He was a small, balding man with a deep tan and perfect teeth. A year earlier, Kitty had put Dino's designs on some Manhattan socialites for a glittering charity event. His name then turned up in the fashion press coverage, after which business really took off.

"We need a wedding ring," Kitty said.

Dino's eyes widened, and he started to make the perfunctory congratulations.

"Don't get excited, honey. I'm not the bride. In fact, I'll *never* be the bride. Or the bridesmaid. I hate marriage *and* weddings. But my best friend here took the plunge." Kitty paused to give Dino a steely stare. "And he needs a *really* good deal."

Dino nodded with understanding and disappeared into the back.

"I get the feeling this man's jewelry is expensive," Ben whispered.

"He's one of the best. Don't worry about the price, though. This guy owes me big time. He'll give it to you for a steal and let you pay in installments."

"Will he check my credit?"

Kitty pushed up her breasts. "Honey, you're looking at Trans Union. I'm all the credit bureau you need. Now relax and pick out what you want."

"You've helped me out so much today I feel like you should list me as a dependent on your tax return."

She reached for another one of Dino's business cards and turned it over. "Jot down your social-security number."

Ben simply looked at her and laughed, assuming she was kidding.

"I mean it," Kitty said. She gestured for him to start writing. "It's in my Palm Pilot to sleep with my accountant every year before tax season starts. That way he gets very creative with my return."

Dino returned with a small tray of rings straight out of *Town and Country*. Square diamonds. Oval-cut diamonds. Hammer-set champagne diamonds. Flower-shaped diamonds. Pavé diamonds set in platinum.

"These are beautiful," Ben remarked with something close to breathlessness.

Kitty seemed nonplussed. "His wife is something of a fashionista," she told Dino. "What do you have that really dazzles?"

He left again and came back with a selection so amazing that it almost knocked Ben to the floor.

"It's an emerald-cut sapphire," Dino explained. "Ten carats, plus two carats in trillion-cut side diamonds. The stones are exquisite."

"I think she might like that," Kitty said easily, as if a new scarf were in question.

Ben remained speechless. The ring, or rather the work of art, was positively stunning. It didn't seem possible that he could actually select it with some degree of seriousness and not be laughed out of the area code.

Dino gave the ring a close inspection. "It is quite lovely."

Kitty turned to Ben. "You haven't said a word. You must hate it." Back to Dino now. "Take it away."

"No," Ben said, jolting forward as if to tackle Dino should he move another inch. "It's breathtaking. I want my wife to wear that ring."

Kitty shrugged. "That was easy."

"I'm scared to ask this, but . . . how much is it?"

Dino diverted his eyes to Kitty. "What can you afford to pay each month, sir?"

Ben worked up a mental budget. He bounced out his first number. Cable cost more than that. Then he threw out the most respectable amount he ever had at the end of each month. "One hundred dollars."

Dino hesitated, eyes still on Kitty.

She gave the jeweler a severe nod.

"That will be fine, sir."

Ben experienced a flood of relief. And disbelief. "One hundred a month? Really? For how long?"

Kitty patted his hand. "Until you die, honey. And even if you make it to be one of Willard Scott's birthday friends, it's the best fucking deal of your life."

Joseph's big table at Villa was bigger than it needed to be tonight.

Sofia was off acting crazy.

Debi was at some kind of board meeting.

Vincent had suffered enough humiliation.

And Aunt Rebecca was on another bender.

That left him, Fat Larry, and Little Bo. *Family dinner my ass.*

Costas hovered, overcompensating for the thin turnout. "For you, Joe, I'm going to have the chef create a very special dish."

Joseph nodded dismissively and gestured Costas away.

"There's one good thing about nobody showing up, boss," Fat Larry said. "More food for us."

Little Bo laughed. "Yeah, boss. More food for us."

Joseph downed a glass of red wine. "What the hell is that supposed to mean? The two of you ever had a problem getting enough food? You calling me cheap?"

"No, boss," Fat Larry said.

Little Bo solemnly agreed.

"Then don't talk unless you got something to say that's worth a damn." The irony still gnawed away at him. He'd sent these yacks to California to whack the boom-box singer. And what did they do? Walk his daughter down the aisle and sign up to be a witness at the wedding! Should he fire them? The thought crossed his mind. But nobody else would hire these dopes, and the boys needed work. So here they were, eating on his dime and grating on his nerves. Business as usual.

Joseph sensed movement and turned to see Tony Langella approaching the table. A huge slab of a man, Tony ruled tyrannically over an empire of trendy nightclubs, upscale strip joints, and slick gay bars. Known to be as ruthless as they come, Joseph had always kept a respectful distance.

"Joe!" Tony said, opening his arms.

Joseph stood up to embrace him and plant a kiss on both chubby cheeks. "How's business, Tony?"

"Couldn't be better now that my little problem's out of the way. You heard about it?"

Joseph nodded. One of Tony's nightclub managers had been mouthing off, talking crap about having enough goods on Tony to send him to prison. On a Thursday he didn't show up for work. On a Friday he turned up dead in his apartment.

Tony had a big grin on his face. "A very clean job."

Joseph read between the lines. Tony had used the Caretaker, every crime family's hit man of choice. Expensive but efficient. The Caretaker's history was the stuff of mythology. No one had ever seen or talked to him. According to legend, a mysterious courier service shepherded the necessary tools for hire. And there were only two—the name of the intended and lots of cash.

"What's this I hear about Sofia getting married? I show up for three weddings and get nothing. Now I come to find out I've been shut out for the real thing."

"You're not the only one, Tony," Joseph said miserably.

"Say no more. I've got three girls of my own."

"This guy she ran off with is a bum. He apes Sinatra and calls it making a living."

"Sounds like you need the Caretaker." Tony laughed and slapped Joseph on the back, charging ahead to join his party.

Joseph's mind began to race. He stared at the empty chairs around the table. *Ben Estes.* The name smoked inside his head. Ever since that creep had come into the picture, there'd been nothing but trouble. Perfect plans turned upside down. A daughter out of control. Family traditions ignored.

Maybe he did need the Caretaker.

Chapter Seventeen

With Taz down on both knees in front of him, new razor in hand, Ben stood naked, massaging shaving cream into his pubic hair. "Thanks for helping out. I just couldn't do it myself."

"If this ever gets around . . . ," Taz started. "I mean, it just doesn't get any gayer, man."

"But this feels so natural," Ben teased. "I once dreamed about you—"

"I've got a razor in my hand!"

Ben laughed. "Just make me smooth enough for a thong."

Taz calmed down. "I will say this. When it comes to size, you've got nothing to be ashamed about. For a white guy."

"Be frugal with your praise. I might get excited."

Taz sat down on the edge of the tub and began to study the Gillette can. "Does this have aloe in it?"

"Get on with the program! This is weird enough."

Taz didn't look up. "You have to leave that on a few minutes to soften the hairs." He tapped the can. "There we go. Aloe." He glanced at Ben. "It reduces skin irritation."

"Thanks, Heloise."

"Maybe I should strip, too," Taz said. "Kitty's after me to pay back that five hundred dollars."

Ben shrugged. "Lather up, Charley."

"I'll see how you do first." He noticed one of Sofia's bras hanging over the shower curtain rod and stared at it. "I can't imagine sleeping with the same woman for the rest of my life."

"The rest of your *life?* You can't imagine it for the rest of the *week.*"

"I'm not that much of a dog. I just don't think I could make the promise to be faithful. My threshold for monogamy is probably three months. And that's just intercourse. Making out and oral sex don't count."

"So you *do* pay attention to politics."

"Huh?"

"That was a Clinton joke."

"I don't get it."

"Never mind." Ben moved closer. "I think I'm ready now. Watch your teeth."

"That's not funny, man."

Ben winced as Taz stroked with the grain to remove most of the hair, then took the blade against the grain to get that smooth, close shave. But so far, only the idea was painful.

"You didn't answer my question," Taz said, concentrating on his task as if it were open-heart surgery.

"You didn't ask me one. You made an observation. About yourself."

Taz held up the razor. "This is a fairly intimate situation here, Ben. You can share."

"I've never had a problem with monogamy."

"*Never?*"

"OK, there was that one time in college. But it was spring break, and I was really drunk. Remember, CZ cheated on *me.*"

"Now, you have to admit, she looked hot last night at Swifty Morgan's."

"No argument here, Charley. But she didn't tempt me. I don't think any woman could." He smoothed a hand over Taz's head. "You're kind of tempting. You've got a sensitive touch."

"Knock that shit off, man!"

Ben laughed. "I married Sofia to save my life. Literally. Every second that I'm with her, though, I realize that doing it saved my life in all sorts of ways I never imagined."

Taz looked up at him. "That was a beautiful thing you just said. Can I use it in a script?"

"Sure," Ben said, making a mental note to remember himself. It could be a home-run paragraph for an apology card the next time he screwed up.

"I'm finished," Taz announced. "Get your wanker out of my face. You better wash with soap and water. Follow up with cotton and rubbing alcohol, too."

Ben gave him a curious look and stepped into the shower. "You sure do know a lot about this."

Taz got quiet all of a sudden and walked out of the bathroom.

Ben turned on the water and shouted, "You're wearing thong underwear right now, aren't you?" He was still laughing when he got out a few minutes later, wrapped a towel around his waist, and joined Taz in the kitchen.

His pallie was staring into the empty refrigerator. "I thought married people kept food in the house."

Ben propped himself up onto the countertop. "What's going on with your screenplay? Kitty mentioned something about you taking a meeting."

"The guy was jerking me around."

"Sorry to hear that."

"Kitty told me he was a loser. I should've listened to her."

"When it comes to business, that's not a bad idea."

"I met another cat, though. A legit one. He used to work with Russ Meyer."

Ben drew a blank. "Who's that?"

Taz shook his head. "Only one of the best filmmakers ever. He made *Faster Pussycat! Kill! Kill!*, *Wild Gals of the Naked West!* and *Beneath the Valley of the Ultravixens.*"

"Oh," Ben remarked. "And to think people make a big deal about this Spielberg guy."

"He says that with a few revisions my script could work as a low-budget B movie. The working title is *Funky Soul Brothers on Mars.*"

Three knocks rapped the door.

Mr. Pickles barked like mad and raced over to scratch.

Ben picked up the creature and locked him in the bedroom while Taz answered. He came back to find the landlord in the living room.

"I know about the dog."

"It's only temporary," Ben said. His voice was pleading.

"So are you."

"I'm married now, Mr. Dunne. We're a two-income household. Rent will never be late again."

Mr. Dunne cut a glance to Taz.

"Not him," Ben said. "He's just a friend. My wife works at Berrenger's."

"Read the terms of your lease. *No pets under any circumstances.* You're in violation of that, which means I'm free to exercise my right to void the rent-control clause and adjust this property to current market rate."

Ben felt physically ill. *Market rate.* To anyone in Manhattan without a trust fund, those were words to fear.

"I also have a petition here encouraging this action that was initiated by Mrs. Townsend," the landlord went on. "Every tenant in the building has signed it." He paused a beat. "Including your wife."

Taz looked at Ben.

Ben looked at Taz.

"No ring," they said in unison.

"This meeting is called to order," Sofia said.

"We're sitting at a table in Starbucks," Debi pointed out. "This isn't a board meeting. It's a conversation."

"I've got thirty thousand dollars," Ricky said. "We should rent a board room."

Sofia nodded. "I like it. A new company has to project the right image."

"Remind me to call a temp agency next time," Ricky added. "Somone should be taking minutes."

"Time out!" Debi yelled.

"That's a sports term," Ricky sniffed. "This is a business."

"OK, how about this word—*bankruptcy.*"

Sofia gasped.

Ricky looked worried. "Already?"

"Very soon if stupid decisions like renting fancy board rooms and hiring staff we don't need are made." Debi huffed a little. "Now, I have a suggestion."

Sofia and Ricky listened intently.

"There are just three of us involved here. Let's work by consensus. Nothing goes ahead unless *everyone* is in agreement. No exceptions."

Sofia pursed her lips. This didn't sound like *her* beauty company anymore. It sounded like *theirs*. But Ricky did have the backing money. And Debi had just saved Jacqueline from chapter eleven. She brightened. Sharing responsibility would give her more time to shop and be with Ben. "OK."

Ricky nodded.

"What is Jacqueline?" Debi asked.

A stony silence hit the table.

Debi rattled on. "What do we sell? Who is our customer? How will we market our products?"

Another deafening silence.

This was like a live version of the *Wall Street Journal.* "Has anyone been watching *Passions?*" Sofia asked. "I've missed a whole week."

"Sofia!" Debi shrieked.

"Stop yelling!" Sofia shouted back. "You've done that twice since we got here."

Debi started to gather up her things—purse, legal pad, calculator. "I knew this would be a waste of time."

Sofia felt the sting of hurt right away. "What's that supposed to mean?"

Ricky cupped his latte with both hands and settled back to watch.

"I think my point is obvious," Debi snapped.

"I'm the dumb sister, remember? Help me out."

"A small business is not a toy that you can just push aside whenever you get bored. It takes passion and dedication and more hard work than I think you're capable of. I'm asking *fundamental* questions that you haven't even thought about! And your *best friend* is sitting right there, willing to put his life savings on the line. If you don't have what it takes to approach this seriously, then forget it! Stop talking about it. Stop calling meetings. Just stop it!"

Sofia sat there, frozen. Her lips quivered. She felt a tear form but flicked it away with a swipe of her hand. "Are you finished?" she asked softly, voice cracking.

Debi took in a deep breath. "Yes."

Sofia tried to compose herself. She could handle the occasional Kitty and CZ confrontation, but conflict with family always made her cry. Though difficult to admit, Debi was right. Sofia had to approach Jacqueline differently. Its success—or God forbid, failure—depended primarily on her. This was a critical moment. Proof that she could be a competent leader had to come through right now. At this table. It was do-or-die. She took a sip of her Italian soda and cleared her throat, willing herself to remain calm, stay focused, and most of all, display a little of that Bliss Girl magic.

Splaying her hands on the table to steady herself, she began. "I appreciate your suggestion to operate by consensus, Debi, but I'm actually opposed to that."

Debi leaned back, stunned.

"Jacqueline is *my* company. I'll solicit as much information from you and Ricky as an issue warrants, and then I'll make a final decision."

"I don't—"

Sofia held up a hand to silence her sister. "I let

you have your say. Allow me to have mine." She reached into her purse and pulled out the tiny Hermes notepad that she regularly scratched musings into. "The two of you have strengths that I'll never possess. I'd like to delegate and turn you loose to do what you do best. Debi, you know the necessary legal requirements for setting up a new business. Take care of those details. And don't forget to join the CTFA."

Debi gave a blank stare.

"That's the Cosmetic, Toiletry, and Fragrance Association." Going back to her notes, Sofia flipped through all the scribbles and doodles. "I think Jacqueline should start small and limit its product line to nail polish. We can position it upscale and sell it for twenty dollars a bottle." She cast a glance at Debi's calculator. "I'm no accountant, but I know this much—high markup means high profit."

Ricky bobbed his head, impressed. "You sound like an accountant to me."

Sofia smiled. "I should slap you for that."

"Tell me what I can do."

She found the page she was searching for. "Research suppliers of dyes, bottles, and caps. Keep in mind that we're selling Jacqueline at a premium price. We need high-quality packaging. Something that makes enough of a statement to capture attention but not so costly that it kills our profit. Delivery terms are important, too. Speed is critical."

Ricky leaned in and put his elbows on the table. "I'm all over it."

"I want the image and mystique of Jacqueline to be fun and self-indulgence." Sofia's pulse started to race as she realized that they were staring back at her with something close to awe. But she pressed on, anxious to make all her points known. "We'll create eye-popping new colors and use the company title in the name to help build the brand. Like Jacqueline Feels Pretty in Pink or Jacqueline Feels Girlish Green."

Sofia stopped to take a breath and another sip of soda. "I've got a strong sense of fashion. People are always coming up to me to ask where I got this purse or that pair of shoes. *I'm* the Jacqueline customer. Show me four fabulous nail polish colors, and I'll show you an eighty dollar charge on my Visa statement. Revlon spends a fortune on market research and analysis. We don't have to bother with that. I *am* the market, and this city is filled with women just like me. It's not that complicated. Let's build something great together, have fun, and get rich." She rose gracefully and fixed a triumphant look on Debi. "Meeting adjourned."

"I'm going home right now to do research online," Ricky announced. He turned to Sofia. "It's time to operate on a higher level. As of today, I'm swearing off Internet gay porn."

Sofia giggled. "Well, the first step is always admitting the problem." Turning to leave, she felt Debi touch her arm.

Ricky made a discreet exit.

"I want to talk to you," Debi said.

Sofia pushed back a tendril of hair from her forehead and just stood there.

"The pitch you just made was brilliant. Where did that come from?"

She looked away for a moment, then back at Debi. "I'm not an idiot."

"I know that."

"You spoke your heart. Do you really think that I

would fritter away Ricky's money or name a company after our mother and let it fail?"

Debi hesitated. "Not intentionally."

Sofia sank down into her chair. "God, I mean, do I come off as that much of a flake?"

"No. Maybe I overreacted. You have this air about you, this invincible attitude that no matter how casually you take things, they'll work out fine in the end. I was worried that you might approach the company the same way. I didn't want to see you get in over your head. There's too much at stake."

Sofia shut her eyes. "I know."

"But after tonight, I have no doubt that you can handle it."

"Really?"

Debi gave her a knowing nod. "You're going to surprise a lot of people with Jacqueline's success. Including yourself. I've got a strong feeling about that."

Sofia pulled her chair closer. "I read once where the way to find your calling is to figure out what you can do for twelve hours a day without looking at the clock or realizing you haven't eaten. That's what Jacqueline is for me."

Debi averted her gaze to play with the calculator. "Don't ever think you're the dumb sister. You're smarter than I am."

"Excuse me, Miss Near Perfect SAT Score?"

"Forget tests. I'm talking about life. You know how to live it. Every day is a chance for you to just hold your nose and jump. Look at how you cut off all your hair, took off for California with some guy you barely knew, and *got married!* Now you're starting a business from ground zero. All I do is stick to the same routine because I'm too scared to find out what's out there."

"That's not true," Sofia said firmly, almost scolding her. "For example, you went to SpeedDating."

"That was your idea."

"But *you* walked through the door. Don't compare your willingness to take risk to mine. I'm a daredevil fool! When you've been sunk in habit for most of your life, small changes are incredible risks. Like going to SpeedDating. Or coming here tonight and knocking some sense into your goofy sister. That takes guts."

"I ate lunch in a new place today," Debi put in, her eyes sparkling. "Hey, I'm dangerous!"

Sofia laughed.

"Here goes another risk. A confession. I'm in love with Vincent Scalia."

Sofia stopped laughing.

"I have been since the eighth grade."

Sofia ransacked her purse for a cigarette.

"You can't smoke in here."

"I know. I just want to hold it. When I can't stand it anymore, we'll leave." She fidgeted a moment. "OK, let's go." Lighting up on the way out the door, she took a drag. What if Debi and Vincent got married? *From fiancé at gunpoint to brother-in-law.* It was frightening. But Papa would be pleased. And all of them were shoo-ins for an appearance on Jerry Springer.

"Are you sure it's love, sweetie?" Sofia asked as they started down the busy sidewalk. "We are talking about Vincent."

"One woman's trash . . ."

"Can very well be another woman's trash," Sofia finished. "That's why I'm against recycling." She took another puff, thinking hard. "Anyway, he's not my trash. I never pursued Vincent. He was forced on me by Papa, so don't ever believe you're getting left-overs."

"But he just thinks of me as a Sofia almanac."

"You've been spending a lot of time together, right? Coffee, the theater, dinner, vomiting in cabs."

Debi nodded, breathing heavily as she tried to maintain the pace.

Sofia slowed the walk speed from brisk to casual. "I bet he's more aware of you than even *he* realizes." She stopped to finish her cigarette. "Who does most of the calling?"

Debi looked embarrassed. "I do."

"How long has it been since you placed the last one?"

Debi looked even more embarrassed. "About an hour."

Sofia flicked her smoke into the gutter, put her free hand around Debi, and set off again. "This isn't a problem. Now you just have to dig deep and find the necessary discipline to pull away, no matter how much you want to call. Throw yourself into something that benefits *you*."

"Like Jacqueline," Debi said.

"Exactly."

"And losing weight."

"For *yourself*, not for Vincent, right?"

"He's not going to want a two-hundred-pound girl-friend."

Sofia froze in her tracks. "Don't say that. Look at Camryn Manheim. She's always with a gorgeous guy on TV awards shows. Why? Because she's got the right attitude."

"And a hit series. Maybe those men are struggling actors."

Sofia rolled her eyes. "Anyway, never change yourself for some guy. I dyed my hair once because my boyfriend, Karl, had this thing for redheads. He wouldn't even trim his toenails for me. I was furious. Color can be murder. I had to spend a fortune on conditioning treatments to get back the original shine and body."

"I'm tired of being fat, Sofia. I don't feel healthy. I can't even walk down the sidewalk without breathing hard. It's time for a life makeover."

"Did you say makeover?" Sofia smiled, running her fingers through her cropped hair. "You came to the right sister."

Chapter Eighteen

The body of an elderly woman lay slumped on the stairwell.

"Oh, my God!" Sofia shrieked, rushing to take a closer look.

It was Mrs. Townsend, dazed, frightened, but still breathing.

Sofia crouched down, cradled her head and spoke softly. "Mrs. Townsend, can you hear me? I'm your neighbor, Sofia Estes."

"Who?" The reply was faint.

Thinking fast, she fished for her cellular and called 911. They promised an ambulance within minutes. In the meantime, she stayed close to Mrs. Townsend, careful not to move her.

"You're going to be fine. The paramedics are on the way. They're going to take you to the hospital." She spoke loudly this time, overly enunciating each word.

"It was dark," Mrs. Townsend said weakly. "I fell down."

Sofia glanced up the abbreviated five-stair flight. The lightbulb was blown, the top step almost invisible. She cursed the landlord and super for such reckless negligence. But that could be addressed later.

Right now she held Mrs. Townsend's hand and gently brushed the hair from her forehead. "You're going to be OK. The doctors will take very good care of you."

The woman grimaced, tears falling, the pain worsening.

Sofia felt so helpless. Out of frustration, she started to cry, then bravely fought back against it, determined to be strong. "Is there anyone I can call?"

"My granddaughter . . . Melissa Townsend . . . My . . . purse."

Sofia stretched to reach the handbag and looked inside to find a weathered address book. Under T there were several numbers for Melissa—hometown, college, many in New York. She called what appeared to be the most recent entry.

Four rings, followed by the beep of an answering machine. "Hi, this is Melissa, Sarah, Allie, and Jennifer. You know what to do."

"This message is for Melissa Townsend," Sofia began clearly. "My name is Sofia Estes. I live in the same building as your grandmother. She has suffered a fall, and we are taking her to Bellevue Hospital." She hesitated, then pressed End praying Melissa got home soon.

"Just hang on. You're doing great. The ambulance will be here any minute."

The old woman stared back like a frightened child. "Please come with me. I don't want to be alone."

Sofia gave Mrs. Townsend's hand a soft squeeze. "I'm not going anywhere. I'll be right beside you."

Sirens screamed in the night. The sound loomed closer and closer. Flashing lights colored the dark sky. And then a team of emergency medical technicians crashed through the door.

Everything happened so fast. The transfer to the ambulance. The ride to the hospital. The nervous wait. When Melissa arrived and Sofia finally learned that Mrs. Townsend had broken her hip but was expected to recover nicely, she took a taxi home.

Ben lay sprawled on the couch in his boxers, sleeping peacefully, *Politically Incorrect* playing on the television at low volume.

She crept over and kissed him on the forehead.

He woke up. "Where have you been? I was worried."

"Mrs. Townsend fell down the stairs. I've been at the hospital."

"Is she OK?"

Sofia nodded.

"Write your cell number on the fridge. I jotted it down somewhere but couldn't find it." He really studied her. "You look tired."

"I am." She sat down on the edge of the couch and smoothed her hands across his chest. "How was your day?"

"Productive. Kitty's helping me pull a real show together, and I got a job. Night gigs, mostly."

"I want to come. I love to hear you sing."

He hesitated. "These aren't places to brag about. It's just a chance to make some cash until the spectacular. Wait for the big show. I want to make you proud."

She kissed him on the lips. "I'm proud just to know

you. I started my beauty company today. It's called Jacqueline. That was my mother's name. We're going to sell expensive nail polish."

"Everybody needs that." He pulled her on top of him and wrapped his arms around her.

"Ricky is investing thirty thousand dollars of his money into the company."

"Ricky has thirty grand sitting around?"

"It's a long story."

"You and me, baby, we've got good friends."

"I was expecting to come home to an empty apartment.

"Why?"

"I thought you'd still be at Swifty Morgan's."

"Someone had to wrap Mr. Pickles in the pashmina blanket and take him outside for a walk."

She giggled, rose up on her elbows, and started to finger comb his hair. "You did that?" Then she gazed around the living room. "Where is he?"

"Hush," Ben murmured. "He's trying to sleep."

"Are you two boys plotting against me?'

"The menfolk have to stick together."

Sofia took a deep breath and rubbed her eyes, still a little shaken up. "Mrs. Townsend was so scared, Ben. I felt helpless."

He threaded his fingers through hers and lightly bent them back. "I'm glad you were there for her." Then he stretched and gave her a wry, crooked smile. "Maybe she'll convince the evil landlord Mr. Dunne not to restructure our rent to market rate."

Suddenly Sofia remembered the petition. And the fact that she had signed it. "Oh, no."

"Taz has his eye out for a new place. He's like a superhero when it comes to affordable apartments.

He moves a lot so that women he's broken up with can't find him.''

Sofia admired Ben's beautiful hands. "But all they have to do is walk into Swifty Morgan's on any given night."

"Taz's dates wouldn't fare so well on *Jeopardy*."

"Well, don't worry about *Mr. Dunne*," Sofia said, dropping the name sharply as an image of the busted lightbulb and dark stairwell flashed in her mind. "We're not going anywhere, nor are we paying a dollar more in rent."

"Listen, baby, I don't want you to find another home for Mr. Pickles. You love him, and the little guy is actually starting to grow on me."

"Mr. Pickles isn't going anywhere," Sofia said, punctuating her declaration by pressing a hand in the center of Ben's bare chest. "In fact, this whole *no pets* rule is ridiculous. I'm having that changed. I talked to Melissa Townsend about it. We think her grandmother needs a cat. They provide great company and are fairly easy to care for. Anyway, now's a bad time for us to move. We're both too busy."

Ben's delectable mouth curved into a secret smile. She sensed something was going on. "What is it?"

"Go into the bedroom and look on your pillow."

Her heart went bang. She loved surprises. Especially those on or underneath the pillow. Chocolates at fine hotels, money from the tooth fairy. She raced away like a little girl.

In the doorway, she froze. The bedroom was immaculate. Candles were lit all around, creating a dreamlike effect and scenting the air with lavender, honeydew, and mulled wine. And there, on the center of her pillow, sat a small, black velvet box.

Sofia walked over to retrieve it, breath trapped in

her throat, heartbeat out of control. When she
opened the box, her entire world careened. For several shocked seconds she just stared, never blinking,
not believing. The brilliance of the sapphire and diamonds hypnotized her. The stones were enormous.
Joan Rivers would approve. She slipped the ring on
her finger. It fit perfectly. She felt like Elizabeth Taylor. Before Larry Fortensky and all the health problems.

"I hope it was worth the wait."

She spun around to find him in the doorway. "How
on earth? . . ."

Ben put a finger to his lips. "That's my secret."

"But there's no way we . . ."

"That ring never leaves your finger." Moving
closer, he held out his other hand. "And this one
never leaves mine." He wore a traditional gold band
and proudly pointed out the engraved wedding date.
"It's official, baby. We're hitched."

Sofia started to cry. All she could think about was
fate. What if she hadn't been working on that Saturday she stumbled across this incredible man crooning
love ballads in Berrenger's Market?

"Make love to me, Ben. Make love to me right
now."

Placing his hands on her shoulders, he looked into
her eyes. "I don't need prompting."

It suddenly dawned on her how completely un-
judged she felt. There was no monitoring between
them, no sense of thinking she should act this way
or that way to keep him wanting her.

She was Sofia. He was Ben. And they loved each
other. It was the truest intimacy she had ever known,
the kind that you dream about. She experienced a

moment of such pure happiness that her eyes welled
up with tears again.

He responded to her emotion by just kissing her
softly on the lips.

"What did I do to deserve this?"

"You smiled."

Sofia's heart moved.

Ben took her hand and led her into the bathroom.
"Let's take a shower. I've got a surprise for you." He
turned on the water.

"Another one?" She gazed at her ring again. Would
she ever get used to its conspicuous size? One second
passed. OK, she was fine with it now.

He took off her clothes while the steam rose, then
divested his own.

Whenever Sofia found herself alone with him like
this, an unashamed animality seized her. How could
a man's body be so completely and so constantly
alive? And she knew every inch of his, every textured
nuance, every warm and wondrous smell.

Tenderly, she fingered the almost invisible scar
above his eyebrow, the one he got from some girl
pushing him onto a rock during a seventh grade
camping trip. "Who's responsible for this?"

"Paige Glover. She grew up to be a model. I think
she was in *Seventeen* once."

Sofia gave him a look of faux menace. "I want to
track her down and destroy her. Anyone who ever
hurt you has to deal with me now."

"You should go in chronological order then. Start
with my parents."

She looked at him seriously now, wondering if he
meant that.

"I'm kidding." He paused a beat. "Although Mom
did take a brutal approach to editing Halloween

candy. She never let me near the homemade popcorn balls.''

Sofia laughed and stepped into the shower, pulling him in with her. ''When am I going to meet your parents?''

''They're on one of those long cruises that takes you to exotic ports of call.''

''So they do exist?''

''Oh, they definitely exist. And I love them unconditionally, as long as there's a large body of water separating us.''

She couldn't take the suspense anymore. ''What's my surprise?''

''Close your eyes.''

Sofia obeyed and arched her back to wet her face and hair under the streaming steam jets. When she opened her eyes, Ben stood there, one hand cradling a jar, the other one twisting off the top.

''What's that?''

''Brown Sugar Body Polish. I saw it in the window of a boutique.'' He scooped out a dollop and began rubbing it onto her shoulder.

''That feels wonderful,'' Sofia sighed, loving the gritty feel of the sugar grains. ''And it smells divine.''

''I'm going to wash you from head to toe with it.''

Sofia moaned as he worked his way toward her clavicle. ''I'm spoiled.''

''Yes, you are,'' Ben whispered. ''But you were spoiled before I met you. I have no choice but to carry on with the tradition. Anything else would go against the tide.''

''Ooh,'' she sighed as he ran the sweet mixture over her breasts. ''Not there.''

''Everywhere.'' He winked.

"If you insist." She swiped a tad with her finger, plopped it onto the tip of Ben's nose, and laughed.

"I knew I was in for it the first day I met you."

"Oh, really."

"You were eating a fruit salad and refused to pour the poppyseed dressing over the whole thing. I watched you dip in each bite of fruit so carefully."

"And this fascinated you?" She sucked in a tiny breath. His hands were moving across her stomach . . . traveling . . . *down*.

"It told me that you were very precise, and I've been around enough to know that precise girls are a handful."

"I have to do it that way because I hate poppyseed dressing on honeydew melon. Don't know why. I just do."

"And that's why I love you."

"Because I hate poppyseed dressing on honeydew?"

"That's one reason. The other reason is that you're impossible. Promise me you won't go on a self improvement kick."

"Oh, I go on a binge about every six months. Read lots of books, make goal lists, craft a new personal mission statement. But my heart's never in it. I'm still smoking, for instance. I was supposed to quit in 1997."

Ben hushed her, softly, and crouched down to rub the exfoliant onto her thighs. He looked up, without his usual glint of playfulness this time. "I love you, Sofia. For no other reason than you are who you are. That's enough for me. It's more than I ever thought I could feel. The songs I sing really mean something now."

Sofia couldn't speak. The words got caught in her

throat. She'd never felt so wanted, so beautiful, so loved. What did a woman say to such a perfect declaration? *Something simple. Don't want to louse it up, you know.* "I love you, too."

One by one, Ben gently lifted each leg to rub the brown sugar delight all over her feet and between her toes, then lovingly moved her under the hot water to rinse it off, stroking her skin as the mixture washed away. "Feel how soft you are," he murmured.

Suddenly she couldn't stand it anymore. So she kissed him. And she didn't stop kissing him until they reached the bed, their bodies still wet. The idea of stopping to towel dry was out of the question.

Ben made love to her tenderly but with purpose. He was quietly ravenous, and she gave herself up completely. Man and woman. Husband and wife. She never imagined lovemaking could be so amazing. It was biblical.

When he fell asleep, she curled up on him like a fetus, her head on his chest, her left leg across the top of his firm thighs. Against her hip she could sense the rise and fall of his breathing. She tucked her hand underneath his arm for warmth and settled, taking in his scent, thinking how perfect life was in his arms.

The next morning Sofia got up at five o'clock and didn't complain. There was so much to do. How refreshing it was to have an ambitious purpose. *Future parenting note number one: Encourage my children to do science projects, homework, and other things I never bothered with.*

She ducked out to the twenty-four hour drug store down the street and picked up several bottles of white nail polish and a rainbow of dyes. Then she popped into Starbucks for two large coffees and headed back.

Turning the living room into a makeshift factory, she experimented with different colors and shades, scribbling down notes and observations after each batch. Minutes melded into hours. Finally, the perfect shade of blue materialized. It was a pale periwinkle. Gorgeous beyond words. She called it Jacqueline Feels Blissful Blue.

Her company's first original nail polish color! To celebrate, she cleaned the competition off her own nails (apologies to Anna Sui) and painted on a fresh coat of her new creation, admiring her ring while it dried.

Quite accidentally, she glanced at the clock. A few minutes past ten. Already? Oh, dear. Late for Berrenger's. *Again*. The free-gift promotion was still going strong. Claire would really let her have it today. She dashed to get ready and nearly collided with Mr. Dunne on her way out the door.

"Is that animal still in your apartment?" he asked tartly, without so much as a good morning.

"If you're referring to my husband, what we do in the privacy of the home is *our* business."

Mr. Dunne's face turned scarlet. "I'm speaking of *that dog.*"

"You need a lesson in priorities. Follow me." She led him down the stairs, stopping on the last flight to point out the faulty lightbulb, emphasizing the hazard of limited visibility on the top step and how that caused Mrs. Townsend's tragic fall.

A few minutes later there was a new pet policy (limited to twenty-five pounds), a promise that Melissa would get the next available apartment, assurance that Mrs. Townsend's unit would be installed with safety rails in the bathroom, and no more talk of this *market-rate* nonsense. As she negotiated with

Mr. Dunne, Sofia noticed that she'd suddenly developed a habit of waving her ring hand in a way that said, "Look at my jewels. Aren't they lovely?" She decided to work on that right away, as potential to be annoying to others was unusually high.

"Thank you for joining us Princess Sofia," Claire hissed as soon as she hit the Berrenger's sales floor.

"I'm sorry," Sofia sighed. "I've been helping the elderly."

"How interesting. I've been helping your customers."

Sofia ignored her. Claire was one of those people who, if she were to win a million dollars on a game show, would only complain about the taxes. Indulging her hostility with nasty comebacks simply encouraged more of the same.

Ricky came bounding in a full hour early. "Did you know that we can produce a bottle of nail polish for under a dollar? And we're going to turn around and sell it for twenty. Now I know what a drug lord feels like. How are you?"

Sofia turned her head and let her wrist fall.

"Sweet Jesus! You mugged Ivana Trump!"

She splayed her fingers and checked the fit for the thousandth time. "He gave it to me last night."

Ricky aped Mae West. "Honey, I thought he gave it to you every night."

Sofia giggled and twirled around. "I have the most wonderful husband in the whole world."

"Not to mention great nails. That blue polish is fierce."

"It's Jacqueline Feels Blissful Blue. I made it this morning."

Ricky made a face. "Here comes fuckhead. I guess we have to stop ignoring the customers now."

Sofia turned to see Howard Berrenger coming their way and moved swiftly to approach a mother and her provocatively dressed teenage daughter. "May I help you?"

"Taffy wants some new makeup," the mother said.

"That's not *all*, "Taffy huffed. "I need other stuff, too. God!"

Future parenting note number two: Be rich enough to afford Swiss boarding school to limit my parent/child contact during this difficult period of adolescence.

"I want that," Taffy demanded, pointing to Sofia's sparkling hand.

Her mother smiled nervously, shrugging off the request. "I don't think the nice lady's ring is for sale, Taffy."

"Not the ring. That's, like, drag-queen gaudy. Yuck! I'm talking about the nail polish. It's *so* cool. Nobody at school has that color."

Sofia's disgust (what did this brat know about jewelry?) and delight (the little snot did know her nail polish) was ameliorated by the presence of Howard Berrenger, who'd stopped to hover and conduct an impromptu sales performance critique, as was his custom with all associates.

"Do you sell that color at this counter?" the mother asked.

"Well, no . . .", Sofia began.

"Where did you get it?" Taffy asked sharply. "I want to buy, like, every color."

"Let's not get carried away, Taffy," her mother said reasonably. "We'll try one color and see if you like it."

"God! I *know* that I do. It's not like Daddy didn't just sell his Internet company for fifty million. *Whatever.*"

If only to save the mother from more abuse, Sofia

came clean. "Actually, I made this nail polish myself. I'm starting my own company."

Howard Berrenger stood statue still.

"God! I don't need your A&E biography," Taffy said. "Just tell me how many colors you have."

Future parenting note number three: Rethink this whole idea about having children. Sofia stared at her nails. "Only this one right now." A sense of pride, of individual accomplishment like none she had ever felt, overwhelmed her. "It's called Jacqueline Feels Blissful Blue."

"Like, how much is it?"

Sofia hesitated. Jacqueline was either open for business or it wasn't. Even with Howard nearby, she decided to take the plunge. "Twenty dollars."

"I want ten bottles to give to all my friends," Taffy said.

The thrill of her first order sent shock waves through her body. "Come back tomorrow. I'll have it ready."

Sofia watched them leave, realizing she had never asked if they were interested in the Aspen line. And then there was the conflict of soliciting product not sold by Berrenger's. Both were fireable offenses.

A stone-faced Howard stepped closer and quietly studied her hands. "Nice rock," he commented.

"I'm newly married." She smiled sheepishly, certain this was her last day at the store.

"Congratulations." His gaze rose up to her face now. "That was an interesting transaction I just witnessed."

Sofia looked to the heavens, shut her eyes, and took a deep breath. "You don't have to say it. I know that I'm fired."

"Oh, you would be, if you had just sold one bottle

to that girl. But you moved ten. That tells me you might be onto something with this Jacqueline Feels Blissful Blue. I'll arrange for counter space. Deliver two hundred bottles by the end of the week."

Sofia fought for calm. Had she heard right? Did Howard Berrenger just place Jacqueline's first retail order?

"I'll pay you eight dollars a bottle."

"Nine dollars," Sofia said firmly. She was excited, not stupid.

So far, the Ben Estes spectacular was spectacularly bad. Kitty had managed to assemble a team more dysfunctional than her own family.

At the piano was Robert Cannon, a rotund voice coach whose training method seemed to be inspired by the Louis Gossett Jr. character in *An Officer and a Gentleman.*

On the floor was Rhythm Nation, a street-tough choreographer sporting cornrows, baggy jeans, and a T-shirt emblazoned with the words ANGRY BLACK MAN.

Off to the side was Tim Rebel, a flamboyant queen in head-to-toe Gianni Versace, complete with feather boa and Elton John–style sunglasses, circa 1970s. By comparison, Ricky Lopez could be the pitch man for the National Testosterone Society.

And then there was Kitty, the woman responsible for this mess, sitting in the back, working two cell phones and typing madly on her Apple Powerbook.

"People, it's not working for me!" Tim sang acidly.

"Kick it like this," Rhythm Nation said. He pushed a button. High-energy dance beats exploded into the small rehearsal space. Then he launched into a dance routine that looked perilous to most internal organs.

Ben just stared at him. "I'm not dancing like MC Hammer."

Robert rose (with great difficulty) from the piano bench. "If you want your voice to last, you'll have to stop smoking today. That's an order!"

"Frank Sinatra smoked," Ben said.

"Don't challenge me!"

Jesus Christ Almighty. He'd been at it for three hours with this crew, running in different directions, each one going nowhere. All the hopes he'd built up for this spectacular were disintegrating fast.

With great relief, he realized it was time to quit for the day. Kitty had booked the "star-making team" in limited blocks, a couple of times a week. He barely waved them good-bye, then made a beeline to confront the publicity shark, herself.

"What the hell is this? A circus? I want a spectacular, not a sideshow."

"Let me call you back," Kitty purred into her cell. "I've got an ungrateful bastard front and center." She flipped the phone closed. "Honey, you have *no idea* what you want. That's why your first rehearsal was a waste of time."

Ben wanted to argue, but an immediate feeling told him Kitty was right. He *didn't* know what he wanted. Damn. Everything had been clear in his mind before that lunch at the Four Seasons. "I used to know," Ben said, more strongly than the sentiment called for. "I wanted to be Frank Sinatra."

Kitty shook her head. "Honey, Frank Sinatra *Jr.* doesn't want to be Frank Sinatra. He was an icon. Nobody can fill those shoes. You know, this idol worship was cute at first, but it's getting old. Anyone can put on a tuxedo and sing 'I've Got the World on a String.' There's a cheesy talent like that on every cruise ship from Miami to the Bahamas. Do something different. You don't have to steal someone else's act. You're a star. Create your own act.''

Ben didn't know what to say. He was touched. "You really believe I'm a star?"

Kitty groaned. "You're not getting melancholy, are you? I don't do melancholy. It's a policy of mine." She snatched a lime green Post-it from her computer screen. "You've got another booking tonight. Here's the address. Ask for Chris." She started to gather her things. "How did your wife like the ring?"

"She cried and told me to make love to her."

Kitty scoffed. "That's why I hate women. I'd give a man the fuck of his life and then ask for a matching necklace."

Ben laughed. Underneath Kitty's ball-buster armor, there was a little girl who'd suffered a lot of hurt growing up. She chose to reveal her tender side in quiet ways, like going to great lengths to help her friends and telling them the truth when they needed to hear it. That's why he loved her.

He scanned the Post-it. The address was in Chelsea. Last night's first strip had been a breeze. Just a bunch of drunk and horny women screaming while he stripped and danced around. They stuffed money in his thong, ran their hands over his muscles, licked their lips, and chanted 'Take it all off!' " But he kept his teeny-weeny underwear on. A man had to maintain some dignity.

"I have to get this spectacular moving in the right direction," Ben said as he followed Kitty to the elevator.

"I wasn't on crack when I called these guys in to

help. They're great at what they do, but they're *tools*. You have to know how to use them. If you tell Robert, Tim, and Rhythm exactly where you want to go, they'll take you there.''

"Is Rhythm Nation his real name?''

Kitty nodded. "He's a huge Janet Jackson fan and legally changed it after the song came out.''

The arrow light blinked, and the doors slid open. "I guess it could be worse,'' Ben said, stepping inside. "He could've been a Madonna fan and named himself Like A Virgin.''

Chapter Nineteen

Sofia read the anonymous letter again.

YOU'RE A PERFECT LITTLE BITCH WITH THE PER-
FECT LITTLE LIFE. BUT NOT FOR LONG.

It was eerie. Her first piece of hate mail. Except
for Columbia House. They were still angry about her
accepting the twelve CDs for a penny but not fulfilling
her contract agreement.

The more she thought about it, the more it un-
nerved her. The letter had just appeared on the
counter. She'd left her typical standing area to answer
the phone (a poor customer looking for girdles but
transferred to Aspen courtesy of a stoned operator),
returned to her perch, and there it had been.

Sofia cast a suspicious look to Claire. Maybe it was
her. *Think like Angela Lansbury.* Claire had opportunity
(standing just yards away), and she had motive (furi-

ous over Sofia being late two days in a row). This case was solved.

She stomped over to Clinique and thrust the type-written page in her prime suspect's face. "I don't appreciate this!"

Claire read the letter. "Me, either. I think you're a bitch, but I *don't* think you're perfect."

Sofia stood there in a speechless snit. Her gut told her that Claire had nothing to do with this. "Did you notice anyone hanging around my counter a few minutes ago?"

Claire handed back the paper. "I only pay attention to Aspen when you're not there."

Relieved to see Ricky returning from his break, she rushed over. "Somebody hates me!" she announced gravely, presenting him with the evidence.

He looked it over. "Claire."

"That's what I thought at first, too. But I confronted her, and she took issue with this assertion that I'm perfect."

"Claire's such a drag. It's *your* hate mail, and she's still complaining." He tried to think. "Who else is there?"

"Well, it could be anyone. I'm under thirty, thin, married to a gorgeous man, and I wear a beautiful wedding ring."

Ricky thought about it. "Now *I* want to write you a hate letter."

"CZ!" Sofia exclaimed. "And Charli Grant! They both have a thing for Ben." Kitty Bishop popped into mind. "I've told you about his friend Kitty, haven't I? She's very protective of him."

"You can't go around accusing everyone. People will think you're crazy. Put it away for now. Maybe it's just a one-time prank."

Sofia felt like it was more than that, but she heeded Ricky's advice for the moment.

"I talked with the supplier," Ricky said. "They offer same-day delivery, so all the stuff should arrive at your apartment this evening."

"What time can you come over?"

"It'll be very late."

"Why?"

"I'm one of the hosts at a birthday party for the bartender at Chances. He's depressed about turning forty."

Sofia tried to map out the night. "I suppose I can get things started on my own." A thought struck her. "I almost forgot. Debi's treadmill is being delivered tonight, too."

"To your place?"

Sofia nodded. "It's a surprise." Another thought came to mind. "Did I mention that Ben is losing his pubic hair? Isn't there a special shampoo he can use?"

Ricky gave her a strange look. "I've never heard of that happening."

"It's not my imagination. There are a lot of things I don't know about my husband, but I definitely know his—"

"Vincent!" Ricky said.

Sofia's expression was sheer horror. "I never even—"

"No, I'm back on the letter now. It could be from Vincent."

She didn't buy this theory. "Not his style. I think a woman wrote it."

Ricky raised his brow. "Or a gay man. It's bitchy enough."

"Well, unless *you're* the culprit, I'm fresh out of guesses."

"Maybe Ben has a male stalker."

This scenario might have merit. "He does get looks from certain guys."

"You wouldn't have all this trouble if you'd just been smart about things and married an ugly rich man."

Ben could hear the party going boogie woogie several feet away from the apartment. Hopefully they were well into the booze. The more the girls drank, the more the girls tipped. He knocked hard to make certain they heard him.

A man answered the door.

"I'm sorry," Ben started, retrieving Kitty's Post-it from his front trouser pocket. "I thought—"

"Are you the stripper?" The man's smile was big, appreciative, and pleased.

Ben glanced beyond to see a room full of guys.

"I'm Chris. Kitty said you were hot." An indecent glance up and down. "She's true to her word. Come on in."

Reluctantly, Ben stepped inside. It's not like he could be choosy. Last night's gig hadn't even covered today's session with Robert Cannon, Rhythm Nation, and Tim Rebel. Whether he took it off for women or men, the money earned carried the same value.

"Hey, boys!" Chris shouted. "Dinner's here! And it's an all you can eat buffet!"

Screams, whistles, and barks from about thirty horny guys punctuated the most discomforting introduction Ben had received in his twenty-nine years on earth. Though part of him wanted to turn around and run, a larger part simply hoped these men carried lots of cash.

He found an open space on the dining table, set down his boom box, and pressed Play. Time to give the boys a thrill. With a theatrical spin, he turned his back to the lions. Lush orchestral strings swept into the room. Swaying back and forth to the music, he slowly removed his tuxedo jacket. And then Frank Sinatra, the master of all masters, began to sing.

"Strangers in the night . . . exchanging glances . . . wandering in the night . . . what were the chances . . . we'd be sharing love . . . before the night was through. . . ."

His shirt was unbuttoned halfway.

"Something in your eyes was so inviting. . . . Something in your smile was so exciting. . . . Something in my heart told me I must have you. . . ."

He turned to face the guys.

The drunkest partier in the bunch sprang from his seat and played with a stereo nestled inside an entertainment center. Suddenly a throbbing dance beat pumped out of the speakers.

"Strangers in the night . . . THUMP, THUMP . . . two lonely people . . . THUMP, THUMP . . . we were strangers in the night . . . THUMP . . ."

He couldn't believe it. The musical underbed of disco fever became as essential as a pulse, an effect so total that it took Ben completely outside of himself. His hips gyrated in perfect synchronization with the beat. Off went the shirt.

The boys went wild.

An insane energy flooded Ben's central nervous system. He kicked off his shoes, peeled away his socks, let the pants drop, and struck a pose like the Calvin Klein underwear model he knew they wanted him to be. All the while, Ol' Blue Eyes did his thing.

"Up to the moment when we said our first hello

... THUMP ... little did we know ... THUMP ... love was just a glance away ... THUMP ... a warm embracing dance away ... THUMP ..."

Money sprouted faster than weeds in a trailer park. Everybody had bills to give away. Ones, fives, tens, even a few twenties. He offered the big spenders the benefit of loading their appreciation in the front of the thong. Those on a budget had to settle for delivery on the side. His body was a cash magnet. By the time the Sinatra classic faded, the rent and next month's payment to Dino were covered.

But the real jackpot tonight was the inspiration. It was like balm for the soul. *Create your own act.* Kitty's words of wisdom were tattooed on his brain. Oh, Charley, did he have an act now! Something kitschy and outrageous. Disco Sinatra! "Strangers in the Night" revved up to shake your groove thing speed. Hot chicks in slinky gowns dancing around him. He could devastate a crowd with a spectacular like that. Really fracture them. What a gas it would be.

These boys sure knew how to treat a man like a pop star. Neighbors up, down, and on both sides had probably dialed the cops to complain about the noise. He decided to collect his fee from Chris and hit the street before the police showed up.

Gathering the scattered pieces of his tux, Ben noticed a familiar face in the back of the room.

Ricky Lopez was staring straight into his eyes.

The realization stopped him cold.

Sofia paced around the living room, smoking like a fiend. The news had gobbled her up like some Godzilla monster. She felt totally consumed, a big helpless thing flopping about in the belly of a beast.

Debi huffed and puffed on the treadmill, sweating, practically dying. "I hate . . . Jane . . . Fonda. . . . She started . . . all this . . . crap!"

Sofia counted eight snuffed out cigarettes in the ashtray. That exceeded her personal limit of six a day. Well, fuck it. She just found out her husband was gay. How could she not have seen it? Great looks. Sharp wit. Stylish clothes. An eye for jewelry. All the signs were there. She smacked her forehead. What did she need? A telegram? Hmmm. Did people still send telegrams? If not, they should. It made a much stronger statement than e-mail.

"Just . . . because . . . he danced . . . for . . . gay . . . men . . . does . . . not . . . mean . . . that . . . he's . . . gay."

"Am *I* dancing for lesbians? Are *you?* Is *Claire?* Come to think of it, Claire probably should. It might bring her some happiness." Sofia gasped. "Maybe Papa knew all along. What if he had a sixth sense about Ben's orientation toward man-on-man love?"

"That's . . . cr . . . crazy."

"No more talking. I feel out of breath just listening to you." She stubbed out number nine and lit up number ten. "This happened to Carrie Fisher. Can you believe it? Me and Princess Leia. Two girls. Two dreams of love. Two gay husbands. What are the odds?"

"How . . . long . . ."

"Now, how could I possibly know the answer to that? Maybe *years.* I've read that some people know as early as six. Two kids in Little League. A lingering glance from third base. It happens."

"How . . . long . . . do . . ."

"Who knows? Maybe forever. If Ricky hadn't called, I might have never found out."

"How . . . long . . . do . . . I . . . have to . . . stay . . . on this . . . thing?"

Sofia barely glanced at her. "Oh, twenty more minutes, sweetie. You're doing great." She surveyed the boxes of bottles and caps, the cases of white nail polish, and the selection of dyes spread out across the room. It rendered the space almost unlivable. But at the core, it strengthened her. This is why she had to soldier on. For that little brat Taffy. For the Jacqueline consumer at large. For America.

Ben walked through the door. "Baby, it's not what you think."

Sofia took one look at him and knew the truth. All the worry, all the nicotine, and for nothing. "I never doubted your manliness, not even for a second."

With nineteen minutes to go, Debi fell off the treadmill.

"Don't sit on the couch," Sofia said. She'd just finished perfecting another batch of Jacqueline Feels Blissful Blue.

"How can I? It's covered in painter's plastic and nail goop." Ben stood in the center of the chaos. "This used to be my living room. What if I want to watch television?"

Her eyes never left her task. "Lie down on the treadmill."

"Why is Debi's machine in our apartment anyway?"

"I'm her personal trainer."

He squatted down on the equipment. "When's the last time *you* exercised?"

"Does running to catch a cab count?"

"No."

"Playing tug of war over a cashmere sweater at a Bergdorf's sale?"

"No."

She thought about it. "Tenth grade."

"Are you almost done?"

"I can stop now. I just wanted to get a head start on this big order for the end of the week." She held out her hands, which were streaked white and blue. "Look at me. I'm a mess."

"I don't know how I'm going to face Ricky again."

"Hopefully with your clothes *on.*"

Ben stretched out and started doing crunches.

"You know, I've been thinking. I don't mind you stripping for gay men. That's harmless. But the idea of my husband taking off his clothes for other women makes me uncomfortable."

He froze the abdominal work. "Baby, just think of me as an actor. It's like a piece of theater."

Sofia's doubts lingered. "Maybe it would help if I saw your show."

"How about tomorrow night? Kitty should have another booking for me by then."

"But I'll be busy with this huge order. Why not right now?"

"Here?"

She nodded innocently. "You have to take off your clothes anyway."

Still in his tuxedo, Ben shrugged, fiddled with the stereo, and started his routine from the top of "Strangers in the Night."

Sofia sat there mesmerized as he stripped in slow time to the music. She wondered what went through the minds of other women. Did they imagine themselves being crushed against his body? Did they yearn to have him deep inside them?

Because she knew what it felt like. And this knowledge brought with it a certain erotic power. Ben Estes belonged to her. Body, mind, and heart. All the spectators could do was fantasize. She could experience the real thing.

Suddenly the music took her away, and Sofia closed her eyes, living the lyrics out loud.

"Ever since that night, we've been together ... lovers at first sight, in love forever ... it turned out so right, for strangers in the night."

"Where have you been?" Joseph barked.

"At Sofia's," Debi said, closing the door. "I left word with Fat Larry."

"Little Bo's the one who knows how to deliver a message."

This week, Debi wanted to add. But she let it go. "Sofia is fine. She's living in a decent apartment in a safe neighborhood."

"Did I ask?"

"I heard you thinking." She stared at the back of his balding head as he sat kicked back in his favorite chair, watching a terrible Cinemax movie. It looked like *Night Eyes 9: Will the Seduction Ever End?* She started up the stairs.

"Vincent called."

Debi stopped in her tracks. For two reasons, one being this shocking turn of events, the other being that the steps were murder on her sore feet, calves, knees, thighs, and buttocks.

"He wants you to call him back."

A formal invitation to telephone. In one word, *lovely.*

"I told him not to give up on Sofia."

Debi wished that she possessed the telepathic power to make objects move at will. If that were the case, the reading lamp would be crashing onto her father's head right now. "Why did you tell him that?"

"Because that bum won't be around much longer."

It's official. Dementia has set in. On the television screen, the star of the movie was taking a gratuitous shower. More women needed to direct bad movies. Normal girls never washed their breasts that way. Disgusted on a number of levels, Debi went up to her room without a word.

She thought about not calling Vincent back until the next day. *How radical.* But deep down, she knew the resolve to wait that long just wasn't in her. The best she could muster—stalling him while she took a shower. When she picked up the phone to dial, she was soaking wet.

"Hello?"

He sounded bored and depressed. Two positive signs for the underdog.

"It's Debi."

"How are you?"

Debi's heart swelled. He was interested in *her!* This man really knew how to give back in a relationship. "Exhausted," she admitted. "I've been working out and—"

"You usually call to tell me about your sister," Vincent cut in.

Disappointment. Humiliation. Self-esteem meltdown. *Everyday high-school experience for five hundred!* "Sofia's married. And she's happy. I really don't see the point to that anymore."

"Your dad told me to hang in there."

"This is the same man who spends the better part

of his weeks with Fat Larry and Little Bo. His judgment is impaired.''

"It's not too late, though. They could still annex the marriage.''

Debi closed her eyes. She was tired and wanted to sleep. "You mean annul. I don't think Sofia and Ben will be incorporating themselves into any existing political units.'' And then it dawned on her. She was tired of *this*. Conversations that went nowhere. Feelings that remained hurt. Giving and getting nothing back.

"You know, Vincent, this isn't working for me anymore. I love my sister, but I'm tired of talking about her. I have a life, too. It's pretty interesting. If you want to know about it, give me a call sometime. If not, well, we'll always have *Annie Get Your Gun*.''

"That's the night you vomited on me.''

"Yeah,'' she murmured wistfully. "Our very own memory.'' Then she quietly hung up.

The crashing storm of regret never came. Maybe she was too fatigued to realize what she'd just done. Or perhaps she really was *fed up*. These were the kind of moments that her cravings for junk-food binges proved undeniable. But tonight was different. Debi Cardinella ate a rice cake, crawled into bed, and drifted into sleep.

And she felt pretty damn good about herself, too.

Chapter Twenty

"Dancing girls? Sugar, baby, cookie, honey, I'm getting a picture of Tony Orlando and Dawn," Tim Rebel said, flicking back his polka-dot chiffon boa. As if faint, he felt his temples with both bejeweled hands. "Now I'm getting an image of the Mandrell sisters. Including *Irlene*. Somebody get me an Advil!"

Frustrated, Ben decided to try explaining his vision a second time.

But Rhythm Nation, whose T-shirt today screamed GONNA KNOCK YOU OUT, beat him to the punch. "I can kick it with some dancing girls. But my flow is some booty club hos shaking what their mama gave 'em."

"I'm still against the smoking," Robert put in. "Drop and give me twenty! Do it!"

Ben gave the men an imperious stare. He knew exactly what he wanted, and this deranged crew of talent shapers was going to help him pull it off. How tough could he get with these guys? With a question in his eyes, he turned to Kitty.

She gestured for him to give her a minute. Once again, the back of the rehearsal space had become her portable office. "Honey, that's what happens when you sleep with a supermodel," she was barking into her cell. "The columns print it. And *everybody* reads Page Six. You want anonymity? Bang your secretary. That's so boring I bet your wife wouldn't even care. Or take me on. I'll give you a tumble. Fine. I'll meet you in the lobby of the Hudson Hotel at noon. And I've heard about you, so know this up front— I'm not taking it up the butt." Kitty closed the phone with a loud clack.

Then she strutted over to the group, admiring her own breasts, testing the firmness of their jiggle. "Jesus Christ. Do I have to provide the sand, the waves, *and* the beach ball?"

Ben opened up his hands in despair. "See if *you* can communicate with Sergeant Bilko, Liberace, and Tupac Shakur all at the same time. I'm a singer, not a nation builder."

"No problem, honey." She turned to Robert Cannon. "Do for Ben what you did for Pia Zadora. He'll be singing and dancing, too. Only better, we hope."

Robert surrendered a brief nod.

Kitty fixed a gaze on Rhythm Nation. "Honey, I need you to focus. You're trying to mix Vanilla Ice with Tommy Tune. A bad combination any way you look at it. Ben can do a few moves, but for the most part we want him to just stand around and look sexy. As for the girls who flank him, you can get a little funky with the choreography, but keep it clean. When the show's over, we don't want anyone waiting around for a lap dance."

Rhythm Nation held up the peace sign.

Now it was Tim Rebel's turn. "Honey, hold on to your boa. The centerpiece of the show is going to be a disco version of 'Strangers in the Night.'"

"Brilliant!" the producer shrieked.

Kitty grinned. "I hope you're wearing a diaper for what's coming next. How do you describe a Ben Estes spectacular?" She paused to heighten the drama. "Harry Connick Jr. meets Cher."

Tim Rebel lost it. "Somebody get me a Depends!"

Kitty smiled at Ben. "You take it from here, honey. I'm off to get laid."

Jacqueline Feels Radical Red was stuck like chewing gum to the living room floor; the factory had overflowed to bathroom, bedroom, and kitchen basin, and Mr. Pickles wore a splotch of Jacqueline Feels Passionate Purple on his snout.

Sofia's cellular rang nonstop. Orders were coming in like crazy. Bloomingdales, Bergdorf Goodman, Saks Fifth Avenue, Henri Bendel, Neiman Marcus. Everybody wanted Jacqueline. She dreamed up a new color to describe her state of mind—Jacqueline Feels *Scared to Death.*

Insane. That was the last few weeks in a nutshell. Miraculously, the company had taken off in ways she never imagined, thanks in no small part to Chrissy Chrissy, the hot new disco singer being promoted by Kitty Bishop. She wore Jacqueline Feels Blissful Blue during a dance club showcase and after the show prattled on about how much she loved the color. The *New York Post*'s Page Six column had picked it up. Apparently, it'd been a slow week.

But the real storm gatherer was Lisa Ling, the smart

and sassy Asian girl from *The View*. She wore the same color one morning on the show, and the ladies gabbed about it for at least two minutes. With no exclusive agreement limiting her to Berrenger's, Sofia was free to take orders from other stores. And Howard was happy to pass along her contact information. He loved being first and trumping Bergdorfs and Saks on a hot fashion item.

Working fast, Debi and Ricky had set up an informational Web site that listed retailers who already carried Jacqueline or would be offering the line soon. As for the tiny apartment that Sofia and Ben shared? Already it was being used for shipping, packaging, warehousing, receiving, and research and development.

Was there anything more frightening than the possibility of success? That was the real road less traveled! After all, failure comes as easily as cell renewal. It just *happens*. And most lives were really nothing more than an extended run of tiny losses.

There was the Rubik's Cube you could *never* line up properly, the cute boy in middle school who refused to ask you to dance (probably gay, but you didn't imagine the possibility *then*), a pair of shoes you would commit treason for sold out in *your* size, the rotten luck to *always* get in the slow cashier's lane at the supermarket.

If Jacqueline had turned out to be a total bomb, Sofia wouldn't have been so freaked. With success came expectations, greater stakes at which to fail in the future. *A truly vicious cycle.* How did Bliss Girl cope? Sofia made a mental note to find out exactly what her name was. Maybe they could power lunch at Le Cirque.

"Come look at this," Debi said for what had to be the kazillionth time that morning, as she pointed, clicked, and pecked away on a laptop Sofia didn't even know how to turn *on.*

"I'm up to my eyeballs in Jacqueline Feels Perfectly Peach." It was almost noon, and she'd been scheduled to show up at Berrenger's before ten o'clock. Maybe Claire didn't have anything to do with the first hate letter, but she'd probably step right up to cosign the next one.

"This is important," Debi said. She sounded really intense. Which, at the moment, was *really* annoying. "We've got to work out cost controls, establish a management system, set up inventory records, track orders, send out invoices, and review the balance sheet."

Blah, blah, blah. That's what it sounded like to Sofia. "As president of Jacqueline, I'm delegating those tasks to you. I'll be in charge of filling and delivering the orders if you do . . . Um . . . Whatever it is that you just said."

"This is the nuts and bolts of any business. You need to show an interest in that side of things, too," Debi argued.

Sofia was bordering on tears. How could she please everybody? Debi wanted her attention. These orders required her time. Berrenger's expected her to honor their schedule. Ben needed her to show a little interest in his spectacular. But Sofia Rose Cardinella Estes could only be in one place at one time.

Ben stuck in her mind. She missed him. It was like they were suddenly living on separate islands. Husband and wife? More like *roommates.* She had the Jacqueline frenzy and Berrenger's schedule; he had rehearsals for his spectacular and stripping gigs. The sum of it all left them no time for each other. Sometimes Sofia longed for those glorious days in Carmel when they were marooned at the Cypress Inn.

But for now, she made a mental list and prioritized based on this question: What's the worst thing that could happen in the next five minutes? She could get fired. It was a no-brainer. "I have to go to work. Assuming I still have a job, that is. Everything else will have to wait."

"This *is* work," Debi said sharply.

"This is a *business*," Sofia shot back. "I've got to make a living."

"Hello? That's what a business is *for*. Jacqueline isn't a soup kitchen."

The point sunk in. "Oh."

"We didn't use all of Ricky's money on start-up costs. If we get invoices out and collect receivables for these orders, our financial situation will be pretty healthy. How much do you make at Berrenger's?"

Sofia had no idea. Most of her check went to pay her house account. And then there were taxes. United Way got a few dollars. Some went into a 401K. Wait a minute. She cashed that out to buy the Cartier tank watch. It was hard to say what her take-home pay was.

Debi got tired of waiting. "Let me make it easy for you. If things continue to go like they are now, you'll make more money concentrating on Jacqueline full time than you will trying to do both jobs. The numbers don't lie."

In answer, Sofia pulled all three of her Aspen lab coats from the closet and placed them into a Berrenger's shopping bag. "I want to tell Howard in person." On her way out, she noticed that a note had been slipped under the door.

YOU'RE A PERFECT LITTLE BITCH WITH THE PER-
FECT LITTLE LIFE. BUT NOT FOR LONG

Sofia scrambled out to the hall. No stalker in sight.
She didn't dare breathe a word of this to Ben. He
needed to focus exclusively on the spectacular. This
was her issue to deal with. The latest letter copied
the first one word for word. She ruminated over this.
A clue! Whoever was behind it must need a thesaurus.

"You're like two ships passing in the night," Jilly
said, presenting Ben with his second drink of the
night at Swifty Morgan's.
"That's understating it. We're not even cruising on
the same body of water. We don't see each other. We
barely talk." He took a healthy sip of Jack Daniel's.
"And my bird hasn't seen any orchid growth in quite
some time."
Jilly nodded miserably. "Mine's only been bloom-
ing about once every two or three months."
Ben grumbled. He and Sofia used to make love two
or three times a *night*. It wasn't just the sex that he
longed for again. He missed *her*. Granted, he was
happy that Jacqueline had taken off so fast. But the
business was all-consuming. Debi and Ricky got more
of his wife's time than he did. In all fairness, though,
he was no Ozzie Nelson. Getting ready for the spectacular was like training for an Olympic event. At the
end of the day, he didn't have much left. And what
energy did remain had been going to women and
men who wanted to see him strip down to his T-back
to the tune of Ol' Blue Eyes.
Could two people give their all to their careers *and*
maintain a successful marriage? A little shower of

guilt started to rain over him. Deep down, he wanted Jacqueline to be a hit but not *too* much of a hit. In Ben's mind, the real fanfare should be his. *Man, I'm such an asshole. I ought to be wishing Sofia the moon and back.* He didn't want to be like so many other guys—supportive only up to a certain point. As much as he loved Sofia, he should go all the way with it.

Ben looked at Jilly for the answers the bartender didn't have. "I should be happy, right? Last night I hit my mark. I made enough dough to quit stripping."

"Hey, will you miss that?"

"All those skirts screaming for me to take off my clothes, pawing their hands all over my body, begging to see my package? No way. It's a bore, Charley."

"I wish I could rustle up some boredom like that. What's this I hear about a recording deal?"

"Kitty lined me up with this Vegas Records outfit. They're just about to go under, so what do they have to lose by taking a chance on one song from a nobody? We cut the disco version of 'Strangers in the Night' with an up-and-coming DJ who really knows his way around the production board. The track smokes, Charley. If somebody out there gave it half a chance, I think it could be a hit. I mean, have you listened to the radio lately? Worse stuff than mine gets a spin. What's a Limp Bizkit anyway?"

"You got me," Jilly said. "Hey, did I tell you I got the night off for your big spectacular? I'll be there."

Ben took another sip. "That's great. Kitty's going all out for the promotion. It's guerrilla warfare. Flyers all over the city, VIP invitations in the mail. They even went out to my father-in-law and Sofia's ex-fiancé. Should be interesting."

"It's at the Charade, huh? Not a bad joint."

"Sofia's friend Ricky helped put it into motion. His

mother's a housekeeper there. She dropped a hint to management, and Kitty closed the deal."

"Speaking of Kitty, where is she tonight?"

"Busting some guy's chops probably. She said something about a big gallery opening."

"And Taz?"

"Working on his movie. The deal's finally coming together."

"Everybody's doing better than ever. So why are you bummed?"

"Call me an ungrateful son of a bitch, but I want more."

"For instance?"

The Jack Daniel's went down. "I want a wife who's talking to her Pops. When a chick's on the outs with her family, a relationship suffers negative effects. It's like a dark cloud that just hovers. On the flip side, I want a father-in-law who doesn't hate my guts. He can dislike me a little. That's only natural. But save the real animosity for criminals and guys named Pete."

"What's wrong with guys named Pete?"

"Every Pete I've ever met has been a fink."

Jilly nodded. "Come to think of it, you're right. The Petes I've known have been real assholes."

"I clobbered a Pete in law school once. Couldn't stand him."

"You fight pretty good, Ben?"

"Not really. My way is to kick a jerk in the ankle and belt him across the chops while he hops on one foot."

"So what else do you want? Pretend I'm Santa."

"I want an apartment, not a twenty-four-hour nail-polish factory. I believe in being supportive of my wife's dreams, but the other morning I woke up and my cheek was Jacqueline Feels Basic Black. A man's bedroom should be sacred. I want to make love to my wife every night, say 'Sleep warm, baby,' and make love to her again the next morning. I want to make big money and find major success at doing something I love. But don't make me work too hard for it. That's just a drag."

"Any other requests?"

Ben pushed his rock glass toward Jilly. "More gasoline. I'm just getting started."

Manhattan girls were gaga over Jacqueline Feels Voulez Vous, a darling little French manicure kit. They were gobbling up the sets like Jurassic Park monsters on speed. Berrenger's was flat sold out, and postcards had already been mailed to push the product during the store's twenty-fifth anniversary weekend blitz. That's why Howard Berrenger was on the other end of the phone right now, begging for two hundred more to meet at least *some* demand.

"I want this celebration to be as close to perfect as possible," he was saying. "Advertising a product not in stock is against everything Berrenger's stands for. I hate to pull this card, but if I have to play on your sense of loyalty, then so be it. Which store gave Jacqueline its first retail order?"

Sofia caved, promised him what he wanted, and hung up. She stared at the nail polish factory that doubled as an apartment. It used to be the other way around. Yes, the mess looked that awful. No matter, there were just enough supplies to build the order. If Debi tore herself away from the laptop to pitch in, and Ricky came by later as planned, they could fill it in time.

She and Debi were working like sweatshop children

when Vincent called. He didn't even *pretend* to want to talk to her. The man wanted Debi on the phone pronto. Sofia was happy for her sister, but she wouldn't have minded just a *smidge* of fawning. After all, thirty was just around the corner. A girl liked to know she could still dazzle.

When Debi hung up, she just stood there, stunned. "I don't believe it."

Sofia remembered seeing her sister in such a state of amazement once before. It was the time Fat Larry and Little Bo finished a word-find puzzle without soliciting help from the neighborhood kids.

"Vincent Scalia just asked me out to dinner. He wants to meet at the Charade's restaurant for a quiet meal before Ben's spectacular. Papa's going, too. Not to dinner, of course, but to the spectacular. Maybe he's trying to make amends."

The happiness on Debi's face touched Sofia deeply. It was the sweet culmination of a practically lifetime infatuation. "Didn't I tell you that playing the aloof card would work? You made it known that you couldn't be bothered, and now he's burning up the telephone wire for *you*."

"I need to go. I want to find something new to wear and get my hair done." The sprawl of bottles, caps, and labels across the floor seemed to remind her of the job in progress. Her face crashed.

How could Sofia ask her to stick around? "Go on, sweetie. Ricky and I can churn this out."

Guiltily, Debi bunched up her shoulders. "Are you sure?"

Even before she could lie and say yes, Debi was out the door. Sofia had never been happier, though. It was high time her sister got the guy, even if that guy was Vincent. But who could judge another's attraction? Crushes were as personal as fingerprints.

Sofia was back at work—still like a sweatshop child—when Ricky called. After explaining Debi's quick exit, she implored him to take a helicopter over if it would land him here a minute sooner. Then something in his pause caused her stomach to drop faster than an elevator with Nell Carter along for the ride.

Ricky's reason for bailing was equally compelling. Cynthia Lopez had called to suggest a family reunion. Mother, father, and son to munch at a Red Lobster in New Jersey (terrible ambiance but nobody had asked *her*), then all aboard the train to the Charade for special table seating at Ben's spectacular. How could she pooh-pooh a family trying to heal in favor of a French manicure for one of Taffy's bitchy (seemed logical) friends?

Well, to call this lousy timing was the understatement of the century. It was worse than a rich relative getting hit by a bus on his way to the attorney's office to declare you sole heir.

Everyone was going to be at Ben's spectacular. Everyone except her. Oh, God, what could she do? Nothing, really. And would he understand? Probably not. Sofia thought back to her third-grade dance recital, the one Papa had missed. OK, at the last minute she'd deemed the costume inferior and refused to go on, but the point was he hadn't shown up. She could still recall the hurt she felt. But she'd been eight years old back then, and Ben was twenty-nine. Certainly he would fare better than she had.

Anyway, it's not like Sofia was being *totally* selfish. There was Debi, practically walking on air over a real date with Vincent, one that *he* initiated. And then

Ricky, finally having a family moment that didn't involve hostile words and late night packing. In a way, she was Joan of Arc, sacrificing herself for noble causes. What had Joan of Arc fought for? Was it the Fourth Amendment? *Hmm. I should know this. Too many notes passed to boys in history class.* A dramatic pause. *Oh, my.* Suddenly she remembered that those dreadful people had burned Joan of Arc. *Yikes! Must find new martyr to compare self to.*

Alyssa Milano! The star of *Charmed* had sued all those creepy people who'd posted bogus nude photographs of her on the Internet. And she'd done it in the name of all celebrities sick and tired of having their images exploited against their wishes. The courage! Alyssa was a martyr who *survived.* Still looking great, doing silly TV, making commercials, etc. Sofia stared pensively a moment. What was the point to all of this?

Ben! Yes, her darling husband and his spectacular. Certainly there would be others. Of course, opening night mattered most of all. That's why he'd forbidden her to show up for any rehearsals. He'd wanted her to see the show slick and polished on the first night.

Sofia stared at the task before her. There was no way she could stop, pull herself together to look fabulous, go to the spectacular, and come back to the apartment with the expectation of finishing the order on time. Without Debi and Ricky to lend a hand, it would take her all night—if she was lucky.

I'm a terrible wife, she thought. *But I'll make it up to him someday, somehow.* In Ben's honor, she put his "Strangers in the Night" demo recording into the CD player, pressed repeat, and let it play over and over, praying he would understand. Then, one by one (tedious as hell but *her* babies) she began to put together Jacqueline Feels Voulez Vous.

Ben held a cigarette in one hand and a Jack Daniel's in the other. His spectacular was just minutes away. He felt a few jitters, but no bone-chilling fear yet.

Kitty and Taz joined him in the intimate dressing area of the Charade's celebrated Star Room. Framed autographed glossies of the entertainers who'd once performed there lined the walls—Rosemary Clooney, Liza Minnelli, Paul Anka, even Tony Danza.

Kitty hijacked his reverie. "After tonight, you'll be up there, too."

"Your belief in me helped make this happen."

Kitty rolled her eyes. "Honey, you have to learn to move past a statement like that and not get sappy. Do I look like Della Reese? Do you see a film crew for *Touched by an Angel?*"

Ben held up his hand, separating his fingers like Spock on *Star Trek.* "I forgot that you were a Vulcan, no emotions and all."

"Go out there and kill 'em," Kitty said, her voice more feisty than ever. "The room is packed—press, VH1 execs, pop-radio music directors, club DJs. This could be the beginning of a wild ride."

And so began the blind terror. And the nausea. And the premonitions of monumental failure. He gnashed his teeth.

"Everyone out there has your press kit with bio, photo, and a promo copy of the 'Strangers in the Night' single. By the way, you met Frank Sinatra back-stage at one of his concerts when you were a little boy. You told him that you wanted to be a singer, and he said, 'Don't give up on your dream, kid.' That's what brought you to this point.''

For a moment, Ben just stared. "But that's total bullshit. It sounds like a rip off of the Mean Joe Green Coke commercial.''

"Honey, unless Kitty Kelley's on the byline, all bios are bullshit. Take those actresses and supermodels who say they never had a date in high school. Ugly ducklings my ass. But it makes for a good story. Sounds better than, 'Well, I've always been beautiful and popular. I can't remember life any other way,' '' she finished in a breathy mock-bimbo whisper.

Taz laughed. "Consider yourself lucky, man. Her first draft had you as the love child of Ol' Blue Eyes and Angie Dickinson.''

Ben gave Kitty another look of disbelief.

She shrugged. "I still think we could've pulled it off.''

His palms were sweating. A man got one chance to sell himself at the right moment. This was his. It bothered him that his wife wasn't around, driving him up the wall with her crazy talk. Nothing made him smile more. "Is Sofia here yet?''

"No,'' Kitty said. "Her father is, though. You know, for an old-timer he's not a bad-looking man. I'd give him some action.''

"Here's an idea—reintroduce yourself to the concept of private thoughts.''

Taz gripped Ben's shoulder. "Need another drink?''

He declined. "I don't want to slur the lyrics. Only Dean Martin could do that with dignity.'' Where the hell was Sofia? His anxiousness jumped up a notch.

There was a bustle outside the dressing room. A few seconds later it graduated to full-scale invasion as Robert Cannon, Rhythm Nation, and Tim Rebel crashed through.

Robert snatched the cigarette and the drink.

Rhythm Nation preened with a certain pimplike flair in white suit, white fur coat, and gold chains as thick as dog collars. "Get out there and *work it!* Wear it out! You know what I'm saying?"

Ben nodded firmly, confident that he had all the moves locked into memory with military precision.

Tim Rebel clasped both of Ben's hands. "Sugar, baby, cookie, honey, this is *your* moment. Embrace it." Behind the rhinestone-encrusted glasses, the producer's eyes misted with tears. "This reminds me of Pia Zadora. She stood in this very room, experiencing similar feelings. I'm going to ask you the same question I asked her."

"Why did you star in *The Lonely Lady*?"

Tim shook his head. "Are you ready to sing from your heart? And do you know what Pia told me? She said, 'You betcha, baby!' " A tear rolled down Tim's cheek. "I get emotional just thinking about it."

"Part of me wants to cry, too," Ben said dryly.

A hotel staffer popped inside. "It's time."

Silence dropped over the room. Ben sucked in a deep breath.

"You betcha, baby," Tim whispered.

Kitty took one hand, Taz held the other, and Ben shut his eyes, hoping he would step out there, look out into the audience, and see Sofia beaming back at him.

Chapter Twenty-one

Four leggy female dancers—extras from *Show-girls*—slinked across the polished floor to the lazy synthesizer intro that was unmistakably "Strangers in the Night." An urgent drumbeat picked up the tempo, and the girls responded with Rhythm Nation's slick choreographed moves—slide, kick, turn, step, spin.

An explosion of applause burst from the crowd as Ben sauntered in from stage right, sheathed in an Armani tux, a headset microphone allowing him total dance freedom.

The girls were well into their routine, but Ben strutted into the fold with perfect synchronization. And then he belted out the first verse, his vocals crisp, clear, stronger than ever. Ripping into each lyric, he wowed them with a searing sexual energy.

The audience responded ravenously, like caged

lions to fresh meat. Their bodies swayed to the trance-like beat, seduced by the new spin on an old favorite, enchanted by the cheeky fun of it all.

Ben felt like Spice Boy. His *guy power* was undeniable.

The song ended. He stood frozen—front and center—flanked by four chicks with smooth moves and nice sets of knockers. There were worse places a man could be.

Down went the lights. Up went the audience. On their feet, begging for more.

He drank in the approval, looking out at all the familiar faces.

Kitty, Taz, and Jilly from Swifty Morgan's.

A radiant Debi seated cozily with Vincent.

Ricky Lopez with his parents.

Joseph Cardinella sharing a table with Fat Larry and Little Bo.

Robert Cannon, Rhythm Nation, and a sobbing Tim Rebel.

Bitch-goddess CZ Rogers.

Even the alluring Charli Grant had made it.

Everyone but Sofia. Her table was conspicuously, heartbreakingly empty.

Somehow, he pushed the disappointment out of mind and delivered the rest of his set like a cat on top of the world. Only on his closing number, "I'm a Fool to Want You," did he sing with the ache and anguish tearing him up inside.

The Ben Estes Spectacular was a smash. The standing ovation told him so. But without Sofia there, the euphoria crashed and burned. That old cliché about success was true. Sharing it with the one you love makes it sweeter.

* * *

The son of a bitch has talent out of this world, Joseph thought.

"He's not so great, boss," Fat Larry said.

"Yeah," the rejoinder came from Little Bo. "He ain't got nothing on the kids from *Fame.*"

"Shut up!" Joseph snapped, straining to hear the conversations around him. There was definitely a buzz. Radio guys talking instant-play list adds for "Strangers in the Night." Club DJs swearing the tune would set dance floors on fire. Video executives predicting immediate heartthrob status.

Ka-ching! This could put Vegas Records in the black. Maybe the no-good son-in-law was worth a damn, after all. It was more than that, though. Joseph knew a torcher when he heard one. Ben Estes wasn't just singing "I'm a Fool to Want You." He was living it, as he stared at the empty table so obviously meant for Sofia, delivering each lyric with more devastation than the last, a man completely fractured by love.

Suddenly Joseph felt consumed with self-loathing. Fearfully, he looked around. The money and the mark had been delivered. The Caretaker could be here tonight, ready to strike. Any minute might be Ben's last. Regret stormed Joseph's heart. Somehow, the hit had to be stopped.

Urgently, he turned to Fat Larry and Little Bo. "You boys listen to me and listen good. My son-in-law is in danger, and I don't want anything to happen to him. Stay on him like white on rice until I say otherwise."

Fat Larry and Little Bo traded confused looks.

Joseph stared right through their eyes and into their guts. *"Got it?"*

"Like white on rice?" Fat Larry inquired. "Is that the same thing as flies on shit, boss?"

"Or water off a duck's back?" Little Bo put in.

Jesus. He fought for a calm, even voice when he said, "Forget all that, boys. You'll only confuse yourselves. Listen to me very carefully. I don't want Ben Estes to take a leak without you two being close enough to hear the piss hit the porcelain. Be his shadow and keep an eye out for trouble at all times. Understand?"

"This is like that movie *The Bodyguard,* boss," Fat Larry said.

"Yeah," Little Bo, seconded. "We're just like Whitney Houston."

"What the fuck are you talking about?" Joseph exploded. "You guys are Kevin Costner!"

Fat Larry turned almost coquettish. "Gee, thanks, boss."

Little Bo giggled. "Boss man thinks I'm pretty."

"BEAT IT!"

A terrible fear closed around Joseph's heart as he watched them take off. He'd try like hell to stop the Caretaker. But what if it was too late?

"I always knew you would make it," CZ said. She was all over him, stroking his hair, touching his arm, giving him the full benefit of her Poison by Christian Dior.

Ben smiled seductively. "Did you really?"

"Absolutely, positively," CZ purred.

"Well, if memory serves, your Dear John letter said—and this is lifted directly from your text—*Quit chasing that stupid pipe dream you pea-brained loser.*"

"You . . . You're taking that out of context," CZ sputtered.

Ben waved his wedding ring in her face. "How's this for context? I'm married."

CZ made a point out of looking around. "To a very supportive woman, I gather."

Ben's face registered the hit.

CZ picked up on this and pressed forward. "Have a drink with me to celebrate your success. Remember how you used to feed me the olives from your martini? I miss that. All I want to do is tell you how fantastic you were tonight. Is that so wrong?"

Before he could answer, Charli Grant floated into his personal space and slipped an arm through his. "There you are," she sang. "I've been looking all over for you. The party is well underway. Shall we?"

Ben gazed at her, a question in his eyes.

CZ stood there in a huff. "What party?"

Charli iced her down with a cold glare. "It's strictly NI where you're concerned."

"NI?" CZ asked.

"Not Invited," Charli explained. And then she pulled Ben away from the bar and led him toward the elevator. "You looked like a man in need of a rescue."

He was impressed. "They trained you well on *Malibu Undercover*."

Charli held up a room key as if it were a ticket to paradise. "I have a suite upstairs."

"I feel like getting smashed."

"That's what minibars are for."

The light pinged, and the doors opened. Ben wavered a moment. There were so many good reasons not to go upstairs with Charli Grant. But he stepped inside the elevator anyway.

* * *

Sofia had just counted off one hundred bottles of Jacqueline Feels Voulez Vous when the phone jangled. She picked up on the third ring, intoning a bleary, "Hello."

"I should come over there and break your head." It was Kitty.

Sofia gasped. "Just for that I'm rethinking your membership in the book club."

"Maybe I should kick that dog of yours so you'll disregard it altogether."

The mere suggestion terrified her. Frantically, she searched the room for Mr. Pickles. Then an idea took hold. Kitty was the person behind those awful letters! Oh, God! Sofia's pulse began to race. "The authorities have copies of your letters," she lied, remembering this strategy being played out once in a Tori Spelling movie on Lifetime. "The phone line is tapped. Police are listening in. It's over."

"Honey, are you *selling* nail polish or *sniffing* it?"

Total denial. Voice equal parts dismay and irritation. And convincing as hell, too. This girl was a pro. Hmm. As far as acting chops go, right up there with Melissa Gilbert. Sofia decided to draw her out. "I'm talking about the letters you wrote that called me a perfect little bitch with the perfect little life."

Kitty sighed. "Honey, I *know* bitches. I've broken bread with the best of them. I *am* one of them, and trust me, you're *not* a member of the sorority."

Sofia felt like she should protest. Kitty made being a bitch sound like a great thing. *Must sharpen bitch skills in near future. Will start with being rude to cabdrivers and people who work the counter at frozen-yogurt shops.*

"And a perfect life you don't have," Kitty went on. "As we speak, your husband is locked up in a hotel room with Charli Grant."

Sofia gripped the receiver tighter and began twisting the cord with her other hand. *Him: cheating bastard!* She lit a cigarette.

"It broke Ben's heart that you didn't make it to the spectacular."

Crashing waves of guilt soaked her to the core. *Her: selfish business mogul!* She took a deep drag.

"Honey, Ben is not the kind of man to keep on a long leash. Women throw themselves at him. CZ already tried tonight, and she's still parked at the bar, hoping for another chance."

At first Sofia couldn't believe it. This was actually a *friendly* call from Kitty Bishop.

"Now get over here and prove to Ben and those sluts that you're his wife!"

Sofia gargled some mouthwash and swiped on a little lip gloss. Five minutes later she was in a taxi. The jeans were ripped, the T-shirt splattered, the hair particularly bad (ghastly cowlick). But the sapphire and diamonds sparkled. Ha! Take that, CZ! Up yours, Charli Grant! This lady's wearing the ring!

A snippy front-desk clerk refused to give out the room number. Something about hotel security policy. So here she was, looking like something that had been dragged in by whatever the cat had dragged in and left with no choice but to knock on every door of the stinking hotel (frustration talking—it really was quite nice) until she found them. This predicament could only be described as SNAFU. *Situation Normal: All Fucked Up.* Or rather, a typical day in the life.

Pacing the lobby like a panther wired on diet pills, she noticed Papa slumped into one of the love seats clustered in the corner, looking like a man who could tell you anything about defeat. They hadn't spoken since that terrible night at the house in New Jersey. Suddenly it all seemed so silly. "Hi, Papa."

He glanced up, eyes gleaming with love. "Baby bunny." His voice was soft . . . and sad. Giving her a once-over, he murmured, "You're a mess."

Sofia settled down next to him and sighed. "Tell me about it."

"Where were you tonight?"

She told him all about Jacqueline and tried to explain about the Berrenger's order.

Papa shook his head. "I remember missing one of your dance recitals because of something like that. Your mother stayed pissed at me for a whole month. Today I can't even remember what the business crisis was. I bet I'd remember your recital, though."

Sofia started to cry. She wanted to bridge the distance between them, to approach him with compassion instead of anger and blame. "I miss you, Papa."

He wrapped her up in his arms, rocking her back and forth. "I miss you, too, baby bunny." For several long seconds, he just held her quietly. "That husband of yours is some kind of talent."

She drew back and wiped her cheek, surprised by the genuine affection in his voice. "You really think so?"

"I sure do. My son-in-law killed them tonight."

Sofia put hand over heart. *My son-in-law.* "Oh, Papa, it makes me so happy to hear you say that."

"Want to hear something funny?"

Sofia nodded.

"Ben's already an important part of the family business. Turns out I own Vegas Records."

They were laughing about this bizarre coincidence

when Debi and Vincent approached, followed moments later by Ricky and his parents. Heavens! It was old home week at the Charade. Everybody raved about the spectacular. Sofia felt like she'd missed the most important event on earth, and her anxiousness to find Ben reached an unbearable level. Considering the fact that Cynthia Lopez worked at the hotel, she dispatched her to pull some strings at the front desk.

Sofia was shocked to find Fat Larry and Little Bo standing vigil outside Suite 1025. ''What's going on?''

''Strict orders to stay close to Ben when he urinates,'' Fat Larry said.

''Yeah,'' Little Bo added. ''That comes straight from the boss.''

With no time to make sense of their latest drivel, she pounded on the door.

Charli Grant answered it wearing a ridiculous midnight seduction number—clingy nightgown, fur-trimmed robe, spiked heels that added six inches. The sex symbol from decades past glowered. ''This is a *private* celebration.''

''That just ended,'' Sofia snapped, blowing past her to find Ben slumped back on the sofa, half drunk, tie loosened, shirt half buttoned. She pointed an accusing finger. ''You creep!''

Ben rose to his feet, a wee bit wobbly but still righteously indignant. ''Go home to your nail polish, baby.''

''Grab your jacket. We're going home.''

''You don't care about me!'' Ben roared.

Sofia rolled her eyes. The Jack Daniel's was pushing cry-baby talk past his lips. And Ben Estes didn't carry self-pity well. Talk about an emergency! This man needed hot coffee faster than Lara Flynn Boyle needed a hot meal. ''Stop acting insane.''

Charli Grant tottered between them. "He's making perfect sense to me."

Sofia gave Charli a head-to-toe glance. The hair could definitely benefit from some of Raymond McLaren's handiwork at Bumble and Bumble. And the shoes? Manolo Blahnik knockoffs. *Tacky.* "What do you know about *sense*? You look like you're wearing Eva Gabor's old wardrobe from *Green Acres.*"

"Charli cares!" Ben slurred. "She came to my spectacular! Years ago she taught me how to make love!"

"Taught you how to make love?" Sofia blanched. She'd underestimated her husband's level of inebriation. Ben was amber-drenched beyond reason. "You had this woman's bathing suit poster tacked up on your wall. All she did was teach you how to entertain yourself with baby oil and a Kleenex."

"You perfect little bitch!" Charli shrieked.

Sofia froze.

"With the perfect little life!"

Slowly, the realization became clear. "You!"

"Watch what you say about my wife," Ben scolded. "Anyone who's seen her credit report knows she's not perfect. Not to mention she doesn't know how to train a dog properly. Or quit her smoking habit. Did you know she's got the worst CD collection I've ever seen? *Physical* by Olivia Newton-John? Come on!"

"We get the point!" Sofia screamed. Then back at Charli Grant. "You wrote those letters!"

"And I meant every word when I said . . . *not for long.*" From the pocket of her robe Charli brandished a sleek, pearl-handled revolver.

Sofia's blood turned to ice water. Maybe Charli had just wanted a pen pal. If only she'd written back!

Ben got real sober real quick. "Easy, Charli."

The gun-toting star from decades past extended her arm. "It's my duty to kill you. It's my pleasure to kill your wife."

Ben stepped forward and shielded Sofia's body with his own.

She swooned, hugging him from behind. He was *so* Harrison Ford.

Ben held out an open palm. "Give me the gun, Charli."

"Don't call me Charli!"

"Okay, Alice, Suzie, Goldilocks, whatever. Just give me the gun before someone gets hurt."

"I'm the Caretaker. They don't pay me to hurt. They pay me to kill."

Sofia yelped. Oh, God! She knew the legend. All this time the Mafia world had thought the Caretaker was a *he!* She just couldn't believe it. "How many people have you murdered?"

"How many pair of shoes do you own?" Charli countered.

Ben glanced back at his wife, worried.

"Ask her if sneakers and slippers count," Sofia whispered. And then it dawned on her to ask the obvious question. Who would put out a hit on Ben? The answer crushed her. *Papa!* But he'd been so conciliatory in the lobby. Maybe a change of heart? Her brain kicked into overdrive. Yes! That's why he ordered Fat Larry and Little Bo to shadow Ben. To protect him from harm. Sofia's heart melted. What a darling man. Hmm. But then he *was* the reason a crazed killer had a loaded gun pointed at them. *Damn you, Papa!*

Sofia burned with curiosity. "I don't understand. You were the star of a hit television show. Why on earth did you become a contract killer?"

Charli gave a diffident shrug. "They cut me out of the syndication profits. I had to do *something*."

"Let Sofia go," Ben implored. "It's me they paid you to kill." He halted and turned back to Sofia. "By the way, who wants me dead?"

"Papa," Sofia whispered.

"One good thing about your dad—a man always knows where he stands with him."

"But Papa feels terrible about it now. In fact, he ordered Fat Larry and Little Bo to keep you safe. They're just outside the door."

"And the killer's in here. Sounds like their idea of quality protection."

"Stop whispering!" Charli hissed.

"As I was saying," Ben said, "My wife has nothing to do with this. Let her go."

"Your wife is young and beautiful," Charli said bitterly. "That's reason enough for her to die."

"I'm really not," Sofia corrected. "Young, that is. I turn *thirty* this year. I don't even get carded anymore. But thanks for saying I'm beautiful, especially in this outfit. You're a peach."

Charli Grant aimed squarely between Ben's eyes. "Any last words?"

"Please return to acting. It's a different world now with cable. You'll find lots of work."

Sofia felt something in her front jeans pocket. A stray bottle of nail polish! Stealthily she scooped it out.

Charli gestured to the balcony. "Let's take a walk outside. I'd hate to get blood on the furniture. The hotel will bill my credit card for the damage."

Just then Sofia rolled Jacqueline Feels Outrageously Orange under the madwoman's foot. Charli's cheap shoe came down on the cap, twisting her ankle and snapping the heel. "Always buy designer," Sofia clucked.

As Charli scrambled to regain her footing, Ben lunged for the gun.

Then Sofia raced for the door, flung it open, and yelled to Fat Larry and Little Bo, "Save my husband!"

The guys wasted precious seconds bumping into each other before stumbling into the hotel suite. But by then Charli Grant had won the struggle. Her trigger hand took dead aim at Ben's chest.

One bullet tore loose.

Sofia closed her eyes and screamed like the pretty girl in any teen slasher movie (the one who runs through the woods in the dark with just a bra and panties on).

When she opened them, Charli was crouched down, massaging her hand. Only when she saw Fat Larry and Little Bo with both their guns drawn did she realize what happened. Like master sharpshooters they'd fired the revolver clean out of Charli's grasp.

"I got the shot!" Fat Larry exclaimed.

"No way," Little Bo argued. "It was me!"

Sofia kissed each buffoon on the cheek. "You *both* got it."

And then she raced to Ben, hugging him as tightly as strength allowed, surrendering a breathless stream of I love yous, explaining in maudlin detail why she missed the spectacular, and imploring his forgiveness for having done so.

"I'll forgive you on one condition."

She watched his luscious mouth expectantly.

"You've got to move the business out of the apartment. It's killing our marriage."

"Already done. I found the perfect little warehouse in the western part of Greenwich Village. *Cheap*. It's not far from Jackie 60, the famous drag-queen bar. I met a wonderful guy named Miss Sonya who's going to be my receptionist. I've never had a drag queen for a friend before. I think everybody should have at least one transvestite in their life, don't you?"

Ben smiled. "Have I told you lately how much I love you, baby?"

"Like a broken record." She embraced him once more. Suddenly an odd thought struck her. "You know, I can't believe Charli Grant won that wrestle for the gun. Maybe you should start working out more."

Epilogue

Funky Soul Brothers on Mars was the worst movie Sofia had ever seen. And she felt confident that it would hold that distinction with anyone else in the room, city, tristate area, country, hemisphere, world, and universe.

The special effects were so low budget that, by comparison, the infamous megabomb *Plan 9 from Outer Space* played like a George Lucas production. And let's not even *start* with the sexist, exploitative garbage factor. Simply put—if an impossibly large-breasted woman was not *naked* in a scene, then she was most certainly *wet* (a lot of rain on Mars, apparently) and *hot* (requiring her to dress in strategically placed fabric swatches).

Sofia sat fretfully clutching Ben's hand. Taz was heading straight for them, his face eager and expectant. This was, after all, his big Hollywood-style premiere. If you could say that for folding chairs, an old projector, and a rickety screen at Swifty Morgan's. What did one say in the face of such dreadfulness? She decided to play it cool and take Ben's lead.

"Give it to me straight," Taz said.

"Charley," Ben began earnestly, putting a hand on his pallie's shoulder. "The movie I just saw represents celluloid crap at its purest. It sucks *hard*, you crazy bastard!"

Taz beamed triumphant. Academy Award winners accepted Oscars with less delight. Then he danced around in search of more critical abuse.

CZ, now hot and heavy with a Wall Street whiz, tottered into Taz's path. "My boyfriend promises to invest in your next film," she said, "if you promise not to make one!" She roared with laughter. So did the stock-market stud.

Taz raised a triumphant fist and partied onward.

"I don't get it," Sofia murmured.

Ben draped a hand around her waist and kissed her cheek. "In Hollywood, you fail *up*, baby. How else can you explain Tom Arnold? Taz is on his way."

The celebration teemed with Swifty regulars and assorted hangers-on, plus the New York society press. The tabs were all over it. Sofia watched a Page Six reporter, her gaze Krazy Glued to Ben, move in on them.

"Can I get your reaction to the movie?"

"Sure," Ben offered. "I'm pissed that I wasn't asked to sing the love theme."

The junior gossip huntress scribbled down the response. "You give good quote," she praised. "What's happening with the next record?"

"More of the same. I put a disco spin on 'Fly Me to the Moon.' The single ships next week. We're shooting the video tomorrow night at Windows on the World. You should come by."

She nodded eagerly. "I will." Then she turned to Sofia, the look on her face saying, 'No harm in throwing the wife a bone.' "Anything new with Jacqueline?"

"Our new lipstick line launches next month." Sofia crossed her fingers. "First year sales were just over two million dollars. We hope to add a new product each year."

The reporter nodded, jotting like mad, impressed. "How does it feel to join the ranks of the BYT crowd?"

Sofia and Ben stared blankly at each other, then back at Page Six girl.

"Bright Young Things," she clarified. "Great jobs, fabulous apartment, admired for your style."

"Baby, it wasn't so long ago that we were *Broke Young Things,*" Ben said, laughing.

The scribe's photographer snapped a quick candid. Media moment over, Ben smiled good-bye. The press loved him because he knew how to play. Sofia did, too, but she strategically kept something sly in reserve. Better to leave them wanting more. A little mystery was good.

It was hard to believe a whole year had gone by since reporters had swept down like vultures to dig up every tidbit on the Charli Grant scandal. But all the fuss had boosted Ben's "Strangers in the Night" CD single *and* sales of Jacqueline. Ever the marketing slyboots, Sofia had manufactured a limited-edition color during all the hoopla—Jacqueline Feels Glad to Be Alive, a gold glitter stunner that glowed in the dark. Club kids went wild for it.

"Baby, I think your purse is ringing."

"Oh," Sofia said, scooping it out to answer. "Hello?"

"So, is he the next Cameron Crow?" It was Debi.

"Let me put it this way. *Funky Soul Brothers on Mars* is so bad that Jean-Claude Van Damme would be offended."

Ben's face lit up. "Taz will love that one." He ran off to tell.

"How do you feel?"

"Very pregnant," Debi answered. "But Vincent makes it bearable. He's painting the nursery now. Did I tell you he was building the baby furniture himself?"

Sofia smiled. Ever since the spectacular, Debi and Vincent had been inseparable. His courtship had been attentive, respectful, romantic—everything her sister deserved. Papa could *finally* call Vincent a son-in-law. And for once, a wedding he paid for actually went the distance as far as the bride and groom exchanging I dos. To think that Debi was pregnant now, that Sofia was going to be an aunt—it filled her up with such warmth. She'd been counting the days until Debi's due date. Forty-one to go.

"Fat Larry and Little Bo stopped by this morning. Fat Larry knitted the baby some booties, but there are no openings for the feet. Just two masses of red yarn."

"I wonder if Papa's called them. I haven't heard boo from him."

"Same here. What a rat. He's been cavorting around Mexico with that Kitty Bishop for a whole week. I still can't get over the fact that I'm *older* than my *father's* girlfriend."

"Don't worry. Kitty changes men as often as I change handbags. I just hope Papa doesn't get too attached."

"Do you think they—"

"I refuse to go there."

Debi snorted. "Maybe he learned some hot moves from those late-night cable movies."

Sofia feigned line trouble. "You're breaking up, sweetie." Papa's sex life (yuck—she even hated to string those three words together) was off-limits.

"Ricky sent me a postcard from Switzerland. How are you managing without him?"

"Claire's been a big help. Can you imagine? We hated each other at Berrenger's. Now she works for me, and we're like sorority sisters. Things are a bit of a mess, though. I can't wait until he gets back."

Ricky had stopped trying to convince his mother to tour Europe without his father. Instead, he extended an olive branch to Juan and invited him to go as well. The three of them were having an incredible time. Not perfect, of course. But family never was.

Debi groaned. "I just clicked on *Court TV*. The Charli Grant trial is on again. There's no escaping her."

"I know. I just read that Susan Lucci signed a deal to star in the miniseries."

"Oh, God," Debi said. "I hope it's not a musical."

"Let's just be thankful that Charli didn't rat out Papa. He could be in serious legal trouble for trying to hire someone to kill Ben."

"It seems like she *would* hold a grudge against Papa, since his job is the one that ended her career as the Caretaker."

"Well, first of all, the woman is *insane*. She made all that money killing people and still bought knock-offs. Don't tell me she couldn't afford designer originals. Anyway, as I understand it, she's a perfectionist and didn't want to be linked to any hit that wasn't successful. That's why people like Papa's friend Tony Langella are behind bars."

"That's awful," Debi said. "Because those Langella sisters are wild. They need their father around. One of them is working as a stripper. I hear she calls herself a pole dancer, though. I wonder where she studied?"

Sofia giggled, closing her eyes, wanting to seal the beauty of the moment. She treasured casual chatter with her sister. They could easily blather on for hours. But life was getting so complicated.

Ben was on his way to becoming a bona fide star. Nothing could stop him. And her dedication to all things Jacqueline had created a profitable yet demanding corporation. Perhaps the most daunting—Debi's baby. An actual living breathing little person to see after!

Deep in her secret heart, Sofia longed sometimes to relive one of the simple days. Eating Cap'n Crunch straight from the box. Watching TV for hours. Laughing with Debi about the silliest things. Gossiping with Ricky about their coworkers at Berrenger's. Arguing with Papa about, well, just about whatever came out of his mouth.

The sensation of warm breath on the nape of her neck tripped her into the here and now. "Hey, baby. You *are* going home with me tonight, aren't you?"

Sofia twirled around with faux indignation. "I'm not some groupie. It takes more than a line and a hit record to get me into bed."

He grinned at her. "How's Debi?"

"She's fine. Remember we're eating dinner with them tomorrow night."

Ben made a face. "That means I'll be stuck trying to make conversation with Vincent."

"He's making baby furniture. You can help him with that."

"I don't know how to build stuff. I even hated Legos as a kid. I guess I shouldn't complain, though. Kitty could end up as your stepmother."

"That's not funny!"

"You know, it really isn't." Ben shuddered. "It's frightening." One beat. "Would you call her mom?"

"Ben!"

He kissed her forehead to calm her down. "I'm teasing. Kitty wouldn't like it if you called her mom anyway."

Sofia jabbed a finger into his stomach.

Ben feigned excruciating pain for a moment. Then he gazed around Swifty Morgan's, looking a bit melancholy.

"I was thinking the same thing," Sofia said.

"What's that?"

"How simple life used to be."

"I know. I remember coming in here almost every night. No pressures, no worries."

"Any regrets?"

"A few."

Sofia experienced a moment of alarm. Did he long to go back to his old life? "Such as?"

Ben's voice went down an octave. "That we lived the first twenty-nine years of our lives before meeting each other."

"I could've been driving you crazy as early as kindergarten."

"I've always had close pallies like Kitty and Taz, but until you, I've never had a best friend. I love you, Sofia."

She touched her heart. It was uncanny how he always caught her off guard. The sweetest things could just drop off his lips with no warning. "I love you, too."

He looked around again, this time with a cocksure attitude. "What does a minor pop star have to do to get a little action?"

Sofia challenged her husband with a passionate gaze. "Sinatra's always brought you luck. Try one of his numbers."

Ben pulled her close. "Here's a ditty just for you, baby. It's called 'Love and Marriage.' " And then he began to sing.

Dear Reader:

I had a blast writing FLY ME TO THE MOON. I actually fell in love with my own hero. Creating the intimate scenes even caused me to hyperventilate at times. Maybe a real-live Ben is out there somewhere. I certainly hope so, because the men I meet can't make me laugh and never pick up their socks.

As for you, dear reader, may there be a Ben in *your* life, a sweetheart so fun and sexy that you just want to squeeze him to pieces. And honeybunch, if you're single, hang in there. Someday your prince will come. That's a comforting cliché that gets *me* through a Saturday night when I'm home alone watching *Walker, Texas Ranger*.

I truly believe that a love like Ben and Sofia's is not just fodder for romance novels. It can be *ours*. Heavens, it could be *mine*, providing I find a man who isn't bisexual (happened to my friend Kate), a total bore (paging my cousin Sheila's husband), or a complete shit (my last boyfried).

I'm hopeful, though. After all, George Clooney is *real*.

Happy Reading,

Kylie

PS Darlings, tell me what you think about my first racy romp! If it's happy talk, I'll send back big hugs, plus my newsletter, *Kylie Says*. If it's negative, I'll simply tell you to write your *own* book and get on with my life. Who has time for complainers? Write to me

c/o Zebra Books
850 Third Avenue
New York, NY 10022

or e-mail www.kylieadams.com